I0663649

MOJAVE
MAN

MOJAVE MAN

BOOK 2 *of the* ARCPOINT SERIES

J.W. Gilbert

MOJAVE MAN

Copyright © November 2022 John Gilbert Wozniak

Book design by DesignWise Art

All rights reserved. No part of this book may be used or reproduced by any means, graphic, electronic, or mechanical, including photocopying, recording, taping or by any information storage retrieval system without the written permission of the author except in the case of brief quotations embodied in critical articles and reviews.

This is a work of fiction. All of the characters, names, and events as well as all places, incidents, organizations, and dialogue in this book are either the products of the writer and illustrator's collaborative imaginations or are used fictitiously.

ISBN 978-1-7344212-3-1

OTHER WORKS BY J.W. GILBERT

Mojave Rock
Published by J.W. Gilbert

Mojave Man
Published by J.W. Gilbert

Mojave Rift
Published by J.W. Gilbert

The Moment
Published by Outskirts Press

Not Your Ordinary Praise and Worship
Published by Elisha Records

Escaping Ignorance – Pursuing Wisdom
Published by Inkwater Press

CHAPTER ONE

Roberto shoved the last chicken nugget in his mouth and moved the Search and Rescue Vehicle into the right lane. His Personal Information Device was repeating a series of tones that identified the messenger as Ranger Dan. Roberto pulled into a grocery store parking lot and grabbed the first spot he saw. He reset the PID and opened his comm-pad. The message read: [Hide Tarzan Now. Keep In Touch. Secure.] *Great. What could've happened?*

He tapped a button on the steering wheel and said, "Call Elaina." He put away the comm-pad and listened to the phone ring on the car speakers. *Come on, girl, where are you? You always have your phone with you.*

He put the SRV in gear, snaked through the lot, and darted back into traffic. There were only a few miles to go, but cross traffic seemed to steal the right of way at every intersection. *Can't catch a break.* At the next yellow light, he stepped on the gas, seeing it turn red just as he passed under it. *Be patient. You don't want any company right now.*

If this was an official concern, he could call in for favored traffic flow or turn on his lights and sirens. *But what would I say? I need help to avoid the authorities?* He slowed the SRV down some, but his mind was still racing. One dangerous scenario after another filled his thoughts.

Could that reporter have found their home address that fast? Would she have called the authorities on her own regarding Arcon? What would Arcon do if a crowd suddenly descended on him? What if he thought someone was threatening Elaina? Roberto hit the redial button. No response. *What if they never made it home?*

He was about to hit redial once more when he heard another tone from the PID. It was Ranger Dan again. He wheeled to the side of the road and opened his comm-pad. The message read, [HAVE LOCATION 4U. SOUTH. 447YB811V].

Roberto breathed a sigh of relief. *Ranger Dan must've located a place to hide Arcon.* At this point, he had no other choice than to trust the Ranger. Roberto got back on the road, mashed the pedal to the floor, and prayed he wasn't too late.

Elaina melted into Arcon's firm embrace. She'd need to explain so much to him, especially how he was a fugitive in this world. *Later.* This moment, this touch, had been a long time coming. She'd feared it never would. Now there were even more things to be afraid of. Ranger Dan ought never to have allowed her dad to have custody of this escapee from the Mojave Forest.

The law stated: "Anything coming from that location must be quarantined until proper judgment can be made by the authorities having jurisdiction for both that area and the locality where that entity may be relocated." Her dad had pounded that rule into her, then surprised her by breaking it himself. *This house doesn't qualify for quarantine. Ranger Dan isn't the authority over this area. What were those two thinking? Neither of them are Judges.*

Elaina believed that, in the eyes of the Authorities, Arcon would be considered innocent. He was a good, kind, honest man. Now that he wasn't dressed like Tarzan, they'd see him as more than just a Mojave man. Everyone would come to see—Arcon is not a leper.

2

She knew no one believed that. But that's how many people viewed the Mojave Restricted Area—like the leper colonies of the Middle Ages. Only it wasn't a physical disease. It was like some form of spiritual leprosy. *Pity those poor people, but don't go near them.* When that thought came to her, she just hugged Arcon harder. Any quarantine he'd have to face, she would endure with him. Her greatest fear was they'd send him back to the Mojave.

Arcon's immediate future was a mystery, but hers was not. She knew the moment they heard her dad's car in the driveway, this embrace would end, followed shortly thereafter by a lecture from her dad. She'd forgotten her shoulder-phone in the car and was long overdue to check in with him. But she refused to stop what she was doing to retrieve it.

After the drama of getting Arcon across the Rift, she'd hoped for a few days of tranquility, a chance to be with Arcon before they turned him over to the Authorities. They'd isolate him in a secure location. He'd be questioned, probed, tested, and watched, trading his prison in the Mojave for another in this world. It was important she had time to prepare him.

Maybe her dad was right. She should never have encouraged him to leave his people. But she firmly believed Arcon would be a free man someday. She just needed to explain the procedure so he could endure the trial. But she wasn't about to end their embrace for that either.

Ranger Dan paced outside the station, waiting for Roberto and refusing to take any more calls. The reporter for the San Bernardino Portal was not satisfied with his 'no comment at this time' routine. *She won't rest until she finds out who rescued Arcon. This human-interest story will morph into a manhunt and an inquiry. Then the news will hit the surrounding states, and those with Calneva Rift alerts on their searchnet device.* He walked across the parking lot and stared at the broad expanse of the Rift.

Why had I been in such a hurry? He'd been prepared—and excited—about the prospect of meeting the Mojave People someday. He'd studied the laws regarding the containment procedure. The population would be quarantined, given physical and psychological exams, and treated fairly. Had he stuck to protocol, the original plan would have let the Authorities judge Arcon, and his fate would've been determined. Then various localities would've sponsored him with a home, job, and—most importantly—supervision.

But Dan hadn't followed the rules. Instead, he'd gotten caught up in the novelty of giving freedom to a naïve, polite, young Mojave man clad in animal skins. Dan had let his own curiosity and excitement get the better of him. The only way to make things right was to recapture Arcon. Dan's plan revolved around the two people who'd assisted Arcon to leave that area. If he could control the actions of Roberto and Elaina, he'd be able to contain Arcon and make things right.

But now Dan had a reporter dogging him. All he could hope for was to get Arcon hidden away before she took the story public. If suddenly confronted with the unknown, any man's instinct is to fight or take flight. Whether a bee or a bear, the panic is genuine. If Arcon felt threatened by an onslaught of news crews, his reaction could be perilous.

At the moment, Dan despised the Mojave Restricted Area even more than usual. The hassles of dealing with those who obsessed about the Mojave People frequently eclipsed his duties as Park Ranger. Anyone, from the casual tourist, clear up to the Peace Regulators that governed human interaction, was biased and afraid of what may lie beyond the Rift. It didn't help that it had once been a desert area called *Devil's Playground*.

As Chief of the Calneva Rift Ranger station, all Rift related inquiries funneled through him. As Authority over the Mojave Forest, they expected him to be in control of what happened around the Restricted Area. The higher authorities allowed only a twenty-four hour window to locate and confine Arcon to a safe location. After that, they would activate the Open Eyes protocol.

Ranger Becca was already gathering video footage for the search algorithms. Stills from the Ranger station cameras of Arcon in his Tarzan suit, his new apparel, even the scars on his arms, were all to be cataloged. So were pictures of Roberto, Elaina, and their vehicles. Becca had already logged the Gonzales' employment with San Bernardino Search and Rescue, as well as their home address.

Ranger Dan glanced at his watch. He had a meeting at 9AM on Tuesday with Sir Nelson, the Authority over Southern California. *I'll request the Open Eyes protocol be postponed until after the meeting.* He knew if Arcon wasn't in a secure location by then, He'd need to be found fast. With a tap on a keyboard, the protocol would activate thousands of surveillance cameras in the radius of five hundred miles. If the cameras spotted any of the images Becca just input, the Rangers would receive an alert.

Dan at least needed to know if Arcon was still with the rescuers. *Why aren't they contacting me? What if they're avoiding the cameras?* He started pacing again, waiting for a response from Roberto.

They cut short their embrace when headlights lit up the curtains like the sweep of two spotlights. Arcon stepped back toward the sofa and watched the motion detector light come on. He heard a loud car door slam and watched as Elaina scurried to open the door for her father. In the window, he could see Roberto's shadow as he sprinted toward the door. Elaina said, "Hi, Daddy, you caught up quicker than I—"

"Pack your bags quick. We need to move out." said Roberto, abruptly. "And turn on your phone!"

"It is turned on, but I forgot it in the car."

As Elaina stepped outside to retrieve it, he barked, "Never mind that now. We're leaving. Pack as fast as you can for at least a week's stay. We may have to camp out, so bring supplies to do that. Come on, girl. I'm not kidding." Then he looked at Arcon. "You, follow me. If I hand you something, put it in my rig and do it fast."

"Dad, what's going on?" Elaina asked, taking jackets from the closet.

"I'll tell you when we're on the road. Right now, just do as I say, please!"

"Which rig? Should I pack my three-wheeler?"

"Yes, we're taking both vehicles. Now hurry." Roberto darted out the front door.

Arcon stared at Elaina, who just motioned in her dad's direction and said, "Go help him." He hurried out the door and saw Roberto waiting for him at the corner of the house. As soon as their eyes met, Roberto disappeared around the corner. Arcon ran to catch him.

Roberto was standing in front of another building, one with a large, roll-up doorway like the one they had at the ArcPoint Facility. When he got close, Roberto handed him a box. "Take this out to the rig and put it in… oh, wait a minute. Follow me."

Roberto ran back to his vehicle and opened the back hatch. "Help me with this, will you?" He started tugging on the super-rope, and the two of them dragged it out onto the driveway. He dumped a few more things out, handed Arcon a rolled-up sheet of something, said, "Take this in to Elaina, carefully!" and went back to the garage.

Arcon headed for the house. Inside he yelled, "Elaina, your dad wants me to give this to you."

She came running down the stairs. "What is it?" As she got a closer look, she grinned. "It's the roll-up monitor." She grabbed it from Arcon and whisked down the hallway.

6

"He said carefully," Arcon warned, but just that quick, she disappeared into another room. When she reappeared, he said, "Elaina, tell me what's going on!"

She answered, "I wish I could, but I don't know," then ran back upstairs. "We're just going to have to trust Daddy. Go help him."

Arcon ran back out and found Roberto near the other building with a small pile of boxes. Roberto told him, "Put these in the rig, and drag that super-rope of yours over here." Arcon did, and for the next few minutes, helped Roberto continue to shuffle supplies in and out of either his vehicle or the building. When they finished, they went inside to see how Elaina was doing.

They found her in her room with some hanging clothes, assorted bags, and a suitcase. Roberto shook his head. "Is this what's going?"

"Yes, this should take care of me. I'll go grab some camping food."

"Well, get the drone unloaded first. Arcon, schlep this stuff to Elaina's car. Elaina, Arcon's riding with you, so we'll put this stuff in your drone trailer."

For the next few minutes, Arcon helped where he could but mostly just watched the other two race around. When they were all through packing the trailer, Roberto instructed, "Meet me at Henley Park, under the water tower. I'll do some final checking and be there as soon as I can. I'll explain everything then. Keep your phone keyed to channel three and on speaker while you're in the car. Now go!"

"Okay, Dad, see you soon." She pointed at the bright blue autocycle, a two-seat utility vehicle. "Arcon, go ahead and get in. I'll do a final check on the trailer hitch."

Arcon climbed into the cramped backseat, moving a few randomly tossed items out of the way. He had plenty of elbowroom but didn't like how the hanging clothes blocked both side windows. When Elaina got in, his front window view got blocked as well by Elaina's substantial amount of wavy black hair. He felt sealed in like a seed in an Acacia pod. With some effort, he located the seat belts and strapped himself in. Elaina did the same from the seat directly in front of him.

"What is channel three?" asked Arcon.

Elaina closed her door, settled her shoulder-phone into its cradle on the dash, then started the autocycle. As she backed out of the driveway, she said, "Everybody has channel one on their phones, but emergency people have three more. Channel two is for all emergency people, like Police, Firemen, and Search and Rescue people like Dad. Since I assist him, they gave me one as well. We all use the same channel so we can work together."

As she stopped at another street, she continued, "Channel three only connects between Dad's phone and mine and works like a walkie-talkie. If Dad has his on, he can hear what we're saying right now."

"And a walkie-talkie is what?"

"It's like a phone, uh, well…Okay, if you and I are using walkie-talkies, then no matter where I'm walkin', you can hear me talkin'."

Arcon thought about that. "Oh, okay, I get it. What about channel four?"

"That one acts as a walkie-talkie among all the Search and Rescue team, including dispatch, but not the rest of the emergency people. That's the one we use when we're trying to rescue someone."

"Like when you were helping me across the Rift?"

"Naah, Dad and I used channel three for that, to keep the conversation private. The earpiece we gave you is what we call a dummy piece. It only works on the channel it's set for."

"Sorry I dropped it."

"Oh, don't worry about it. Rescue buys those by the dozen."

They weren't too far from the house when a crackling of static came from the car speakers. "Hold it a second, Arcon; it sounds like Dad is connecting. Big D, is that you?"

"Affirmative, Girl," he responded. "Are you on the freeway?"

"Almost."

"Well, don't get on it. Take the surface streets instead, okay?"

"Okay. Around Hesperia?"

"Affirmative. You can mute if you'd like, but if you see anything unusual, give me sound. I'll do the same."

"Understood. Girl out." Elaina tapped the mute button and moved her seat forward a notch. "There's a little more room for your legs. I suggest you try to get comfortable and sleep if you can. You've had a very long day, and it may not end soon. I'm sure Dad will explain what's going on when we get to the park."

"I'll try," he said and slouched down until his knees rested on the back of her seat. "You call him big D?"

"Right. Rescue people give each other nicknames. We call them call signs. I used to call him Big Daddy, and I was Baby Girl. We've shortened it over the years."

"I just had one more question. Why do you call it a shoulder-phone?"

"Uhh, maybe because it's a phone, and we wear it on our shoulder?"

"Oh. I guess that was a stupid question. But in ArcPoint, we only spoke face to face."

"Sorry. You didn't have *any* phones?"

"Hmmm. In the Room of Remembrance, we had something called a cell phone, but it looked nothing like your shoulder-phone. The sign on it read 'We carried this everywhere,' but it didn't say why."

"Well, I've seen those in the archives. People used to carry them in their pockets and had to hold them in their hands to talk. But a long time ago, someone invented super-capacitors. We call them caps for short. They can store a lot of power in a tiny disc. Guess they got rid of the display screen to keep it less bulky. Shoulder-phones are tiny and mount on our shoulder so we can hear them better. We program it to make unique sounds so we can identify callers without looking at it. And it does have a tiny camera for recording video."

"You mean like a movie?"

"Yeah, it's motion video, but not as long as a movie. It only holds about five minutes of footage; then it continuously erases the older stuff to make room for the new. If it records something you want to keep, you just tap a button, and it shuts off, keeping what was just recorded. Make sense?"

"I think so." Arcon leaned forward in his seat. "If I'd have been wearing one when I tightroped across the Rift, I could have a movie of smashing into the cliff."

Elaina chuckled. "If you could've tapped the button quick enough. With all the shaking around, it may have been hard to see what happened. But that's definitely the type of thing you'd want to save."

Arcon settled back in his seat. "I remember seeing people tapping their shoulders when we were back at the Rift. I wondered what they were doing."

"Uh-oh. That means there's shoulder-phone footage of you."

"Is that bad?"

"Hope not. Anyway, there's one more thing I want you to understand about these phones. The shoulder-phone connects to a bigger device that we call a comm-pad. It has a screen we can look at and a keyboard to enter text. It has bigger caps and does all the heavy work. We can upload the video from the shoulder-phone so we can look at it, and it has a program to take out all the shaking. Then we can clear the cache on the phone, uh, empty the memory chip. Let's just say that's how we keep the video."

"Okay, I think I get it. The phone grabs it, the comm-pad keeps it."

"Right, and one more thing. There's an earpiece for private listening. All three of them work together. Some of us, like Dad or Ranger Dan, also have a personal information device, or what we call a PID. It's a super secure thing that only works with our own comm-pad."

Arcon pointed to the dash. "Why put the shoulder-phone up there?"

"When it's there, it charges the cap, and channels the sound through the car speakers so I can hear it better. It also disables the screen on the comm-pad, so the driver isn't distracted by it. That's an annoying safety feature." Elaina sped up as they left Hesperia. "Aren't you getting tired? Why don't you try to get some sleep?"

Arcon was dead tired, but he wanted to learn everything he could about this new world. He wanted to know what had Roberto so stressed out. *Are some outsiders still dangerous? If they are, Elaina isn't acting like it.*

Elaina. So badly he wanted to just relax with her, to talk with her about this outside world, about her, and about them. He still had so many questions he'd never been able to ask with Morse code.

The hug. He wanted to go back to that moment. Even though he was still confused about what a romantic relationship might be like, he knew it felt good just to hold her. And it was comforting to know she seemed to like it as well. Arcon rested his head against the clothes hanging next to him. With everything going on in his head—and the pain in his arm—he didn't think sleep was possible.

The next thing he knew, he was waking up to Elaina's voice saying, "We're here."

As Roberto backed out of the driveway, he looked both ways down their street. He didn't recognize the car parked two blocks down. He left in the opposite direction Elaina had taken, just to drive past that vehicle. He glanced as he went by but saw no one in it. *I'm just being paranoid.* He watched it from the rear-view mirror, just in case. It didn't move.

Roberto pulled into the parking lot of his favorite restaurant. It was just after closing time. He parked at the far end of the lot, where there weren't any cars. Grabbing his comm-pad, he reached in his shirt pocket and pulled out Ranger Dan's business card. He typed in a code that was scribbled on the back.

There was no response, not even after a few minutes. He wasn't sure if Ranger Dan would check his PID after-hours. He had to know what risks he was facing. He was about to put the comm-pad away when a response came in. All it said was [RANDAN. SECURE?]

Roberto responded, [BIG D, SECURE. RISK ASSESSMENT] and waited. The screen eventually read, [RISK LOW NOW, HIGH IN AM. PRESS MADE SBS&R RIG. EXPECT TO BE TRACKED. UPS WON'T PROTECT TARZAN. WORKING ON IT. HAVE YOU CONTACTED SAFE HOUSE?]

Roberto thought about the ramifications, then responded, [NO. WILL IN ONE HOUR.]

Ranger Dan replied, [FINE. MAKE ARRANGEMENTS. THEY WILL CONFIRM WITH ME. NEED NO MORE COMM FROM YOU. RANDAN OUT.]

Roberto responded, [THANKS. BIG D OUT.] He started his vehicle and headed toward the freeway.

CHAPTER TWO

Henley Park was a quiet place late on a Saturday night. During the day, it was a popular trailhead with restrooms and picnic areas for day hikers. But there was no camping allowed, and it was too far from a highway to be used as a rest area.

Elaina drove straight to the parking spots designated for emergency personnel. The tower provided water for fire fighting, so out of respect, she didn't park directly under it. She went to her usual spot to the left of the tower, more out of habit than necessity.

She recalled assisting on a minor rescue here. Some tourists got turned around after straying off the main trail. Search and Rescue located the hikers with the drone and directed them to the right trail. Tonight was her first time here without the drone in the trailer. It felt strange. She unbuckled her seat belt. "Did you get some sleep?"

"I think so," Arcon responded. "How long since we were at the house?"

"Let me see." Elaina checked her comm-pad screen. "It's ten after nine."

"I'm not sure how long that is."

She thought about that. "How do you usually tell time?"

"I look at the sun or my grandma's cuckoo clock. Sometimes a sundial."

"Oh, okay. About an hour ago."

"Oh ... yes, I slept."

"Let's get out and stretch." Elaina opened her door, got out, and did exactly that as Arcon slowly crawled out of the back. She pointed to the other side of the parking area. "Those are porta potties by those other cars if you need to use one."

"What are ..."

"Sorry, I mean, toilets." Elaina watched Arcon as he stretched his arms up as high as he could. Then he leaped in the air over and over. When he finished that, he reached one hand down to the ground and then stood up. Then the other hand. Then the first hand again. She scrunched her face and asked, "What *are* you doing?"

"I'm stretching."

"It looks like some kind of routine."

"Well, yeah, it's part of an exercise thing us hunters do."

"Explain."

"Well, we have different exercises for different activities. We call the first one I did Reach for the Branch. The next one was Jump for the Branch."

"That makes sense. But I don't get the last one."

Arcon laughed. "That one is called Pick Up Your Machete."

"Ha, I get it. Are there more?"

"See if you can figure this one out." Arcon alternately pumped his arms and legs while looking toward the sky. He stopped and asked, "Do you get it?"

"Uhh, no."

"I'll do it again. Watch my hands."

Elaina watched closely. She noticed his hands were cupped. "You're climbing a tree!"

"Astute observation," he joked.

"Any more?"

Arcon looked around. The last car was leaving the parking lot. "I rarely do this one in front of other people. Try to guess what it is." He held his arms straight out from his side, then began walking in a meandering line while thrusting his shoulders and hips in different directions. Halfway across the parking lot, he stopped, turned back toward Elaina, and did the same thing in her direction. "Are you going to guess?"

She had no idea. "Are you trying to attract a female monkey?"

Arcon threw his hands in the air. "We don't have monkeys in our jungle."

Elaina hugged her belly and bent over laughing. "Do it again."

"That's not happening. We call that one Walk the Branch. It helps us limber up. If the ground wasn't so hard, I'd show you the one we call Fall Off the Branch."

Elaina's body convulsed as the tears streamed down her face. She hadn't laughed this hard in years. "Are all the Mojave People as funny as you?" she asked.

Arcon's laughter slowed to a stop. He turned away from her and stared toward the lake. *I messed that up*, she thought. *I should have called them ArcPoint.* Trying to recover, she said, "Dad should get here soon, I hope."

She saw him look at his surroundings. He walked out into the middle of the parking lot. He looked up at the sky and said, "It may seem obvious to you, but those are our stars out there. I recognize them. I see the big and small ladle, the snake, the coyote footprint, and the goat's head. I remember Jarden pointing them out to me as a child. I haven't seen this many of them for a long time."

"Why, were they blocked by the trees?"

"No, I was asleep. We always sleep at night unless we have a night job. Besides, the stars never change. If they do, the sky watchers let us know, and then we look. Here it's different. There are so many more stars to see at once." Arcon looked at Elaina and asked, "What are you thinking?"

Elaina didn't want to tell Arcon what she was thinking. She hadn't seen her dad this concerned and tight-lipped since her mom died. Whatever this trouble in their life was, her dad probably wouldn't talk with her about it until the moment was right. She looked up at the stars and made small talk.

Roberto's world was spinning out of control. Not a single thing had gone according to plan this entire weekend. He'd known it would be dramatic but had expected Arcon to be in the custody of the authorities for his own safety and theirs. All he'd wanted to do was to ensure the Rift crossing didn't have a traumatic effect on his daughter. Right now, those two should be miles apart; her at home in bed, Arcon at a Containment Center. They'd visit Arcon until judgment was passed on his future. Hiding from the Authorities was not part of the plan.

He tried to force the arrest scenarios out of his mind. No one was in trouble for anything yet, and with the help of Ranger Dan's connection, they should be able to transition Arcon into modern society. In a few hours, he'd turn Arcon over to a complete stranger for protection. Elaina would insist on sticking by Arcon's side. That was the way she operated.

Whenever they rescued someone, Roberto would deal with the apparatus, the paperwork, and the authorities. His daughter would stick by the rescued people until the last moment. In that respect, she was very much like her grandfather, focused on the needs of the hurting individual, not on the paycheck.

He had to remind himself Elaina was old enough, and capable enough, to take care of herself. He trusted Ranger Dan, and he was beginning to trust Arcon. He'd find out soon if he could trust this stranger at the safe house. But ultimately, he'd put his faith in God to alert him to danger.

As long as he continued to have inner peace about the decision, he'd allow this current path to continue. He'd return to work in the morning as if nothing had happened and hope nothing ever would. If word got out, all he could do was take the blame for allowing it to happen.

He glanced down to see how fast he was driving and eased off the accelerator again. He wasn't far from the Park and didn't need the Traffic Flow Sensors spotting his vehicle ID chip. Any other time, the TFS units were his friend, easing traffic ahead so he could cruise without lights and sirens. But they would also verify the emergency with Rescue dispatch, and in this case, he didn't want that to happen.

Roberto was in a hurry to talk to his daughter and quiet her fears. She was the type of person who could bury her natural reactions in order to complete an arduous task. But he'd discovered the hard way that Elaina had a breaking point if pushed too far. Better to pry feelings out of her than to wrap her in protection. Arcon wasn't capable of looking out for Elaina's best interests. At least, not right now.

His foot grew heavier on the accelerator again.

Arcon rested his hands on the steering wheel of the autocycle. Elaina sat in the back, describing what all the dials and instruments were for. She was explaining how the foot pedals worked, when the headlights of a car flashed in the window. Arcon was feeling around, trying to find the door handle, just as Roberto pulled up alongside them. A pair of wide eyes stared at them as they crawled out of the little car.

Roberto lowered his window. "You are *not* letting him drive!"

Elaina stifled a laugh. Her dad looked serious. "Oh no, Daddy, of course not. Arcon just wanted to know how I did it. He told me his people don't have cars, just a lot of parts."

"Okay. Good. No offense, Arcon, but driving is not as easy as it looks."

"I understand," said Arcon. "It seems at least as difficult as picking fruit while swinging on a rope through the trees."

"You got that right," said Roberto. "And slamming into a hunk of steel is a lot worse than falling into sticker bushes." His brow furrowed. "You two get in. I'll fill you in on what little I know. I'm afraid you may not like it."

With his wife gone, Ranger Dan went to bed early. But after nodding off fitfully a few times, he rolled out of bed, moved to his favorite recliner, sat in the dark, and prayed.

As the authority, he had jurisdiction over the public lands of San Bernardino County outside of city limits. That included the Calneva Rift and the Mojave Forest. It was a lot of land to govern but involved very few people until yesterday. One solitary person had crossed the Rift, turning Dan's world upside-down. It troubled him.

His actions today transgressed the laws regarding the Mojave People, laid down over a hundred years earlier by Central Authority. As a child growing up within miles of the Mojave Forest, adults had drilled those rules into him. No one was to cross the Calneva Rift. Jesus himself declared the entire Mojave National Preserve off-limits to everyone other than the Mojave People. Where the Rift didn't block access, the basic rule was, if you could see the Acacia trees, you were too close.

Dan recalled the Bible verse in Hosea, a verse people believed applied to the Mojave People: "*For this reason I will fence her in with thorn bushes. I will block her path with a wall to make her lose her way.*" The thorns across the Rift were blatantly obvious to anyone with a pair of binoculars, and the Rift did block everyone's path like a wall.

He reminded himself once again he hadn't broken the rules Jesus had laid down. His rules didn't restrict the Mojave People to their area. Humans required the detainment of anyone whose feet touched that soil, but his service was to the highest authority.

He leaned back in the recliner, clasped his hands behind his head, and closed his eyes.

As a young man, he'd yearned to know what was across that Rift, even thought that one day he'd formally petition Jesus to enter it. Now he was in authority over that area, tasked with keeping people out, including himself. Ironically, that daunting responsibility had allowed him to make the request of a lifetime—permission to use a drone to fly over the Mojave—and explore the area without touching his feet to the soil. The perfect compromise.

He'd faithfully followed all of man's rules regarding the restricted area until he saw a young man teetering across the Rift. Then the Mojave man's safety was his only concern. Rules never came to mind—they'd fallen by the wayside until that reporter questioned him. Now he prayed for guidance. *Did I break the rules out of rebellion, or had my response to help the Mojave man been prompted by the Holy Spirit?*

Dan wasn't comfortable with formal prayer. He preferred talking with God throughout the day while going through his normal routine. While he shaved in the morning, he'd ask what the day would bring. During breakfast, he'd ask for wisdom and guidance. On his drive to work, he'd ask God to open his eyes and keep him alert.

Throughout the day, he thanked God for life itself, and for the ability to be aware of it, and aware of Him. Prayer had become so automatic; he wondered now if he'd forgotten it yesterday. He must have. He'd received no warning in his spirit as to the disruption his actions would cause. Now he was at a loss to know how to correct the situation.

CHAPTER THREE

Elaina walked around to the driver's side of her dad's Search and Rescue Vehicle. "I am not getting in your SRV until you get out and give me a hug."

Roberto clambered out of his seat and into her waiting arms. "Oh, girl, I'm so sorry."

"You should be," she said. "You didn't even say "Hi" when you got home. What's got you so flustered?"

He kissed the top of her head. "Get in, and I'll tell you about it. Arcon, you can get in the back seat."

Arcon got in while Elaina ran around to the passenger side. When they were all in their seats, Roberto said, "You're probably both wondering why I called this meeting," hoping a little levity would soften the news he was about to share.

"I know I am," said Elaina. "What's going on?"

"Well, to start with, I've had people asking me about the tightrope walking kid. I gave them a lot of 'No Comments.' Some asked if walking a rope was an official Search and Rescue technique."

"What did you tell them?" asked Elaina.

"No comment. Then I had a reporter pestering me back at the Ranger station."

"A real reporter?" asked Elaina. "I had a lady reporter bugging me last Friday when I was studying the Rift."

"You did? You didn't tell me about that," said Roberto.

"Well, it was just small talk about the Rift. When she said she was a reporter, it made me nervous. I left."

"Wonder if it was the same person. What did she look like? Short with Asian features and—"

"With dark reddish hair?" added Elaina.

"Exactly."

"Natural, not colored?"

"I didn't look that close, but it was pretty. Well, anyway, it took a long time to get out of there, but nobody tried to stop me. Then, as I'm driving down the freeway, I get this text from Ranger Dan. I'd given him a secure code so he could text my PID, and it said, 'Hide Tarzan NOW.' I tried to call you right away but didn't get an answer."

"Sorry about that," Elaina moaned.

"Well, never mind that now. Dan's text told me to keep in touch and keep it secure. I didn't like the sound of that at all. I kept trying to get through to you, but to be honest, I didn't know what to tell you if I would have. Anyway, a while later, I got another text. That one said he had a location for us and gave me a code to another secure PID."

"Have you connected with that number yet?"asked Elaina.

"No, not yet. I was too focused on getting home, and I wanted to discuss it with you two first. I was concerned that a certain reporter was figuring out who I was and where I lived. I felt we needed to get out of there quickly and go anywhere. When you left, I watched to make sure no one followed you, then hid in Mama Rose's parking lot to contact Ranger Dan."

"I like Ranger Dan," said Arcon from the back seat.

"And well you should," said Roberto. "He saved your hide once, and now it sounds like he may risk his job to do it again."

Elaina tapped her dad's arm. "Were you able to get through to Ranger Dan?"

"I did. I asked him for a risk assessment of our situation. He said the risk was low tonight but would be high in the morning.

He didn't say why. I'm not sure if that's because of the reporter, the authorities, or SBS&R. More than likely, it will be all three. Something's bound to happen in the morning when people show up for work. It depends on what that reporter does."

"Why is that?" asked Arcon.

"If she waits till she gets official news, we're fine. But if she broadcasts that a Mojave person is out roaming the streets ... we just don't know how the public will respond."

Elaina poked her dad again. "Was there anything else?"

"He said upper management with the Rangers won't protect Arcon, so we're on our own. He's working on an official solution, but for now, I think the two of you should wait at the safe house until further notice."

"So where is this safe house, and who runs it?" asked Elaina.

"I don't know that yet. All we can do is trust the Ranger. But before I call, I want you both to be prepared to do this without me. The best thing for me to do right now is go to work this morning as if nothing happened. I need to make the drone available for sure. But I also want to be there if any trouble brews over my having flashed my badge at the Rift. I think I can run interference for you best from the office."

"Are you going to be in much trouble?" asked Elaina.

"I think there are extenuating circumstances that'll benefit me. I'm sure this could go all the way to the Judges, but I have faith in the system. The question right now is, do we trust Ranger Dan and whatever solution he's come up with? Or do something on our own, like camp somewhere? I say we contact this person and then decide."

"I say we trust Dan," said Arcon. "I have a peace inside of me about him."

"I agree with you both," said Elaina. "Let's call this person."

Ranger Dan sat in the darkness of his den, trying to listen for an answer from God. A little guidance would sure help. The silence should have at least allowed him to relax and get some sleep, but it made him nervous.

When he had issues that troubled him, he'd usually share them with his wife. She seemed to have an especially close relationship with God. But tonight, she was visiting her sister in Oregon, unaware of the day's events. He let his mind drift. One thought kept recurring. He was hungry. His stomach growled as if agreeing.

In all the commotion, he'd missed lunch, and without his wife, there was no dinner waiting. It was time for a late-night snack.

Dan climbed out of the recliner and walked to the refrigerator, pulled out his uneaten sandwich from lunch, and poured himself a glass of milk. At the kitchen table, he unwrapped the sandwich and just stared at it. He thanked God for providing it and then realized; had he taken the time to eat it sooner, he may have sought God's help sooner—maybe lived the day with a little more wisdom.

Midway to his first bite, he heard a voice say, "Do you mind if I share that with you?"

Ranger Dan froze. Just as quickly, his spirit was flooded with peace. He didn't need to see the intruder's face. Dan stammered out the first thought that came to mind, "You ... you want to share my sandwich?"

Jesus smiled at him and took a seat in one of the kitchen chairs. "I was referring to the burden you're carrying."

Dan choked back his emotion, even as he felt a weight lifted off his shoulders. It may have been his imagination, but his worries felt like they'd literally been weighing him down. He hung his head and said, "I'm sorry, Lord."

"Can you tell me what it is you're sorry for?" Jesus asked. "Do you know what it is I called you to do? Did you disobey that call? Do you know why I'm here?"

Dan realized he couldn't answer a single one of His questions. Dan opened his mouth to speak, but nothing he could say seemed adequate.

"Dan, listen to me. My sheep make laws for others in my flock to follow. I said *my* laws would be in your heart. Arcon, the one you call Tarzan, is my child. I have guided him to you for a purpose. You were faithful to my Spirit as you cared for him."

Dan trembled with emotion as Jesus spoke. He'd only seen Jesus once before, at a gathering of the judges and authorities. He remembered the awe and respect he'd felt to be in the physical presence of the Creator of all things. As a newly appointed authority, he'd been told to expect a personal visitation if it was warranted. None of that had prepared him for this moment. "How can I serve you, Lord?"

"You've already served me well," Jesus responded. "Since you were a child, I have called you for a specific purpose. Tonight that calling will end."

Dan didn't know what to think. Even more perplexing, he didn't know how to feel. He'd failed Jesus somehow. His heart was nearly pounding out of his chest in anticipation of what Jesus would say next. He wanted to respond, to encourage him to continue, but he couldn't speak.

Jesus hesitated for only a moment. "Who gave you dominion over the Mojave?"

Dan didn't know how to answer, but he knew one was expected. "The County of San Bernardino did?" As soon as the words left his mouth, he felt foolish.

"The County of San Bernardino gave you authority," Jesus replied, "but I give you dominion. This is the purpose I called you to and is now complete. From this point on, I am sending you. I need you to stand firm for the land and for the people of the ArcPoint Community. You are to serve them as you serve me."

"I ... I'm honored, Lord. But I don't know how to serve them."

"Arcon is their ambassador. I will give him the wisdom to help you, Dan, as I gave Joseph, Daniel, and Moses wisdom to help their rulers and the people of the land. Do not fear what men can do or say. Just seek my face as you have need, and my Spirit will guide you." Jesus looked at the sandwich, still suspended in Dan's trembling hand. "That looks good, though. Now eat and get some rest. Your days will be full."

Dan hung his head and stared at the sandwich. He couldn't bring himself to take a bite, even though he was still hungry. As Jesus had spoken, Dan's mind had filled with a sequence of visions. He'd seen the Forest, Arcon, a large group of people, and other various places and events. The images had swept through his mind so fast he'd had no time to fully comprehend each one.

The visions regarded the future, that much he knew. They certainly weren't memories. Somehow, he knew understanding would come. Dan looked up to say something to Jesus, but his chair was empty. And so was the glass of milk.

CHAPTER FOUR

Roberto opened the console of his SRV and grabbed his comm-pad. He located the PID code Ranger Dan had given him and copied it into a new message. "I'm sending a request for contact. If Ranger Dan gave me a good number, whoever gets this will see my Search and Rescue handle on his PID. He should acknowledge, if we've got the right person."

Arcon tapped Elaina on the shoulder and whispered, "What does that mean?"

"The person getting Daddy's message should know it's coming. Whoever this person is must trust Ranger Dan a lot. Hope this works."

Roberto heard a familiar chirp in his ear and said, "We got a response." He looked at his comm-pad to see the message. All it said was [TARZAN SECURE?] "It looks like we have the right person," said Roberto. "He's looking for Tarzan."

"I sure can't wait to find out why people call me Tarzan," said Arcon. "Or maybe I don't want to know."

"Don't worry about it, Arcon," said Roberto. "You just remind us of something from a long time ago. But they're fond memories."

"And everybody has those memories?"

"Pretty much."

Arcon looked over Roberto's shoulders. "He wants to know if I'm secure?"

"No, he's asking if the connection is secure before he relays any sensitive information. Okay, I sent a message that said, [HAVE PACKAGE FOR YOU.]"

Elaina looked at Arcon. "We have an encryption tool in the PID that scrambles the message before it sends, so only these two devices can communicate. Most people respect the privacy of others, but we're dealing with the press here. They believe it's their duty to investigate others."

"Okay, here's his response," said Roberto. "It says, [HAVE RABBIT HOLE RESERVED. SHIP 2 BBL SURVIVAL]. I wonder what that means."

They grew silent for a minute. Elaina blurted out, "I know what that is, Dad. When I was scoping out the Rift on the maps, looking for a way for Arcon to cross it, I saw this business pop up called Big Bear Lake Survivalist Camp. Do a search for it."

Roberto connected to the Web and typed in BBL Survival. "Looks like you're right." He clicked on a link for the camp.

They read about a survivalist enclave made of shipping containers buried in the ground. "It appears people fled to this place during the Tribulation and then abandoned it later. Someone is now renting out space in these containers so people can experience the survivalist mentality of yesteryear. The only things visible above ground are the holes for entering the containers."

"Rabbit holes!" exclaimed Elaina.

Roberto tapped away on his comm-pad. "I'm checking to see if there's another one available." After a few minutes, he heard the chirp and checked the message. "It appears there's another hole for you, Elaina, so you two will have separate quarters. You'll be able to sleep better that way." *And so will I.* "Let me confirm we have everything correct." He typed [TARZAN AND JANE SEPARATELY CONTAINED?]

They waited a few moments, then saw the response, [AFFIRMATIVE. ARRIVE AFTER 8AM. NORMALCY. OUT.] Roberto responded with, [ACK'D, OUT.]

"Well, it sounds like you two are in excellent hands," said Roberto. "They want you to show up after 8 AM, which must be the earliest check-in time. If it's near Big Bear Lake, that's a long drive for me, but I see why Ranger Dan chose it. It's in his jurisdiction, not all that far from his Ranger Station, and completely isolated from the public. He probably has a direct line of communication already established with the owner, so no one would get suspicious."

"Dad, can you bring up a map and plot the course for us?"

He started tapping and swiping his finger on the comm-pad. "Okay, I'll put in Henley Park, destination Big Bear Lake Survivalist Camp. Directions. Oh, that's simple. Just go down the hill here and hit Highway 138, then take that to Highway 18. Follow 18 until it meets with Highway 330. See that? Looks like the spot you're looking for is somewhere near that intersection. Hopefully, there are signs."

Elaina studied the map closely. "Dad, I'd like to stop and get Arcon some more clothes. There should be stores near the intersection of 210 and 330 in Highland. Do you think that'd be okay? I could take I-15 or 330 and then drop down Highway 18. He needs something to wear besides the Ranger's baggy pants."

"Oh, yeah, you're right. But I don't know about going to regular stores. Remember, he has no ID. A lot of stores are membership only, and you have to scan to get in. Why not just go to one of the resell shops? The clothes are cheap, so you could grab some quick and get out. If it doesn't fit, so what? You could probably find a suitcase there, too. Make him look touristy."

"That's a great idea," she said. "Search for a Shop Again in Highland." She waited as her dad tapped away at the comm-pad. "Oh, good. See, there is one. It's a little ways off of 210, but I can find it."

Roberto brought up their website. "They open at 8 AM on Mondays. That'll put you late at the Survival Camp, but that should be okay. Besides, you need some sleep, girl. Don't want you doing that while you're driving."

Elaina chuckled. "You either, Dad."

"How about if we car camp here for the night?" asked Roberto. "We'll recline the seat in your car for Arcon. You can join me here in my car. But I'll need to kick you out by 5 AM."

"At this point, I'll take anything I can get," said Elaina, yawning.

"Sounds good," said Roberto. "If you get to the Shop Again at 8 AM, shop a while, then go straight to the Camp, you should get there before 10 AM. I'll send this guy a message to let him know."

Noreena Chan sat at her dining room table, scrutinizing tidbits of information. She'd printed off the info-net what she could find about the Mojave People, circling words like "survivalists" and "religious cult." She'd found the names, Lee Franklin and Dr. Norman Ashford. She circled them.

She grabbed another handful of papers she'd stapled together. The top page outlined the official action by Central Authority establishing the Mojave Restricted Area. It didn't amount to more than half a page. Central Authority had extended the existing Mojave National Preserve to the Rift, then closed the area, allowing only those who currently lived there to be in the area.

The rest of the papers concerned the Act of Congress establishing the Mojave Preserve in 1994. She would need to read that in order to understand its original boundaries. People complained the Mojave People were building too *close* to the Preserve, not *in* it. If that were true, then they should be located somewhere *between* the old Preserve and the Rift. That was the best theory she could come up with.

She'd hit a dead end with San Bernardino Search and Rescue. None of their crew had been involved with any operation at the Rift. It was not contrary to policy for employees to use SBS&R vehicles for personal use, though. Whoever these searchers were, they'd been on their own time. *Gone rogue, maybe.*

Noreena had one resource as a member of the press. She knew all government vehicles were monitored by time and location. Every place that vehicle had traveled—as well as its speed—could be discovered. All she needed was a legitimate cause, which she lacked at the moment. But if she could discover with any certainty that there'd been a violation of the Mojave restriction, she'd have all the authority she needed.

Authority. That was a tricky aspect to getting this story. Alert the authorities too soon, and they'd react publicly—every news agency would be onto her story. This news could be explosive enough to get everyone's attention—and she wanted to be the one to break it.

Ranger Dan Wilson. Another confusing element. As the authority over this area, wouldn't he be the one to provide answers and give her information? He'd seemed so friendly in the observation tower, but now he wouldn't even speak to her.

The girl in the blue autocycle. Mystery number three. The more she thought about that girl, the more she was convinced the Mojave man left with her in that little vehicle. *Snuck him right past me, I'll bet. That girl could very well be the key to finding that man, and he was key to what the world wanted to know—how dangerous are the Mojave People? Is there evil across that Rift?* She was certain the big story—human interest or otherwise—pivoted around those people.

CHAPTER FIVE

Jarden stood alone in apartment number twelve, where Arcon had lived until his twenty-seventh year. In the ArcPoint Community, there were always at least two people who had the job of dividing the belongings of a recently deceased person. First was the nearest of kin to that individual since they now owned that property. Second was the Chief of Procurement, who handled resources for the Community. Whatever the kin didn't want would need to be divided amongst others.

Jarden was fulfilling both jobs since he was the designated guardian of Arcon. It would be difficult to do alone, but not because it was a big job. Nobody in the Community owned many personal items. He simply didn't believe Arcon was dead. He hoped he would return someday. He wanted to leave the apartment the way it was—preserved for that day. He'd told the elders to do just that, but they'd insisted the Community needed to move on. So, here he stood, staring at what remained of Arcon's history.

Through the years, he'd spent as much time in the Franklin family log home as he had in his own, and had helped Arcon move out of it after his grandmother died. He wanted the Community to turn the home into a museum, but that wasn't practical since the Room of Remembrance already served that purpose.

Not many years before that, he'd helped Arcon deal with the tragic passing of his parents. It was a time of loss and guilt for him and Arcon. On that fateful day, both had been swinging in the forest when sounds of an explosion rumbled through the trees. It had taken eight men to keep Arcon and Jarden away from the chemistry lab.

Death may have been instant for Zoreb and Sasha Franklin, but it was the most painful loss the Community had ever experienced. Jarden doubted anyone in the Community beyond Arcon revisited that pain as often as he did. He'd lost his two best friends that day.

Now, as Chief of the Procurement Division, it was Jarden's job to assign living quarters. Two different young men had requested Arcon's apartment. One was Raymo, who at twenty-five should be first in line. But he and Arcon had never had a good relationship. Raymo was a staunch Separatist like his parents, who believed the ArcPoint Community should remain isolated. Arcon had always been on the far opposite end of that argument.

Jarden knew there'd been a more powerful conflict separating them. Raymo had his sights on Brina Ashford, but she'd never had feelings for him. Raymo most likely blamed Arcon for that, since he and Brina had been friends their whole life. For the entire history of ArcPoint, the Franklin and Ashford families had been close, even setting up their tiny homes near each other. *Sorry, Raymo. You'll just have to wait for another apartment.*

Tawny was the other young man needing his own place. He was still a teenager, but Jarden knew Arcon wouldn't have minded losing his apartment to him. Tawny wanted to be like Arcon, even begged to train as a hunter way before he was old enough. If the Community wouldn't honor Arcon and preserve his apartment, Tawny would.

Yes, normal procedure was for family to make decisions like this, but Arcon had none. So Jarden had taken a leave of absence to take care of the matter himself. He'd look through everything in the apartment and be emotional for Arcon—his self-appointed god-son.

Most things could stay for the next occupant. Tawny would appreciate the extra-long bed. Jarden had built this bed for Arcon—fashioned from Acacia branches. He set it up and surprised him with it one day. Brina wove extra-long blankets for Arcon soon after. Jarden picked up one of the blankets and stared at the bed. It almost seemed sacrilegious to let someone else use these. He folded them—they would keep. The other bedding and furniture were less meaningful—all there when Arcon had moved in.

There were quite a few books. The largest stack would go to the Clive Barrows Electrical Library, the rest to the main library. Jarden bagged Arcon's clothing and decided to have them washed. He'd keep them in his own apartment. *Someday, son, you'll want these back. I'm sure of it.*

Arcon had left behind a lot of memorabilia, most of which had belonged to his parents. Jarden carefully sorted through every item. There were things the Community needed to keep in memory of the Franklin family. Those items would be submitted to the committee in charge of the Room of Remembrance.

On a closet shelf, he found a notebook. Jarden scanned through it and realized he was glancing through Zoreb Franklin's random thoughts and notes regarding his work in the chemistry lab. His wife, Sasha, had added some notes as well. He decided to give the notebook to the lab for their library. Arcon wouldn't mind.

Certain items had deep meaning for Jarden himself. He put those in a separate sack to keep in his own apartment.

Then there were those items he knew Arcon cherished. On the nightstand, his grandma's old Bible. Tucked away in the closet, he found a small pile of partially polished rocks. Arcon had made them for his grandma over the years and reclaimed them when she'd died. *He'll want these stones back if he ever returns to ArcPoint.* Jarden took them to keep in his own apartment. Someday, he'd let Arcon decide what he'd want back.

Then there was the matter of two tables worth of assorted electronic parts. The existence of these components had intensified the controversy once again about contacting the outside world. There'd been a recent discussion with the Elders about the crystal radio and transmitter. It had been a close vote, but the consensus was, these pieces should be rendered inoperable.

Jarden had caused an outright uproar when he'd suggested they be included in the Room of Remembrance. It'd hurt to hear some elders state that Arcon himself shouldn't be remembered, let alone honored. But, as their Chief of Procurement, all unclaimed material fell under his jurisdiction. He'd keep the radio and transmitter as a memorial in his own apartment. The rest could go back to the Electrical Division.

Last of all, Arcon's hunter's gear. He'd divide these items between Chad and Tawny. Chad was one hunter who truly understood Arcon. Tawny, on the other hand, had only been Arcon's partner for a short time, but that was all it had taken for Tawny to want to emulate him. He was more like Arcon than any of the other hunters, including his being a tall boy. Tawny would put Arcon's tools to good use and may even come to appreciate being mentored by a short old man, as Arcon had.

"Do you have everything you need?" asked Roberto, at ten after five in the morning. He yawned.

"Yes, dad. You better get moving. Don't worry about us; we'll stay out of sight until we hear from you or Ranger Dan. And I mean it, Dad. *Don't worry.*"

"I promise, baby girl. If I start to worry, I'll start to pray. You do the same."

"I will, Dad, for certain," she said, hugging him.

"Me too, Mr. Roberto," added Arcon, shaking his hand.

Roberto got into his SRV and backed out of the parking spot. He turned and looked at his daughter standing with someone who, technically, she'd only met yesterday. Why he felt comfortable leaving his only daughter in a remote place with this stranger, God only knew.

The more he thought about it, the more he wanted to text the Survival Camp to reserve a container for himself as well. But those thoughts gave him no peace at all. He prayed, "Father, once again, I turn this situation over to you. I'm sorry I keep having to do that, but she's all I have." The prayer didn't stop him from worrying about her, but it diminished the weightiness of protecting her all by himself.

On their way to the community of Highlands, Elaina stuck with a fast-food drive-thru for breakfast so they could nod off for a few minutes in the parking lot. The thrift store called Shop Again didn't open until 8 AM, and they were both dog-tired, Elaina dangerously so. It was only a couple of hours of sleep, but it did the trick.

It was a unique experience taking Arcon shopping. It was the first large public building she'd taken him in, and nobody knew who he was or seemed to care. Elaina appreciated the anonymity, but it made her nervous the way Arcon would stare at people, presumably at what they were wearing or at their different hairstyles.

His first choices for clothes were very colorful, and Elaina had to explain, quietly, that only females wore skirts. She got what they needed quickly and got out of there.

They found a good suitcase at the Shop Again, but Arcon was uncomfortable carrying it. He preferred one of the backpacks, but Elaina thought it would attract too much attention. They'd settled on a duffel bag and clothes to fill it. Elaina also found Arcon a cheap watch but saved taking time to explain how it worked until later. Arcon waited in the autocycle while she ran into a department store to get him other essentials like a toothbrush, shaver, and the most difficult of all, underwear. She realized how self-sufficient her dad was in some scenarios.

When she climbed back into the autocycle, she learned Arcon would prefer to do some things himself, when he asked, "When will I be able to get my own things?"

She answered, "You'll need to get officially recognized by the authorities. Then they'll set you up with an exchange account, and you can start filling it with credits. When you go into a store, you exchange the credits for what you need."

"How'll I get these credits?"

"Usually, people have jobs performing some kind of work, and credits get put in their account for doing it."

"How do I get a job?"

Elaina could tell by Arcon's tone that something was troubling him. She wished she had a suitable answer but thought his needs might go deeper than simple employment. Taking a guess, she asked, "Are you wanting to know when you can get out on your own?"

Arcon squeezed Elaina's shoulder from the back seat. "I'm not looking to get away from you," he said. "I just want to provide for myself and for others if I can."

"Oh, okay," said Elaina. "Try not to worry about that too much. It'll take some time, but it's a painless process. We have identification centers that scan you for uniqueness, and that information gets logged into a centrally accessed database." She watched from the rearview mirror as Arcon's brow furrowed, then scowled. "Is something wrong?"

"Do I have to get some kind of mark?"

"What do you mean?"

"In the Bible, it said people had to get a mark to buy or sell, and it was an evil thing."

"Oh, I understand," she said with a smile. "No, not at all. Jesus killed the Beast."

Arcon's eyes went wide. "He did what?"

Elaina started up the car. "The Beast was a covert worldwide system of control. I guess it made sense at the time, since no one could profit from criminal behavior or squander resources, which was happening a lot, long ago. In reality, Satan was using world leaders to control the physical world, pulling strings behind it all. When Jesus came, he shut Satan down. He didn't kill Satan, but he removed him and his demons from this world. Satan doesn't control things anymore. Didn't you know any of that?"

Arcon settled back in his seat and buckled up as they pulled out of the parking lot. "I'm figuring out that we in ArcPoint missed out on a lot of things." He stared out the window. "If Satan controlled being marked, why do you still do it?"

"People don't get marked. They're just scanned for unique things God created us with, like fingerprints or facial features. The mark of the Beast was what humans created to identify everything, including people. Then Satan maneuvered people he controlled into positions of authority in government. But he didn't do it all at once. He started with little things."

"Like what?" asked Arcon.

"Well, I guess it started with some kind of electronic tag that alerted when someone tried to steal something from a store."

Arcon nodded to himself. "We had some of those tags in the Room of Remembrance. They were on the packages."

"Right. Then they injected them into their pets so they could be located if they ran away. There were also numbers and stripes placed on everything, so each item was uniquely identified. Eventually, everything was tracked and identified in the same way, including humans."

"What's different now?"

"Now, everything is recognized for what it is. Cameras and computers see what you're buying and see who you are. Some things have ID tags, but not humans. The most important thing is, it all has to be managed by someone who isn't corruptible. Only Jesus could do that."

Arcon leaned forward to hear Elaina better over the road noise. "All by himself?" he asked.

"No. He gets help from the First Resurrected. You know, the ones who died for Him during the tribulation times. There's nothing you can offer people like that to do something against the law. God gives them a lot of wisdom and discernment, so they make judgments fast. We refer to them as Central Authority."

"Hmmm. Wow. So how would I become part of this system?"

"There are official scanning locations for that," she replied. "Your face gets scanned, your eyes, your fingerprints. First time around, it's complicated, but after that, it's easy. We just need to get a new face scan every so often. We also get a card we can hand to other people like friends or dependents that lets them buy things with our credits."

"What if you don't have any credits?"

"Then you'll just have to be a nice person," said Elaina, turning onto the main highway. "People give each other credits all the time. As soon as you get your ID, we'll give you some credits to get going, and we trust others will help as well. Then we'll see about a job for you and all that. But right now, we need to hide you until we can figure out how to start the process correctly."

CHAPTER SIX

Ranger Dan awoke with a start, assuming he'd overslept because he felt completely rested. He couldn't have slept over four hours tops, though. He pivoted to look at the clock. He'd beat the alarm by six minutes. He spent those extra minutes thanking God for giving him the rest he needed for the day that faced him.

At 10 AM, he was scheduled for a teleconference with his superiors regarding the escapee from the Mojave Forest. Before that happened, he hoped to receive a message from Big Bear Lake Survivalist Camp. He needed confirmation that Tarzan and Jane had arrived. Besides the Camp, only he and Roberto knew where they were. He hadn't even told Ranger Becca yet. He'd do that this morning. Dan's intention was to keep it a secret until he could come up with an acceptable integration plan.

His decision to use the Camp was perfect. He'd be able to inform his superiors that Arcon, the young man who'd emerged from the Mojave Forest, was isolated from the public. Better yet, he could tell them Arcon was *contained*. As he thought about it, Dan realized Arcon was essentially quarantined. Somehow, he'd unintentionally done precisely what he was supposed to do, so long as Tarzan and Jane followed his instructions.

The Victorville offices of San Bernardino Search and Rescue seemed normal for a Monday morning. Evidently, no reporter had been poking around yet. Roberto went about his day like any other. If the subject of Arcon ever came up, he'd tell his superiors they'd discovered him while testing the drone.

Roberto would apologize for carrying out a rescue mission without first contacting the 24/7 dispatcher. He'd simply gotten caught up in the moment with his daughter, and worked with the Calneva Rift Ranger Station, since they were the local authority having jurisdiction for that area. All of that was true, more or less. He hoped Ranger Dan could come up with an official repatriation scheme for Arcon before the news services pounced on the story.

This would be a long day. Barely an hour had elapsed before he told a co-worker he was nervous for his daughter—she was on her first long-distance road trip to visit with a friend who'd suddenly become disoriented. That also was true, more or less. But the co-worker hadn't noticed he was nervous; he'd just blurted it out. That's the typical modus operandi for a guilty person, to state your alibi before someone asks you for it.

He dropped into his office chair and stared at the monitor of his computer. After a typical rescue, he'd normally input the information such as it was. There were fields for time spent, risk assessment, and materials used. There was additional info required if other agencies were involved and more regarding those who were rescued.

Roberto didn't enjoy doing paperwork, but he understood its value. That's how he earned credits to compensate him for time spent. In this case, he didn't need the compensation. He just wanted to know how to answer the questions. When was the call received? *I don't know, eight years ago?* Requestors ID. *Arcon doesn't have identification yet.* What SBS&R resources were used/consumed? *This one's easy. Drone 17B. Unauthorized use.*

What happened at the Rift could not be ignored, but Roberto saw no drop-down menu item for illegal Rift crossing.

He knew two things were likely to happen. He probably wouldn't receive any credits for the rescue, and the entire affair would need to be examined by the judges. His only saving grace would be Ranger Dan Wilson. As the Authority involved, he could alter the outcome.

Roberto stood up to look over the walls of his cubicle. Everything around him looked perfectly normal. *Why am I here?* He sat back down and shut down his computer. He could wait at home to be dispatched to a rescue. He could do paperwork there. And it would be a more comfortable place to worry about Elaina.

Elaina turned off Highway 18 into a rather busy tourist strip mall. There were shops for skiers, hikers, hunters, and fishermen. Nothing for survivalists, fugitives, or people who swung through trees for a living.

She double-checked with Arcon, and he remembered the same instructions, so they both scanned for the specific address. When they found it, all they saw was a small, nondescript real estate office. If this place wasn't correct, maybe someone there could provide directions.

As they got out of the autocycle, a large woman with short-cropped hair came out of the office carrying a box. She didn't resemble a realtor. Wearing bib overalls, a flannel shirt, and a camo jacket, she looked more comfortable than they were in the chilly mountain air. Elaina met her halfway to the pickup truck she was headed for. "Excuse me. We're looking for the Big Bear Lake Survivalist Camp."

The woman stopped in her tracks. "I know of it," she said.

"Is it around here?" Arcon wandered over.

"Not likely," she responded, setting the box in the back of the truck.

Sounds like she's having a bad day, Elaina thought. "I'm sorry to bother you, but our directions say it should be right here. Do you know how we might find it?"

"You'd probably have to ask the right person the right question."

Elaina thought about that and understood that wherever this place was, it was still off the mainstream radar. "The man we're looking for is supposed to know Ranger Dan Wilson. Does that help?"

"Well, that's certainly not the right person," the woman said.

"Is there someone in the real estate office?"

"Not at the moment. She's busy talking to someone."

This is going nowhere. How will we find this place? Elaina looked around the mall and the parking lot. They were the only people carrying on a conversation. She looked back at the realty office. *Security Real Estate.* "Wait. Are you the realtor?"

"That's me. How about if I ask you a question?"

"If you think it'll help, sure," Elaina answered timidly.

The woman looked at Elaina, then looked Arcon up and down and asked, "Are you Tarzan and Jane?"

Elaina was feeling set up, but she played along. "I've heard of them before, but who would you be?"

"My name is Patty Abrams, proprietor of the Big Bear Lake Survivalist Camp."

Coolly, Elaina said, "Never heard of you. Sorry, we'd better be going." She rounded for the autocycle and saw Arcon's look of confusion. Turning back to Patty, she added, "How did you know it was us?"

"I was told to watch for a blue autocycle with a trailer carrying a Hispanic girl and a tall, pasty-faced fellow. We don't get that combination up here very often."

When Elaina heard that statement, she knew it was Ranger Dan that had made the arrangements. Between relief and exhaustion, her eyes welled up. She walked up to Patty and hugged her.

Patty wrapped her arms around Elaina and hugged her hard enough to lift her toes off the ground. "Welcome to the Big Bear Hug Survival Camp, Jane." Then she went over to Arcon, who blinked, looking more confused than ever. "Do you want in on this action, big boy? I certainly have enough to go around."

Elaina grinned at Arcon. With her nod of approval, he walked up to Patty, and they hugged. The look in his eyes suggested he'd never been hugged like that before. Patty picked him up and walked him ten feet into the parking area. Then she let him down and said, "They named the lake after me."

"Really?" he answered.

Elaina laughed and said, "I can see we're in excellent hands."

"That I can guarantee," said Patty. She glanced around the parking lot. "Even better is where I'm going to hide you two. But let's not talk about that here. Come inside for a minute."

They followed Patty into the office. From the outside, the place had looked run down—the inside wasn't much better. With no furniture to speak of, they sat down on a ratty-looking sofa while Patty sat behind the only desk. "I need to tell Ranger Dan you're here. He's a tad worried."

She sat down at her comm-pad and read out loud what she typed. "Package has arrived. Ready to make deposit." She waited for a few moments and then read Dan's reply, "Perfect timing. RanDan out." She stabbed a key with her index finger.

"Okay, looks like we can take you to your new hole away from home. She chuckled at her own joke. "I can see you're anxious, but the Camp is still an hour's drive away. But if it were easy to get to, it wouldn't be secure. Just stay on my tail, and we'll get there."

Ranger Dan Wilson quick-stepped to the lunchroom to microwave his mug of coffee before the meeting started. When he returned, Ranger Becca was already in her seat with a clipboard, jotting something. She looked up. "Did you hear from Patty?"

"Just now." Dan sipped his coffee and exchanged a glance with Becca that spoke volumes. Neither one of them was looking forward to this meeting with their boss. He set his over-filled coffee on a coaster. "We're all set." He lowered his voice, even though he and Becca were the only ones in the room. "We better talk later."

"Great. Here comes Dwight."

"Sorry I'm late." Dwight sat down to Dan's left, opposite Becca.

The enormous teleconference screen flashed to life. "Good morning, Ranger Wilson," said a voice from the sound system. "We hear you had some interesting activity down at the Calneva Rift viewpoint."

"Nothing trivial, Sir Nelson," said Dan.

"Are the rumors true? One of the Mojave People crossed over?"

"That's true, sir."

Sir Nelson's voice was all seriousness and concern. "Has he been quarantined? Please tell me you've kept a lid on this."

Ranger Dan imagined Elaina and Arcon holed up in a bunker at the Big Bear Camp. "I can state for a fact that the Mojave man is completely contained."

"Whom did he come in contact with?"

Dan thumbed toward Becca and Dwight. "The three of us in this room, two SBS&R officers, and now Patty Abrams over at the containment facility."

"You're sure? No one else?"

"Yes, sir. One of the SBS&R officers has been at his side since he arrived and will remain with him in confinement, as will Mrs. Abrams."

"What about the other officer?"

"I just contacted him. He is self-isolating at his home."

"Verify that for us and have him stay there until we can have the young man examined. Can we have the names of the individuals involved for our records?"

"Yes, sir. I believe you have our names. The officers are Roberto and Elaina Gonzales, and the Mojave man's name is Arcon Franklin."

"Are the officers related?"

"Yes sir, father and daughter."

"Okay, nothing wrong with that. Just seems odd. I'm assuming you debriefed this Mojave man, uhhh, Mr. Franklin, before he left your custody."

Dan straightened his tie, wishing he could take it off. "I debriefed Mr. Gonzales, sir. It appears they had been planning to help Mr. Franklin get across the Rift for quite some time."

"Is that so? For how long?" Sir Nelson leaned forward, his face filling the screen.

"I don't know, but they claim to have been communicating with Mr. Franklin for about eight years."

"What? Oh, my Lord, how did we not know about this? You didn't know, did you?"

"No, sir." Sir Nelson may as well have jabbed Dan in the chest. His nerves bumped up the volume of his response. He lowered his voice. "I mean, no, sir. Can I add something?"

"What is it?"

"At no time did the officers step foot on Mojave soil, sir. The whole event was carried out on our soil. Ranger White can explain what she observed. Becca?"

"Hi, Mr. Nelson, sir," said Becca. "The Mojave man— Arcon—sustained some minor injuries during his escape from the Mojave Restricted Area. Most were caused by the thorns associated with the Acacia trees. He also had an abrupt meeting with a cliff when he fell from a tightrope stretched across the Rift."

Sir Nelson chuckled. "I like your details better already."

"Thank you, sir. Well, Arcon appeared in good health, other than the injuries, none of which required further medical attention. He seemed intelligent and good-natured, even witty at times. He showed no violent tendencies or erratic behavior," said Becca.

"Okay, that's good. Ranger Wilson, you didn't follow proper procedure concerning this individual, but I see no reason for an official reprimand. Provide this man with a physical examination by an Authority approved physician. And you understand he needs to remain isolated until the results of that examination come in. You three should practice social distancing as well, until he is cleared."

Ranger Dan straightened in his chair. "We understand, sir."

"Fine," said Sir Nelson. "Keep me updated on a daily basis, and sooner if anything important should happen. Unless anyone else has anything to add, I need to get to another meeting."

"We're busy too, sir. Could I ask one question before you go?"

"Sure, if it's quick."

"Is there any indication of what will happen to this man after the testing?"

"Depends on the test results, of course. But we only have two choices; assimilate him into our society or send him back to his own people. Gotta go. Have a nice day." The screen went blank.

"That was pretty painless," said Becca, turning off the monitor.

"Yeah," said Dan. "I can stop sweating now."

Becca elbowed him. "Well, we always said it was the Mojave Forest that made our job exciting."

"I said interesting," Dan countered. "I don't enjoy exciting. By the way, do you remember who that reporter was that was asking all the questions? Did you get her name?"

"Yeah, Noreena Chan," answered Becca, "She works for the—"

"San Bernardino Portal," interrupted Dan. "I remember meeting her. That's a small online news site, isn't it?" Becca nodded. "Yeah, they cover San Bernardino and the surrounding area."

"Right, and she does human interest stuff. Dwight, would you mind checking their site to see if they're posting anything about this?"

Dwight got to his feet and rolled his chair back under the table. "Sure, boss. I'll let you know if I see anything."

Dan smiled at Dwight. "Aren't you glad we mentioned nothing about the trip to the restaurant?"

"I was hoping Lord Nelson wouldn't hear about that, sir."

"I'm sure you were. We don't plan to tell him. I think some folks were recording the crossing with their shoulder-phones, and that reporter might get her hands on that footage. Check closely for that," said Dan.

"Will do, sir."

As Dwight left the room, Becca waited, watching Dwight leave, then added, "Privacy Rules won't allow just anyone to use the footage. They'd have to get permission from those being recorded, *and* permission from us, *and* Search and Rescue on top of everything else—and maybe from Tarzan and Jane."

"I know that, but you see the problem, right?" Dan asked.

"I guess I don't follow," said Becca. "Seems like you're in the clear."

Dan stood up. "They'd have to *contact* Search and Rescue. What Roberto did was completely unauthorized. We can't lie about it, so all we can do is stall for time. And if the Spirit convicts me, I won't even be able to do that."

"Oh, I see what you mean," said Becca. She watched Dan push his chair under the table. When he looked back at her, she could see the stress on his face. "Let's pray about it," she suggested, getting to her feet.

"That's a good idea, thanks." Dan walked over and took Becca's small hand in his. "Father, we bring this issue before you. We don't want to be a part of deception and lies. We want to state the truth when we're asked. We simply ask that you help keep people from asking until we have time to do this right. In other words, we want it to happen in your timing. I do believe he's your child. Help us help him, please."

"I agree," said Becca, letting go of his hand. "By the way, have you told Meredith yet?"

"Oh ... no, I haven't." Dan hung his head. "Great, thanks Becca. Now I'm sweating again."

"Why?"

"I promised her I wouldn't see any of the Mojave People until she could join me. I'd better call her and tell her what's going on." *And do I tell her about meeting Jesus? Do I dare tell Becca? Not right now.* "Do you mind if I blame everything on you?" he joked.

Becca crossed her arms. "You better not. Blame Roberto and Elaina. This really is all their fault, you know."

"Good idea."

CHAPTER SEVEN

Elaina took another hairpin turn fast enough to make Arcon slide to one side of his seat. He leaned into the momentum and pulled on the armrest. He understood gravity and inertia from his swing training, but having Elaina in control of it was making him nervous. At first, he'd enjoyed the view, but now the side of the road was disappearing into an expanse of sky. He wanted Elaina to stop. She'd just told him, for the third time, that she couldn't stop. Not until Patty did.

By the time Patty pulled over, Arcon was feeling woozy. He crawled out of the backseat, clinging to the car and standing on a shoulder barely large enough for two vehicles. Patty waved them over, so they walked to Patty's truck.

"Are we getting close?" asked Elaina.

"We're closer than we were," said Patty vaguely. "I wanted to show you two something first. Follow me."

They followed, walking up a rugged trail that meandered up a steep hill. Elaina heard a noise behind her. She turned just in time to see Arcon slip and flail his arms to keep from falling. "You okay?" she asked. "Those boots are too new. They'll be better once they're broken in."

Arcon didn't want to break his shoes. "Thanks for getting them for me. I don't think these rocks will break them. They're much stronger than my moccasins."

"Well, watch your step," said Patty. "There are some good trippers on this trail."

Arcon looked around him. "Sorry, there's just so much to see."

"You don't have to be sorry, just careful," said Patty. A little farther up the trail, she stopped. "Now, when we crest this hill, I want you to look far out into the distance. Okay?"

"Okay," said Elaina.

"I agree to your terms too," said Arcon.

Patty wiped her brow with her forearm. "That's good," she said, laughing a little—until she realized he wasn't kidding. "Nobody's going to tell you what you can or can't look at, kid. I'm just saying, don't miss the view. It's not much farther, but this last bit gets steep and rocky." Arcon watched Patty's foot placements closely.

The worn footpath reappeared just as they crested the hill. Elaina's first response was, "Wow, what a view." After a few more steps, she said, "Oh my, is that the Rift?"

"Yes, it is," said Patty. Arcon came up behind them. Patty pressed a hand to his shoulder and said, "Welcome to one of my favorite views of the Calneva Rift. Do you see how the end of it sort of breaks apart near Twenty-Nine Palms?"

"I don't see the palms," said Arcon.

"Right." Patty pointed as she spoke. "You can see where it cuts across the flats and disappears in the hills."

Arcon studied the view, trying to get his bearings. He couldn't match the views with the memories of the maps he'd looked at on Elaina's computer. "Where's the I-15?"

"That's too far away to see from here. You can sort of make out the Mojave River. It starts in the hills behind us, then flows out toward Victorville." She pointed to the north. "After that, it turns due east, follows the I-15 for a ways, then dumps into the Rift near the Viewpoint. If the stories I heard are correct, that's where Ranger Dan picked you up."

Elaina laughed. "*Literally* picked him up."

Arcon stared into the distance. "I forgot to thank him for that."

"You'll get your chance," said Patty. "Dan said if he can work things out, he'll come visit you here in a few days."

"That'd be great," said Arcon. "I like Ranger Dan."

Patty turned to walk back down the trail. "Well, we'll see," she mumbled quietly to herself. It was too soft for Arcon to hear, but Elaina heard Patty's comment, and it worried her. This place of safety had better not turn into a trap. She had no reason yet to distrust Dan, but trusting Patty was not coming easy. And it seemed odd that a person of Dan's rank would travel to this remote place just for a visit. Elaina determined to keep a watchful eye and have an exit plan, just in case.

Roberto sat in his home office, monitoring his emergency scanner. He was hoping for any reason to be distracted for a while. Elaina usually did that for him, both the scanning and the distracting. He made himself some lunch, but Elaina usually did that as well and was better at it. *C'mon, baby girl, contact me, so I know you're okay. Baby girl. She's twenty-one years old and so far has proven she's a grown woman.* A wave of loss swept over Roberto. What would he do if Arcon returned to his people with Elaina at his side? He hadn't considered that until this moment.

He set his half-eaten, condiment-challenged ham sandwich back on his plate. Just as his pity party was getting started, he heard the PID chirp in his ear. Ranger Dan. He got out his comm-pad, hurrying to see what the message was. He read [RanDan. Secure?] Roberto typed, [Big D Secure. News?] After a minute, [Sorry For Delay. Package Received And Contained. FYI— Monitor SB Portal For Possible T&J News. Out.]

Now Roberto was certain he knew which press outlet the reporter worked for. He responded, [TELL JANE TO CONTACT D. OUT.] Asking Ranger Dan to poke Elaina to contact her father might at least get a text out of her. Any word at all would help quell the uselessness he felt.

Elaina watched Patty make a quick U-turn and did the same maneuver, sticking close behind. After a couple of kilometers, they veered onto a one-lane gravel road that went up a seriously steep incline. About a half-kilometer up the hill, the road leveled off, but it was still very narrow. She hugged the side of the hill, avoiding the steep drop off on her left. Patty stopped her car and got out, so Elaina did the same.

They walked along the edge of the road toward each other and met in front of Elaina's autocycle. "Normally, I warn folks ahead of time about this section of road," said Patty, "But you're not my normal visitors. This hillside is too steep to build a switchback, so we had to be creative. Can you drive that thing backwards with that trailer?"

"Well, of course, but how far are we talking about?" asked Elaina.

"Not far, maybe a hundred meters. But it's up a steep, rugged road. You'll have to be good at backing up that trailer with your mirrors. Don't worry, I'll show you where to go. Tarzan can walk up and help guide you."

"Okay, I can try it. Where are we going?" Elaina was nervous because this was a narrow road on a steep hillside. There was no turning around, so even if she wanted to leave, she'd have to drive backwards down to the main road. Having a trailer on the back would make it difficult. This was looking a lot like a trap.

Patty pointed up another narrow road that intersected the one they were on. "That one?" Elaina asked. She walked closer to look at it. "But I see a dead tree in the way about ten meters up."

Patty chuckled. "Oh, really? Watch!" She pointed at the downed tree and clicked something in her hand. The log twitched and then rose up out of their way.

"Oh, that is so cool." She yelled, "Arcon, come here!"

As Arcon climbed out of the autocycle, Patty clicked the remote again, and the log dropped back down over the road. When he got near them, Patty pointed up the hill and said, "Do you think you're strong enough to move that dead tree off the road?"

"I ... I can try." Just as he approached the log, she raised it again. He jumped and nearly fell down the hill. As the other two laughed, he looked the log over.

Then Patty yelled, "Drop back down!" She clicked the remote. Arcon rested his hand on it as it dropped. "You have trees that obey your command?"

Patty laughed and said, "Only my command. No one gets in or out without me. I told you this place was secure." She clicked the remote again.

Then she looked at Elaina and said, "Watch how I do this—how I back my rig up this road—then you do the same." She looked at Arcon and said, "And you, big guy. You make sure she stays on the road. I don't need her tumbling off the hill and blocking my access." Patty hopped in her rig and pulled up in front of the road. She maneuvered backwards until she was lined up just right. Then she gunned the engine and went racing up the hill backwards. Soon she stopped, then drove forwards part way up another road, and stopped again.

Elaina looked up the narrow road and said to Arcon, "Don't expect *me* to do it like that."

"I'll be impressed if you can do it at all."

"Thanks for the vote of confidence," said Elaina sarcastically. She knew he probably meant it as a compliment, but unfortunately, she agreed with him. She knew she had to do it somehow. The steep edge on this road frightened her, but not nearly as much as trying to negotiate a fast escape would. *So much for an exit strategy.*

She lined up with the road and started backing toward Arcon. She hoped he'd help direct her, but he just stood with his hand on the fake log. At one point, the trailer arced to the side, and the edge was too close for her to correct. When she stopped, Arcon ran down and tried to push the trailer toward the middle of the road. She slowly moved forward until he let go, then lined up with the road again.

The next time the trailer went crooked, she heard Arcon yell, "Hold it." He reached under the trailer's frame, picked it up, and moved it over. "Okay, now try it." After two more attempts and Arcon's adjustments, she made it all the way to Patty's truck.

As Patty dropped the log back on the road, she said, "Who needs brains when you have brawn?"

Elaina put her hands on her hips. "Thanks a lot."

"Now you see why no one comes up to this place unless they go through me. Not even Ranger Dan can get up here unless I welcome him. But I always have."

"I like Ranger Dan," said Arcon.

Patty didn't respond verbally to Arcon's statement, but the look on her face spoke volumes. There was something about Ranger Dan that Patty was hiding. It tempted Elaina to drive away and take her chances elsewhere. But she didn't know where she could flee to, and there was a log in her way.

Ranger Dan settled into the fire watch chair and rested. Off limits to the public, he was alone in this room at the very top of the tall observation tower. He found it hard to believe all that had happened since he'd operated a spy drone from this chair just over a week ago. At that time, the Mojave People were a complete mystery. Now he'd met one of them. He stared at the forest of Acacia trees far in front of him. Then he tapped his shoulder-phone and said, "Call Bronwen."

Dan's sister-in-law answered, "Hello?"

"Hello Bronwen. Is Mery handy?"

"She sure is," quipped his sister-in-law. "Thanks for loaning her to me. Would you like to *talk* to her?"

"As long as I'm on the phone, sure," said Dan.

"You're such a jokester. Let me get her for you … hold on while I walk you back." After a moment or two she handed the phone off. "Here she is … Mery, it's for you. It's your Danny boy."

"Hi, Dan, hold on," said his wife. Dan heard footsteps for a few seconds. "Oh, that's better. Had to get away from the paint smell. Hi there, honey bunch. Miss you. How are things going down there?"

"Interestingly, for sure," said Dan.

"What do you mean?" asked Meredith.

"Well, I don't know how to tell you this, but I violated one of the agreements we made with each other."

"You went to your mother's house and ate?"

Dan laughed, loving his wife's quick wit. "No, nothing like that. But that sounds like a good idea. Just kidding. I've only missed a couple of meals. But I'm getting ahead of myself. Guess again."

"Good or bad?" asked Meredith.

"It's good. Actually, for me, it's very good. Only bad because you weren't with me— like we agreed to. Does that give you a clue?"

"That's a clue, huh? What were we supposed to do together? Just about everything, except work on Bronwen's house."

Dan whistled a non-tune. "I'm waiting."

"Oh, my … did you go into the Mojave Forest?"

"No, but close. The forest came to me. Well, actually, one of the Mojave People did."

"You got to meet one of the Mojave People? When did that happen?"

"Yesterday."

"And you're just now telling me?" exclaimed Mery. "Why didn't you call me?"

"Things have been pretty crazy since it happened. Actually, a lot crazy. In fact, if you'd been here, maybe it wouldn't have been *as* crazy."

"I may just get on the next tube train home. What happened? How did you meet him?"

"Well, let's see. The first time I saw him, he was getting ready to tightrope across the Rift down by the viewpoint."

"What? Okay, wait a minute. This is all a joke, right? There's no Mojave person."

Dan started laughing. "Hey, I just won twenty credits. I bet myself you wouldn't believe me if I told you."

"Well, you can double your money. I still don't believe it."

"I swear on my mother's dinners, I'm not lying. I couldn't believe it myself. This guy was balancing on the rope with a stick; he was wearing animal skins; I had to lasso him; he fell into the Rift ... and that's not the half of it. Last night I ... I ..."

Meredith waited for more, but the line was silent. "Dan, are you there?" More silence. "Dan, talk to me."

Dan cleared his throat. "Sorry, hon. Got a little emotional. Let me tell you everything that happened. Are you sitting down?"

"I can be. Just a minute." Meredith walked back to the bedroom. "Bronwen, I think this'll take a while."

"Is Dan okay?" asked Bronwen.

"Yeah, he's fine. He's just got a lot to discuss. I'll come back when I'm through."

"Let me know what's going on if you can," said Bronwen.

"Sure. See you in a few." She headed toward the back door, feeling a little worried. Her husband didn't usually sound this upset. "Okay, Hon, I'm back." She went outside and sat in a patio chair. "What's going on?"

Dan told his wife about helping the SBS&R officers, lassoing the Mojave man, tending to his wounds, that his name was Arcon, and he swung through the trees. He told her how he made Arcon look civilized with a shave, gave him his clothes, and snuck him out of the Ranger's office in the back of a tiny three-wheeler. She laughed hard when she heard about Dwight in a caveman suit and got concerned when Dan hadn't eaten lunch or dinner. She really got worried when he told her he let Arcon go, and some reporter was now trying to find the Mojave man.

"So now I'm tossing and turning," Dan continued. "Don't know how I'll deal with the Mojave People overall if it comes to that. Both Lord Nelson and the reporter are after me to produce this Arcon. I have no clue who the authority is over those people."

"Well, before you got involved, Jesus was," said Meredith. "You'll probably have to talk to him about it."

In a trembling voice, Dan replied, "Already did."

"You have? How?"

"Remember, I said I couldn't sleep? I thought it might be because I was hungry, having missed two meals." Meredith grumbled her disapproval, and he continued. "About one in the morning, I got up to eat the sandwich from my lunch. I got a glass of milk—remember that, it's important—and I was at the kitchen table worrying over my situation. I tell you, Mery, I was so concerned I'd failed somehow. I was supposed to contain anyone from the restricted area. Not only did I let him go, I helped him escape. It was weighing so heavily on me I couldn't eat. You know that's not normal for me."

"As if any of this was normal."

"No kidding. Anyway, I'm sitting there, holding this sandwich, and I hear a voice say, 'Do you mind if I share that with you?'"

"In your head?"

"No, in the room with me."

"Didn't that scare you?"

"It petrified me. I didn't recognize the voice. But then I was flooded with peace. It's hard to explain, but somehow, before I turned around, I knew it was Jesus."

"Wow. How did you respond?"

With a nervous laugh, he said, "I asked him if he wanted half of my sandwich."

"No, you didn't."

"Made sense at the time. I couldn't think of what else I had to share with him."

"Sounds like you. What did he say?"

Dan was quiet again. In a shaky voice, he continued. "He said he wanted to share my burden. Then it felt like a weight lifted off my shoulders. Kind of like when they take the lead vest off you in a dentist's office."

"It felt that real?"

"Absolutely. Anyway, there's more. When are you coming home?"

"I should be able to finish up tomorrow. Pick me up Tuesday at the station?"

"I can do that. I'll finish the story then."

"At least tell me the rest about meeting Jesus."

"It's rather emotional. Wouldn't you rather watch me blubber in person?"

"No—*now*. Tell me."

"If you insist." Dan told her how surprising the conversation was. He now had a completely different perspective on the restricted area and its people—and why things happened the way they did. "Even the glass of milk helped me understand," added Dan.

"How did that help?"

"It confirmed to me I wasn't dreaming," said Dan, with a chuckle. "You know how I sip milk when I eat a sandwich. There's no way I'd guzzle down a glass of milk and not know it." Dan was silent for a moment. "Mery, he was really there. I'd been told by higher authorities to be prepared for a visit from Jesus. They'd said if I needed special understanding for a troubling situation, he'd be there to help. I must have sounded desperate in my prayers."

"For a long time, you've worried about how to deal with the Mojave People. Do you feel more confident now?"

"I poured myself another glass of milk and ate my sandwich. What does that tell you?"

"Sounds like you're back to normal."

"Even more normal than normal, if that makes sense."

"Well, I can't wait to see the new normal. I better get back to Bronwen. Make sure and call me if anything else happens."

"Will, for sure. Love you, hon."

"Love you, too."

CHAPTER EIGHT

Jarden stopped and inhaled a deep breath of Acacia tree fragrance. He looked behind him at the large Facility building in the distance. *That building unites us, this forest sustains us, and here I am, in between.* He wanted to climb a tree and hide for a while. His conscience rejected the notion. He was a leading member of the ArcPoint Faithful—those who labored to keep the Community together, regardless of personal desires.

The Separatists were stirring up trouble. They were part of the ArcPoint Faithful, but Jarden didn't think this splinter group was being faithful to the original vision for the Community. The Founders would never agree to disagree. They sought unity and peace until everyone agreed. A central part of that unity was trusting God to maintain their peace with the outside world. Separatists preferred to give God some help.

Jarden knew someone would have to unite them all again, but it couldn't be him. He could not be impartial on the subject of Arcon's departure. He turned back toward his destination, Ashford Hill. That tree-less spot stood bright, even with early afternoon clouds. He welcomed the hard climb up the hill to the Ashford home. It invigorated him and had done so for most of his seventy-nine years. He grabbed the handrail next to the first step and silently began counting down the steps; *ninety-nine, ninety-eight, ninety-seven ...*

Jarden stopped at the halfway bench to rest and enjoy the shade of the last trees before the clearing. *How does Lars do it? Brina says her Grandpa Lars rarely stops to rest. He just walks like a turtle, slow and steady, all the way to the top. Of course, she's always there to steady him. Twice a day, she walks him down the one hundred stairs and through the forest to the Facility.*

He got to his feet to continue the climb. He needed to discuss the Separatist problem with Lars before he and Brina took their afternoon walk. As the son of Founders Norman and Sabrina Ashford, Lars had the respect of the Separatists. He leaned toward maintaining isolation from the outside world but was a man who would listen rationally and weigh the facts wisely.

At nearly 120 years old, Lars was the only person left who remembered all of the Founders. He was still sharp in his mind, and everyone knew it. Jarden hated to bring Lars into the discussion, but a few words from him could stop months of arguing. As Jarden crested the hill, he could see that the door to the Ashford log cabin was wide open, indicating they'd seen him coming.

Life would've been so much simpler if Arcon had taken Brina as a life partner. She was attractive, smart, a hard worker. Perhaps too many had told Arcon that uniting with her was meant to be. He always seemed intent on proving them wrong. Arcon had confided to Jarden he felt there had to be more to a relationship than just being the descendants of Founders.

Brina met him at the door. "Hi, Mr. Jarden," she said, with her usual perky attitude.

"Hi, Brina. Is your grandpa available?"

"Sure, c'mon in." She handed him a glass of water. "He's sitting in the greenhouse."

Jarden nodded thanks. "I don't blame him. It's a bit cool outside." Jarden walked through the house and out to the greenhouse made of car windows. He'd spent a lot of time in that place as a child, intrigued by the various plants. It was still a fascinating jungle.

As he walked around a large tree philodendron, he heard, "Hey, little Jimmy Arden! What brings you by these old bones?" Lars was one of the few people who still called Jarden by his given name, James Arden-Merrick, and the only one who wouldn't stand corrected for saying it. "You need to come visit more often. You're getting flabby."

"I can't argue with that." Living on this hill had kept Lars lean and his heart strong. Only his deeply creased face betrayed his age. "I've come to get your input on a concern I have."

"Well, that's something I'm still good for." Lars marked the page in the book he was reading and set it down. "What's burdening your heart?"

"Did you and your father Norm ever talk much about the days before the Founders came here?"

"Oh sure, at times. He'd get emotional, though, and clam up. He said governments were corrupt everywhere. People were breaking into stores and burning them down. Diseases were striking worldwide. I guess it was pretty scary. What upset Dad the most was the way adults abused children back then. They'd strap bombs on them, sell them to the sex trade, even kill them before they were born." Lars grimaced. "I learned not to press him about it. Upset him too much."

"Did he come here to escape all that?"

Lars thought for a minute. "That was probably a big influence. But he always told me God was pressing him hard to do it. All of the Founders said the same thing. He said they'd often doubt what they were thinking, and then they'd test God with a fleece of some sort. God always acknowledged their ideas were correct in some miraculous way, beyond what they expected."

Jarden looked Lars in the eye and asked, "Is that something you'd be capable of, throwing caution to the wind and walking by faith into the middle of the unknown?"

Lars squinted at him. "What's your point?"

Jarden took a sip of his water. "Remember when I was young, how I didn't do things the way I was told? I searched for a different path, a way that was maybe better than what we had."

Lars chuckled. "You weren't one to keep your feet on solid ground, that's for sure. I was certainly opposed to your tree hopping, but it seems to have worked out."

"You weren't the only one who thought the butter had slipped off my noodles," chuckled Jarden. "But I firmly believed God wanted me to do what I did, and He gifted me to accomplish it. When that happens, you have to be obedient to it." He then looked squarely at Lars. "I believe Arcon was obedient to his call, just as I was, just like the Founders were."

"Well, it doesn't really matter much now, does it? He's gone."

"It does to some," said Jarden. "There are those afraid Arcon will bring back an invading army and force this Community to join the outside world. They'd like to tear up more of the railroad tracks and close some of the trails. As Chief of Procurement, I can't allow that to happen."

"Don't you think it may just be a lot of idle chatter?" asked Lars.

"They're organizing," replied Jarden, shaking his head. "You used to go to the meetings of the ArcPoint Faithful, correct?"

Lars nodded. "Sure. Still do once in a while. If you spent time listening to the Founders, you'd always be faithful to this place."

"Oh, I understand. I still go myself. But there are a few young men who sit off by themselves. Some of their comments are pretty radical. I believe they're forming a splinter group."

"So, who's their leader?"

"Raymo," answered Jarden.

"Oh. I understand. I think he's still bitter with Arcon regarding Brina," he said, softening his voice. They both looked toward the main part of the house, but Brina didn't appear to be listening. "When everybody was pushing Arcon her direction,

Raymo felt he was better suited for her hand. He's probably intent on making sure Arcon is never part of her life again."

"To be honest, I know she'd have been Arcon's first choice for a life partner. But he felt this calling to the outside world. He couldn't take her with him, and if they were life partners, he couldn't leave her behind. But I also know he didn't think Raymo was right for Brina."

"Sounds to me like Arcon was wiser than I gave him credit for. And Raymo does seem to be going against the grain."

"Would you consider having a discussion with him? I just want to head off a problem. We all need to stick together."

"Sure. I'll give Arcon's absence some time to blow over, and if it doesn't, I'll intervene."

"Thanks a lot," said Jarden. "Sorry to involve you with this, but I know Raymo respects you."

Jarden stayed with Lars and talked about old times. Lars had some interesting stories about Lee Franklin.

Noreena paced around her small home office. All the evidence to this point confirmed to her that a young man had escaped from the Mojave Restricted Area. What still made little sense were the reactions from the other people who were involved in the incident.

Rescue personnel were usually excited to explain how they'd helped someone survive a dangerous incident. They might be reluctant to share personal details about who they'd rescued, but never their own participation. This rescuer, whatever his name was, acted nervous, like he was guilty of something. *And who was the girl in the autocycle?*

Rangers were usually free-flowing with information. When she'd first met Ranger Dan Wilson, he'd been warm and friendly. Now he wouldn't take her calls. *Why?* So far, she'd only asked a few questions, not accusing anyone of doing something wrong.

The rescuers and the Rangers had to have conspired to get this man out of the Mojave Forest. They'd worked out the details ahead of time. How could they do that? Turning to an empty chair in her living room, she said, "Hey, look! A man on the other side of the canyon. What he needs is a tightrope. I'll go grab one out of my truck."

They must have talked to the Mojave guy. She went back to the notes spread out on her kitchen counter. *The Mojave People have been isolated in that Forest for well over a hundred years. Communication technology is different now than anything they would have access to. From every source she could find, those people should not possess any modern-day communication device, period. That means they must've smuggled a device over to him, and that violated the restriction. That's a good reason to be acting guilty. It also gives me a legal basis for gathering sensitive private information.*

No one could lawfully relocate from the Mojave Forest. She'd checked. Or even be allowed to travel in or out of that area. Noreena had recently moved to San Bernardino, so she knew how the system worked. People were free to move around however they desired, but relocation required the availability of housing and a means of earning credits in the new location. All she'd had to do was contact Relocation Services, and the details of her move were worked out.

Eventually, this Mojave man would be incarcerated pending release or sent back to where he'd come from. If allowed to remain outside of the Mojave, all sorts of information regarding him will be in the relocation database. But she wasn't about to wait that long.

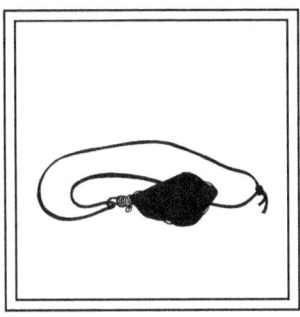

CHAPTER NINE

Elaina followed Patty's car up and over the crest of a hill, past an abandoned cement factory, and into a flat area with sparse vegetation, a couple of porta potties, and a lone trucking container painted in camouflage. She pulled her autocycle next to one of four other vehicles parked by the container. When she got out, she heard Patty say, "Come in here, you two, for a few minutes." Elaina glimpsed Patty as she disappeared into the trucking container.

They followed and found her sitting at a long steel table with a lot of chairs. "Have a seat," she said. "This is where you'll occasionally have your meals, when you get tired of the MRE's."

Arcon blurted out, "Hey, I know what MRE's are! Meals Ready to Eat."

Patty's mouth dropped open. "Where did you see those?"

Arcon thought about that and then said, "Northwest of here, on the other side of the Rift."

Elaina shook her head and nodded at Patty. "Yes, he's always that literal."

"Okay then," said Patty. "Let me tell you both how this is going to work. Normally you'd get this speech before you show up, but now is fine, too. First, I'll need you to empty your vehicle and your pockets. Dump all the contents on this table."

"What!" exclaimed Elaina. "What's that for?"

"Security reasons. I need to know what enters this property. I'll confiscate and control anything I consider dangerous to other individuals."

"But we don't have anything," argued Elaina.

"Then you have nothing to lose," said Patty. She nodded once. "This is what they did in the lawless 21st century, and it's the law in this place. I will also confiscate all communication devices."

"But ... I need to keep in touch with my dad!"

"And you will, but through me. Regarding that, I'm in contact with Ranger Dan, and he's in contact with your dad." Patty got up from her chair. "You'll get everything back before you leave. If that doesn't work for you, I hope you remember your way out."

"Well, we don't have much of a choice, but isn't it a little severe?" asked Elaina.

Patty walked over to the container door and closed it. Then she turned and pointed at Elaina. "Your situation is a little severe, young lady. The Mojave Forest has been a forbidden place for over a hundred years. *No one* is to come or go from that place, and Jesus himself laid down that law." She pointed a thumb at Arcon. "Tarzan here broke the perfect record we had going. For some reason, Ranger Dan wants to protect this man, and I agreed to help, under my terms only. And trust me, my terms are reasonable when you consider the alternative."

"Is Ranger Dan going to get in trouble for what I did?" asked Arcon.

"No," answered Patty. "He'll get in trouble for what *he* did. I want to make sure we don't make matters worse for him. So, here's what we need to do. The rule is, anyone coming from that area must be quarantined until they can be certified as disease-free." Patty stared at Arcon. "Do you understand what quarantined means?"

"Yes," said Arcon. "Our hydroponics workers would quarantine plants. You isolate them by themselves, away from any other plants."

"Exactly. Around you are a bunch of containers just like the one we're in now. You don't see them because they're buried completely in the ground. I'm going to lodge each of you in one of those containers. You're not to come in contact with others at this camp. The authorities will consider this place enough of a quarantine; hence Dan will be trouble-free."

"Will Arcon and I be able to see each other?" asked Elaina.

"It's far too late for you, young lady," said Patty. "If jungle boy here has some horrible disease, you're already infected. You might as well hang out together." Her stern gaze widened into a big smile. "I have you in connecting containers, so you never have to see anyone else, and you can still see each other."

Elaina looked at Arcon, who nodded at her. Then she looked at Patty. "I think your terms are reasonable."

"That's good because they're not negotiable. Now, let's get your vehicle emptied onto this table. I'll work on getting a message out to your dad right away. Then I'll show you to your new homes. One word of caution, though. They're not sound-proofed like this container. If you want to talk about anything private, use Arcon's container. It'll be at the end of the row."

The three of them emptied the autocycle of its contents. Clothes, sleeping bags, food and camping supplies, even blankets went on the table. "See this propane cylinder?" asked Patty. "Can't have fire in the containers. Confiscated. Flares? Confiscated. Tools? If you need to fix something, talk to me. Confiscated."

Elaina pulled something from her pants pocket. "I suppose you'll want this."

"What's that?" Patty examined it. "Hey, that's a nice multi-tool. Never seen one that small. What's this? SBS&R? That's right, I heard you were a Rescuer. It's got a knife, saw blade, pliers, screw-driver—confiscated."

Arcon took the rock out of his pocket and placed it on the table, then did the same with the necklace from Jarden.

"What are these?" asked Patty as she picked up the rock.

"Please don't take those," pleaded Arcon. "They're all I have left from my Grandma and my friend Jarden."

"I just want to look at them," said Patty. "My husband collects rocks in his off-season. This one is beautiful. Did you find it?"

"Jarden found both of those. He polished the one on the necklace, and I polished the other."

"They look like some kind of agate. Nice job on the polish, by the way." She handed them back to Arcon, then rifled through the rest of the items.

When Patty finished, she walked out of the container for a final inspection of Elaina's car. "Cute little three-wheeler," she said as she opened the doors. "Mind if I sit in it?"

"Not at all," said Elaina.

They watched as Patty squeezed into the driver's seat. "Can't believe I can actually fit in one of these things." When Arcon asked her if she'd like to try his seat in the back, she said, "I'm never going back *there*. If I ever travel in one of these, *I'm* going to be in control." All three of them laughed. Elaina understood that statement completely.

After she'd extracted herself from the car, Patty looked at her guests. "You two look like death eating a cracker. Why don't we get you situated into your private luxury condos?" As Patty locked away what she'd confiscated, Elaina and Arcon moved the rest back to the car. Then Elaina picked up her suitcase, and Arcon grabbed his duffel bag.

As they walked across the flat landscape with its sparse vegetation, they saw access hole covers here and there. Stopping at one, Patty said, "Arcon, this one is yours." She reached down and opened the cover, revealing a deep hole with a ladder on one side.

Arcon peered down the opening. "This is my rabbit hole?"

"Call it what you will," said Patty. "The important thing is, there's a comfortable bed waiting for you down there. Go ahead and climb to the bottom, and you'll see a door. Open it and go on inside. We'll follow."

Climbing down, Arcon seemed unsteady at first. "It's like stepping on tiny branches."

"But these rungs don't move," countered Patty.

When he got to the bottom, he saw an opening in the liner of the hole and rippled metal beyond that. He pushed on the metal, and it opened. A light came on, revealing a furnished room.

"Hey, Arcon," yelled Patty. When he returned to the base of the ladder, she yelled, "Catch," and dropped the suitcase and duffel bag to him. "Set them inside. We're coming down."

When all three were in, Patty meandered toward the back of the container, pointing as she spoke. "That is a motion detector that faces the opening. It alerts you to intruders, but it won't trigger if you're walking around in here. You have a sink with running water." She whirled on Arcon and Elaina, and they stopped in their tracks. "Don't waste water." When they'd nodded and promised, she continued her tour. "A refrigerator, a microwave, a two-burner stove, no oven. Down this hall are two bedrooms. The bathroom has a shower, no tub. It has a composting toilet. There are porta potties on the surface if you would prefer not to clean up after yourself." She stopped and watched Arcon, who was lifting the lid on the toilet.

"We had these," he stated. "We used them at the Outposts. We called them push-buckets." He looked inside another bucket and picked up a handful of sawdust. "We used crushed leaves for compost."

Patty laughed. "I see I don't need to explain any more about that. That's good because being in quarantine, you'll have to use one." She turned to Elaina and said, "You, honey, have the option of going topside. He doesn't. Okay, one last thing. Here is the back door. You'll see it's connected to the adjoining container— which is yours, young lady—with only one tube between them going to the surface. You can use this pathway to contact each other, but it's also an emergency egress path in case of a fire or something."

Arcon walked back to one of his bedrooms. He stared at the bed and then tried lying down on it. He got comfortable, so the other two moved on.

After explaining a few more things to Elaina, Patty found Arcon, who was still lying on the bed. "That's all the important stuff I need to tell you so you can get some sleep. I'll help your girl here get settled in, then we can discuss other things tomorrow. Okay?" She got no response. She looked at Elaina and whispered, "He's obviously comfortable here."

Elaina grabbed her suitcase while Patty turned the lights down to night-light mode. Then they quietly moved to Elaina's container.

Noreena Chan pored over the information on her two large computer screens. On the left side was all the archived information she could find about the land where the Mojave Restricted Area was located. *If the information survived the archival process, it must be good, or at least benign,* she reasoned. As a person who sought the good in people, she was glad the internet was reborn in the late 21st century. With a new protected protocol, no corrupted or misleading information could be found on it. Only what was true, good, and worthy of praise.

Officially, the area had been a protected area of the Mojave Desert in the 20th century. Known as the Mojave National Preserve, it was set aside for recreational use with limited development. *Why would anyone want to recreate in a desert, let alone live there?*

In the early 21st century, a business called the Renewable Energy Development Consortium, or RED-C, set up testing grounds just outside of the Preserve. Experimenting with drought-tolerant plant varieties, they hoped to produce a viable bio-fuel source. Research was abandoned because of resistance from environmental groups over genetic modifications performed on the plants.

All of that was interesting, but she wanted to know about the Mojave People. She scanned the right-hand monitor. A different article talked about a group of people who moved into the abandoned buildings of the RED-C. *The trees that grow there now must be the ones experimented with by the RED-C. But who were these other people? Why did they move there?*

The only name appearing in the article was Lee Franklin. She'd have to start there. The locals consider them a religious cult, so maybe she could pursue that angle. There must have been a religious reason Jesus restricted the area.

More than anything, she wanted an interview with the young man who'd escaped the area. He must have a powerful story, and she wanted to be first in line to tell it.

Arcon struggled to wake himself, to remember where he was and why he was sleeping fully clothed. He thought it appeared to be getting light outside until he remembered he wasn't outside. He was underground, with no reference to the outdoors. The dim lights he saw were on the wall, and his surroundings helped him recall where he was. But now, he didn't know where Elaina was and struggled to remember when he'd last seen her. *We were getting a tour of our space.*

His hunter training taught him, when you become disoriented, stay still. Look around, listen, and get your bearings. He strolled around the room and then recalled the hallway that led to the adjacent container. *Elaina's container. Elaina is right next door and probably asleep.*

He walked to the steel door leading to her space. He pressed his hand against it and prayed. *Father, thank you for Elaina. She is a good person, as you showed me she would be. Give her good sleep.*

She needs it and deserves it. His mind and his nerves calmed down, and he remembered Patty. She was in control of his situation right now. It'd be wise to enjoy her protection, at least until he was fully rested. *Thank you also for the others I've met. They've all been good.*

Even though he'd completely woken himself up, he was still exhausted. He went back to the bedroom and saw someone had placed a bottle of colored water on a table, so he drank some. Then he took off most of his clothes and crawled into bed.

He lay there and thought about the past few days. He liked Elaina and Roberto. He hoped to see Ranger Dan again and Ranger Becca. Patty was sort of gruff but likable. He thought about how he liked everyone he'd met. But right now, he mostly liked this bed. It was softer than the one in his apartment. It was a little shorter, but it was wider, so he could roll to either side without falling out. He fluffed his pillow and buried his head in it.

It wasn't as dark in the room as his apartment in the Facility was, but it was much quieter. He could sleep through the noise of the Facility, but here it was so quiet his own breathing was keeping him awake. He rolled onto his back and stared at the ceiling. He thought about what he'd been through and all the things—and people—that nearly stopped him. He thought about Jarden, and Brina, and his Grandma. He remembered his parents, and wept.

CHAPTER TEN

Roberto scanned the website of the San Bernardino Portal, searching for mention of the Calneva Rift. Like most news sites, major news anywhere trumped local news like traffic jams and lost hikers. That irritated him, but today he appreciated it. Normally he'd enjoy seeing his face in the background during a newsworthy rescue, but right now, he wanted anonymity.

So far, he'd only found stock historical data on the Rift, but no breaking news. It was the same with Calico, so he typed 'Mojave People' into the search field. He got a hit in an unlikely place. Under 'Help Wanted,' he read: *Looking for any information regarding the sighting of one of the Mojave People near Calico on Sunday. Video footage appreciated. Please contact Noreena Chan at the San Bernardino Portal, ext. 210.*

Now he was convinced Noreena Chan was the press person Ranger Dan was alerting him to. *If she's begging for witnesses, she must not have seen Arcon cross the Rift herself. She must have heard about it in Calico.* Thankfully, this was an obscure post in a small news source. But the fact remained, she's working on a story about Arcon.

He faced a dilemma. Should he wait her out, hoping for an official solution before her investigation hit critical mass? Or should he try to dissuade her from the pursuit? It was a classic fight-or-flight scenario. *I'll have no control unless I'm in the fight.* He'd contact her and pray God would help her understand.

Arcon had investigated what his new living quarters had to offer. Many things were like the tiny homes at ArcPoint, but here everything worked. First on his list was the shower. He conserved water like they did at ArcPoint. He turned it on till he was wet, then turned it off until he was ready to rinse off. The water was chilly in the beginning, then suddenly got hot in the middle of rinsing, which was painful on his many puncture wounds. He had no more skin patches but decided he'd be fine without them.

He stuck his head above ground once but didn't see anybody. He ate some food he had in his pack rather than the MRE's he'd found in the cupboards. He'd found the light switch in the bathroom and then determined to find them all. He figured out how to turn on the hot plate, which wasn't oil-fired like at the Facility. With this one, part of the countertop got hot, right where his hand was.

His greatest discovery was a disc player. It was similar to what they had at the Facility, which he'd been able to get functional for a while. It was already attached to a television. A user manual and remote lay on top of it. In a cabinet drawer, he found the disks, most of which said "Classic" on them.

He was bundled in a blanket—watching something called Popeye—when he heard Elaina's voice calling to him from the back of the container. "Yes, I'm awake," he responded. "Enter!"

He watched Elaina sneak down the back hallway. She hugged herself and said, "Do you mind if I turn the heat on?"

"You can do that?"

"Of course, I can," she snarked as she walked over and tapped a box on the wall. "What *are* you doing?"

"I was just keeping busy until you arrived." He picked up the remote. "Now that you're here, I'll shut it off."

"What is it you're watching?"

"It's called Popeye. I think it's for children, but it's funny."

"No, I mean, what is the machine you're watching it on?"

"In ArcPoint, we called it a television. We had a pile of them, but only three that worked."

Elaina put her hand on her hips. "I know that. The black box next to it. What's that?"

"It's a … What do you mean, what is it? This is your world; you should tell me."

"I haven't seen one before," she responded.

Arcon tipped his head and said, "I've fixed one before. Without it, the televisions were useless. I could only make one work for a short time. We didn't have enough spare parts."

"How strange," said Elaina. "I'll have to ask Patty about them. It probably has something to do with the nostalgia element of these containers."

"What do you mean?"

"They set these containers up with old books and furniture like things were during the Tribulation period of history. People fled the cities and hid in these containers from the anarchy and violence. So, they must have been used back then for entertainment. That's way before my time. What did you call them?"

"We called them disc players." He pressed a button on the remote, and a drawer slid out of the machine. He picked up the disc. "You lay these discs into the tray, then slide it into the player. The disc spins, a laser shoots light at the disc, the machine reads the information, and… well, anyway, it's all pretty simple. And the discs don't really wear out if you handle them right. But other parts do."

"That's interesting," she said as she looked over a disc titled 'Bug's Life.' "It seems rather bulky for two hours of entertainment." She looked at Arcon and said, "I came over to remove your bandages so you could take a shower, but it looks like you beat me to it."

"Yeah, sorry, I just couldn't sleep anymore. I didn't want to wake you." He glanced down at the ground, then back at her. "Besides, I wanted you to see me in a good way for once."

Elaina blushed. "Arcon, you always look good to me."

"I appreciate the compliment," he said, "But be honest, I do look better now."

She looked him up and down. "Good enough to have almost been worth the interruption."

"What interruption?" he asked, but all he got from her was a sly look. Then it hit him. "Oh, right, when Roberto came home." He walked over and pulled her close. It still felt good when she rested her head on his chest, but his mind was more distracted. He felt he was in the right place, with the right person. But he had no clue how to go beyond this spot in time, and he had no one to talk to about it.

Jarden sat down at the foot of the long conference table. At the opposite end stood Petra Valerio, the elected leader of the ArcPoint Community. Petra kept things in order, but that would happen anyway. Everyone knew their place, did their job and worked with each other. Petra was just a figurehead, and he was comfortable with never being needed. Arcon's exit had just stripped him of that comfort. Jarden knew that and was there to help.

"Can we bring this meeting to order?" said Petra to the Community leaders gathered around the table. "We have important things to discuss." He waited while the heads of the various departments found their seats. When their attention was settled on him, said Petra, "I want to thank you all for taking the time to come to this unscheduled meeting. We need to get a few things straightened out before the upcoming State of the

Union meeting, which, as you know, is right around the corner." He nodded to the woman next to him. "Karen?"

"Sure," she responded, and all that had gathered lifted their right palm skyward. "Lord God, we seek your wise council today. Speak to us by your one Spirit, so in unity, we can discover your will and our path forward." Karen's voice softened in reverence. "You alone have full knowledge of our needs and are able to provide. At this moment we seek your wisdom, in the name of Jesus."

Everyone said, "AMEN!" in unison, with enthusiasm.

Staying seated, Petra said, "Jarden, share with us your understanding."

Jarden stood and said, "Thanks again for the opportunity." He nodded at Don Denton, his former boss. "Every year at the State of the Union, the Head of Procurement gives an accounting of Community supplies, and every year there's a need for something. We receive advice, ideas, supplies, and volunteers to meet those needs. And every year, we ask God's blessing on those supplies and the suppliers."

Jarden walked around the room, picking certain people to make eye contact with. "Every year, God has met those needs, and you all know He's done it His own way—not necessarily as we expected or asked. Some needs are never met, and we eventually discover why we really didn't need them. He's also given us the skills we need to overcome the limited resources this place provides."

Walking back to his place at the conference table, Jarden picked up a Bible and held it out toward the others. "God created this physical world to meet our physical needs. He intended to meet our spiritual needs Himself. But evil spirits persuaded evil men to do evil things with what God originally said was good." He held the Bible close, running one hand over its cover. "Our Founders asked God to separate us from that evil and to once again become our sole source for things of the spirit. Now here we are, in a place that's good."

Jarden returned the Bible to the table and picked up a small, flat, rectangular object. "We don't know if the outside world is still evil, or if it's good, or some combination of the two." He held the object up. "If this thing worked, it could probably tell us. The Founders called it a smartphone, and back then, everybody had one. Some people even gave up life in this Community because they couldn't part with this device. Doesn't sound smart to me." Many people laughed at the comment. He waited for them to quiet down again.

Jarden took his seat and leaned forward, resting his forearms on its rustic wooden surface. "This time every year, since I was a boy, we've taken a vote on whether we should investigate what's happening in the outside world. Should we send out spies, as Moses did? Or should we ignore it until we simply can't survive here? For years now, we've been divided on our decision. That should tell us we don't have the unity of His Spirit regarding this issue."

Jarden filtered through some papers in front of him. "This is my first year as Head of Procurement. I want to thank Don Denton for the excellent job he's done for us over the last twelve years. If not for his tenacity to coordinate our supply and demand, we may already be gone from here." Spontaneous applause rumbled through the Franklin meeting room. Don stood and bowed a few times, then motioned for everyone to quiet down.

Jarden cleared his throat. "My report looks grim. You all know we lost our secondary generator this past year. Without parts from the outside world, we now have only one working generator. If it fails, we have no way to operate our refrigeration compressor. Besides other things, that means we'll have no way to store fresh milk, meat, produce—you get the picture. If we lose it, our lives will transform dramatically. Our mechanics say it's functional for right now, but it's worn out."

A scattering of voices could be heard in the room. Jarden shuffled his papers again, then laid them on the table. "Many of you know that's not why I called this meeting. We have reached the point where procurement has gone from difficult to impossible for some important needs. That's the conclusion Don and I came to." All eyes turned to Don Denton, who nodded agreement.

"This year, we won't need to vote on sending out a spy. Arcon assumed that role of his own volition—contrary to my counsel and the rules of the Community. I was able to locate him on his journey and discover his motives. I am now convinced that God was his motivation. If God is for him, we mustn't be against him."

"In my address next week, I will ask the Community to pray for Arcon, that he'll be successful in finding the truth and in returning here safely with it." Murmuring in the room slowly got louder. Jarden held up his hand. "Let me say one more thing before we open up for discussion. Don and I believe it is too risky to operate without a backup generator. In the outside world there may be vast resources that could improve our lives. So, too, may be dangers that could destroy us."

Once again, Jarden concentrated his focus on certain individuals—those with profound influence on the Community. "For the first time, the Procurement Division was going to be insistent on sending a spy into the outside world. True, Arcon was disobedient in leaving before the Community was in agreement. But rather than condemn him, let's unite around God who has kept us His own for all these years. Whether we rejoin the outside world or stay separated from it, it's important that we are one in God's Spirit and obedient to His will. With that, I hand the meeting over to the wisdom and understanding of others."

CHAPTER ELEVEN

Roberto heard the chirp of his PID and recognized Ranger Dan's code. He checked the message. It read; [PHONE CONNECT?] He responded by sending Dan his Channel One number and then waited. After a few minutes, it rang, and he answered, "Roberto here."

"Hi Roberto, this is Dan Wilson. How are you doing?"

"Doing fine, considering," said Roberto, with a nervous laugh. "How about yourself?"

"Very well, and I want you to know the kids are fine. I've been in communication with the gatekeeper, Patty—she has a good handle on the situation. Now I'd like to talk with you about how we proceed."

Roberto felt an immense weight lift off of him as Ranger Dan spoke. "I appreciate knowing," he said. "So, how is it we need to move forward?"

Ranger Dan laughed. "I don't think anybody knows. The rules for quarantine from the Mojave were laid down over a century ago. No one I can find knows what to do about it or what to do after the quarantine. That may help us."

"How do you mean?" asked Roberto.

"If the two of us come up with a plan that makes common sense and has some obvious wisdom involved, we could probably plot our own course."

"I like the sound of that. Have you been working on a plan?"

"I've started on one," said Dan, "but it so heavily involves Tarzan that I'll need to discuss it with him. I'd like to have you there when I do."

"Elaina as well?"

Dan laughed. "At this point, I don't think we can separate them. Of *course,* she can be there. I was planning on heading down to the Camp to visit them this weekend. Where are you located?"

"I'm in Apple Valley, near Highway 18."

"Would you like to meet me in Lucerne Valley on Saturday? We could meet for breakfast around 7AM at the Junction Restaurant. Then we can go there together in my car."

"Well, if we take your car, then breakfast is on my account."

"Great, it's a deal. Between now and then, I'll have a doctor friend of Patty's do some testing on Arcon. Requirements of the quarantine statutes."

"Who's Patty, again?" asked Roberto.

"She's the owner of the Survival Camp. I thought you spoke with her."

"We only texted. I just assumed ... "

Dan laughed. "One thing you never want to do with Patty is assume anything. You'll probably be wrong."

"She sounds like an interesting lady."

"There you go, assuming again," said Dan. "Okay, see you at 7 AM at the Junction. I'll confirm everything with Patty and Arcon and let you know for sure on Friday. As they say in the rodeo world, hang on tight."

Roberto chuckled and said simply, "Will do."

Patty knocked on the door of Arcon's container. "Is anyone awake in there?"

"I'm awake now," she heard Arcon yell. "Enter!"

As she walked through the door, the motion detector light came on. She could see they were watching a black and white television show. They got to their feet, and Elaina walked over and gave her a hug. "I assumed you'd be awake," said Patty, "since you got here about 6 hours ago. Soon it'll be time to go to bed again."

Arcon looked at the watch on his wrist. "Then this thing can't be right."

Patty gave him a quizzical look and said, "What's it telling you?"

"It says one-fifteen, but without any windows, I don't know if that's AM or PM."

"Sorry about giving you a container without windows. They aren't all like that. It's about 5:30 PM, so either that watch doesn't work, or it was set wrong."

Arcon slid it off his wrist, looked it over, and said, "I don't know how to set it."

"If you don't mind me asking, why are you wearing a watch if you don't know how to set it to the right time?"

Elaina blushed and said, "That's my fault. I got him the watch, but I didn't have time to explain how to use it. That was on the agenda for today."

"Well, in this place, time doesn't matter much. We try to do things here like they did in the Tribulation times. Back then, they used the sun to tell time because the EMP fried a lot of the fancy phones people used."

Arcon brightened, "In the forest, the only thing we use is the sun."

"But you knew how to read the hands on the watch?"

"I've got my grandma's old clock, so I figured it out. The Community uses a sundial in the south courtyard as the official timepiece. But us hunters use the sun itself. I'll use that."

Patty nodded. "I still recommend you learn to use that watch. You'll have plenty of time to do that tomorrow. I hate to say it, Arcon, but I still don't want you to go topside when other people are around. Just so you know, tomorrow I have a doctor scheduled to come and do some testing on you. She'll draw some blood from you, take a urine sample, the usual. She'll want to ask you about any medical issues you've had or been exposed to. Don't worry; it's all routine. If you have any objections, let me know now, and I can postpone it."

Arcon looked at Elaina. She didn't seem worried about any of that. "It's a good thing, right?" When she nodded approval, he asked Patty, "Will the testing end the quarantine?"

"The testing will let us all know if you're safe to be in society," Patty responded. "It will also let us know if you need to be treated for something before we can allow you to interact with people."

"You don't seem too afraid to be around me."

Patty snorted. "Honey, I'm not afraid to be around anybody. But if they find something serious, they may want to quarantine everyone who's had contact with you, including me. I don't think it'll come to that. Diseases like that haven't been seen for over a hundred years."

"So, if I test out okay, when will the quarantine go away?"

"Well, it usually takes up to 48 hours to get all the test results," said Patty, "so that'd mean late Thursday or Friday we should get the all-clear. That's what we're shooting for because I have something special for you on Saturday."

"What's that?" asked Elaina.

"You two will get a visit from your dad and Ranger Dan Wilson!"

Patty hadn't realized how much Elaina missed her dad. With tears streaming down her face, Elaina gave Patty another hug, this one tighter than the first. She patted Elaina on the back and said, "Don't thank me." Patty started to pull away but changed her mind. "Oh, what do I care? If it gets me a hug and makes you feel better, thank me all you want."

Patty couldn't help but notice how Arcon's countenance had dropped. "Hey there, Tarzan. I thought you'd be excited to see them."

"I am ... I'm excited they're coming," he responded. "I just didn't mean to cause so many problems."

"Aaaahh, you're fussin' over nothing. Those are tears of joy on Jane's face, and I don't think the men mind. This may be the most interesting thing that's happened to them in a long time. Besides, I know a little secret about Ranger Dan."

"What's that?" asked Elaina.

"He's been wanting to meet one of the Mojave People for a long time. Ranger Dan's got a whole lot of questions for you. To be honest, so do I. How about you and me sit down sometime and share some notes about the good old days?"

"What... what do you mean?" asked Arcon.

"Well, from the stories I hear, your people fled into those woods during the Tribulation times. My ancestors fled to this place for the same reason." Patty motioned around the container. "That's how I inherited this junkyard."

"Really?"

"Yeah. I thought maybe I could pick your brain about what you know, and I'll tell you what I know about those days. Maybe between us, we can discover the truth."

"I know a lot," said Arcon. "One of my ancestors was the Founder of the Community, and we have a Room of Remembrance where we have a lot of stuff from that time period."

"Well, there you go," said Patty. "One of my ancestors built this place, and I had about twenty rooms of remembrance. They were called containers full of trash. But I found a few diaries and photos and such. Anyway, we've got some time over the next few days. I'll stop by, and we can reminisce."

"I'd like that," said Arcon.

Patty had questions, but she was mostly fulfilling a request from Ranger Dan to get some historical information out of Arcon. Dan wanted to know who these people were, how and why they ended up there, and any psychological profiling she could get about him or others in that community.

Patty was a master at doing that sort of thing because everybody trusted her. She maintained that trust by never violating it. But she wasn't a respecter of persons. Arcon would get the same respect that Dan would until something proved to her he didn't deserve it. Beyond all that, this intelligent but gullible young man intrigued her. She knew she would enjoy his company, and toying with him when she could.

Noreena Chan took another sip of her hot chocolate as she scanned the screen on her laptop. *Still nothing.* She tapped away on her keyboard, entering another name into the ancestry archives. She tried to find someone on her list who had *not* disappeared during the Tribulation times. There had to be somebody still alive who was familiar with the Mojave People. Once more, she threw her hands in the air when her search hit a dead end.

She glanced at the clock. *I should have been in bed two hours ago.* This mystery kept her too wound up for that. In her mind, she saw frightened people—men, women, children—clutching each other as the land broke apart around them. Scrambling back and forth, trying to find a way of escape, cut off from their families by a massive canyon. Then being forced to eke out a living for, what, over a century? *How is that possible?* She had to know.

She leafed through a folder on the table, picking up an overhead photograph of the RED-C research facility. She'd found it in the government archives attached to a building permit. She'd also found satellite photos of that area. All of them showed a desert landscape. She could find no photos of an Acacia forest in the Mojave area. No information about that area or its people that was less than a century old. *Fascinating.*

Also fascinating but disturbing, was the time period associated with the RED-C. That period in earth's history was the most devastating to man's existence. By the time it was over, a third of the population of the planet was gone. More than half died at the hands of other people because of religious conflict, political upheaval, or indifference to human life. Many others were killed in record-setting natural disasters and a worldwide pandemic. Lost in the chaos were multitudes that simply disappeared.

With all Noreena's research, she was learning a lot and not enjoying any of it. Genealogy websites showed many family trees with stripped and broken branches. She tried not to think about the horrors of that time period. The Mojave People appeared to fit into the category of those who'd disappeared, but what number had gone was unknown. She could certainly understand why they'd fled society.

She found the names of ten people associated with the building in the photographs. They'd signed a 99-year lease with the owners of the property and paid in full. Those same ten people were named in correspondence with the County regarding building permits, but soon after, the Rift destroyed the freeway, and there was no more correspondence.

She focused her investigation on those ten individuals. It was a long shot, but maybe their relatives outside of the Mojave Forest survived. Then the archives would help her track down any that might still exist.

Mentioned most in correspondence with San Bernardino County was Lee Franklin. He seemed to be the primary contact person for the group, at least as it concerned government entities. Noreena began a search for his name in every archived document the County possessed, for ten years before and after the signing of the lease. She'd let her computer churn away at that, then check what was discovered in the morning.

CHAPTER TWELVE

Patty jumped up from the chair in her office when she heard a bell tone from the emergency communication system. A single tone meant nothing, so she waited. Three tones meant someone needed help. Five tones meant 'intruder alert.' She walked toward the comm room and heard another single tone. If she heard two more at once, it was something special. She walked closer to the panel, then heard two tones. *Arcon is awake and wants to talk about old times.* She reached for button number fifteen and tapped it twice to let Arcon know she was on her way.

She walked back into the office meeting room, where a dozen guests were enjoying breakfast. "You folks don't need me, do ya?" she asked as she put on a light jacket. She didn't expect a response and got little more than a grunt or a wave from a few. These were regular visitors who knew if they asked for anything, she'd say, "Get it yourself." She grabbed three huge cinnamon rolls and a jug of milk from the table, then headed for Arcon's container.

As she walked across the barren landscape, she turned her back to the chilly wind. She thought about the Rift and the land that lay beyond. Sanctuary of the Mojave People—Arcon's people. She was excited to learn more about them. When she got to the door of his space, she knocked twice and walked in. She found them sitting on the sofa and said, "I brought your gourmet continental breakfast. Come and get it."

They both stood up. "What's that?" said Arcon.

She set the rolls and milk on the table. "Probably the best cinnamon rolls you've had since you got here."

"I've never had sinnanin rolls."

"Then I was right," said Patty, as she walked to the cupboard and grabbed two glasses.

"It's pronounced sin-uh-min," said Elaina. "Have you ever eaten cinnamon?"

"I don't know."

"Oh, you'd know it if you had. There's nothing like it."

Patty handed him one. "These rolls have a *lot* of cinnamon, just like they did back in the day. Try it."

Arcon sniffed it, then took a large bite. "Oh, mibe memmer han mumting nike dis."

Patty laughed. "Didn't your momma ever tell you not to talk with your mouth full?"

Arcon's countenance fell. He turned and took a few steps away from them. Patty looked at Elaina, who just waved her hand and whispered, "Sore subject. Just give him a minute." Then, in a normal volume, "These are superb, Patty. And they're huge."

"Uh, yeah, they're from a recipe I found left in one of the containers. Somebody must have stockpiled a lot of cinnamon when they went into hiding." She looked at Arcon, who was taking deep breaths. *Must be trying to compose himself.* "I think some of the regular guests come back here just for these rolls."

Arcon turned toward them. "I know I'll be back." He took another big bite.

"No need to," said Patty as she handed him a glass of milk. "I'll bring you two some of these for breakfast every morning until the quarantine is lifted. Then you'll have to get them yourself. I don't do room service. You're an exception, but you'll have to pay a price."

"What's that?"

"Telling me the story of your people. Of course, I've agreed to tell you about this place, too. How about if I go first?" She sat down in the wicker chair facing the sofa. She wanted Arcon to have an example of what kind of information she was looking for without making it look too invasive.

"That'd be great," said Arcon, as he and Elaina sat back down. "I've been wanting to know what this outside world was like in the bad times. The information I have is as old as the Rift."

"What you get from me will be old as well," Patty replied, "but it'll be from a different perspective, and that'll help give us clarity."

"Like depth perception," remarked Arcon. "It's hard to swing through the trees with only one good eye."

Patty laughed. "I don't know. Your story sounds more interesting already."

"No, it's already agreed," said Arcon. "You go first."

"Okay. What do I know about this place? Do you remember that abandoned factory we passed on the road up here?"

Elaina said, "Yeah, that was a concrete plant, right?"

"Sort of right. They manufactured cement that was used to make concrete. It employed about two hundred people. Some of them were the ones who initially built this place." Patty paused and took a bite of her roll. "One of them bought a used shipping container from the company and set it up as living quarters, so he didn't have to commute from San Bernardino. A few more joined him. Others were set up as summer places because of the lake."

"How did they get all this stuff up that little road?" asked Arcon.

Patty just laughed. "There used to be a big road in from the plant. But when it shut down, they decided they needed this place to be more secure. So, they took dynamite and blew up the old road. By that time, fuel was so scarce nobody was driving much, anyway. That road we came up was only a trail for motorcycles and horses. Over the years, it's gotten wider, but I plan to keep that little backward driving trick."

"Why put the containers in the ground?" asked Elaina.

"Originally, it was to keep warm," responded Patty. "As you see, it gets cold up here. Somebody put two containers together for more space; then another couple did the same right next to them. The containers were backed up to a natural berm, so they brought in overburden from the mining site and buried them with just the front sticking out. It caught on. Do you know why they're so close together?"

"So they didn't have to use so much dirt to cover them?"

"Maybe, but that's not the main reason. If you pile a lot of dirt against the side, it'll buckle. We learned that the hard way."

"When did they start doing the survivalist thing?" asked Arcon.

"A local tragedy struck. Someone in the group had a relative get killed by a maniac couple who shot up a County meeting in San Bernardino. The incident forced them to consider what the future looked like. In one of the diaries, I read government leaders were promoting lawlessness, and law enforcement was forced to let it happen."

"The same thing happened with our Community," said Arcon. "Most lived in Los Angeles. I don't know how bad it got, but when they got this opportunity to move out, they did."

"How did they end up in the Mojave Forest?" asked Elaina.

"It wasn't a forest back then," said Arcon. "I've seen old pictures. It was desolate—not a place where anything grew. That's why we were there. To grow trees."

"What do you mean?" asked Elaina. "With no water? In a desert?"

"The founders were scientists—researchers working on special trees for bio-fuel. These trees could grow in the desert where there wasn't much water. They grafted buds onto a certain rootstock." On and on, Arcon spoke about how the Community got started, how the trees went wild, how the rhizomes trapped them there, and how they'd devised ways to travel over them.

Patty didn't even try to interrupt him. She was getting exactly what she needed with no coercion. Arcon seemed to be proud of what that group of people had done, and there didn't seem to be any mention of the evil rumored to be there.

When Arcon reached a stopping point, Patty asked Elaina, "Did you know any of this before he got across that Rift?"

"Not at all. We couldn't communicate much." Arcon and Elaina exchanged looks, grinning at one another. "I hate to admit it, but when we saw him dressed in animal skins, it fit our image of the Mojave People more than a lab coat would have."

Patty laughed and asked Arcon, "Were all the people that moved out there scientists?"

"Oh, no," answered Arcon. "From what I was told, the only real connection between them was my ancestor, Lee Franklin, who built buildings. He gathered people he thought might want to create a safe place to hide from the world. There were some that worked on the bio-fuel project. Others were farmers or in construction. No one knew it would turn into what it did."

Patty decided it was time to ask the question Ranger Dan wanted an answer to. "It doesn't sound to me like the group was a religious cult or anything. Was it? I mean, originally?"

Arcon shook his head. "Grandpa Lee hated religion, and especially the thought of us being called a cult. My grandma explained it to me with Bible verses from Galatians five. It lists all the bad things we should avoid, and one was factions, which I didn't understand. But one of her Bibles said it differently— the feeling that everyone else is wrong except those in your own little group. She said that's what cults do that tends to separate them from the rest of society. Grandpa Lee said we should all be united by God's Spirit, and that's what the rest of that chapter is about."

Patty smiled and nodded. "I like that. Sounds like Lee Franklin was a wise man. Let me tell you what I found in a diary someone left in a container. This lady complained about not having a church to go to. She wrote about it often. I got the feeling she needed someone to tell her what God wanted from her. She sounded lost and desperate. It was sad."

"I have a confession," said Elaina. "When we first figured out where the Morse code was coming from, it scared Daddy that it was from the Restricted Area. I didn't know why, so I looked the Restricted Area up on the Searchnet." She looked at Arcon. "A lot of the results called your people a cult. I don't know where that idea came from."

"Is that why you stopped beeping to me?" Arcon scowled at her, and then smiled.

"Daddy made me stop. But in school I took this voluntary class called *History of Religion*. It explained how people would follow some slick-talking person, like sheep after a shepherd— even in Christian churches that you think would know better. Their leader would face the altar and talk to God, then turn to the congregation and supposedly talk *for* God."

"Whoa, I hadn't heard that." said Patty. "That's a bit dangerous, being the go-between like that. But then, those were strange times. It's easier for us, because Jesus is here in person again. Back then, maybe they needed someone to speak for God."

"But they didn't," argued Elaina. "In the book of Hebrews, it says God did at one time have to use prophets to speak to man. But when Jesus came, He became that spokesperson, and has been ever since. Until He returned, He spoke through His Holy Spirit. But Arcon, isn't that the way you say it was for the ArcPoint people?"

"Not at the very beginning," said Arcon. "I read in my Grandpa Lee's writings that there was some kind of religious argument that almost broke up the whole Community. In fact, he was ready to leave if people weren't willing to give up their religious baggage."

"So, how did they settle the argument?"

"I don't know for sure, but it sounded like instead of each person thinking they were right, they all agreed they could have been taught wrong. That's what Grandma told me, to understand there's always the possibility I'm wrong. She said it's more interesting to learn what God is doing with someone else than insist they conform to your viewpoint."

Elaina asked, "When you say Grandma, do you mean Lee Franklin's wife?"

"Oh, no. She was my mom's mom, so she was only a Franklin by marriage. She insisted on reading the Bible to me every day. It was a special time we had together. Lee Franklin was actually my great-great-grandfather."

Patty then asked him, "You haven't told us about your parents. What are they like?"

Arcon hung his head and was silent. Then he mumbled, "I think it's your turn. I've talked enough. Finish telling me about this place."

Patty saw she'd struck a nerve again, so she didn't press the issue. "Sure, where was I?"

Elaina swallowed a bite of cinnamon roll. "You were talking about some maniac couple who shot up a meeting."

"Ahh, yes. We were talking about religion? Well, those two were religious extremists. Anyway, one of my relatives, sort of a way-distant cousin, was one of the people with a container home here. He'd fallen into some family money and was quite a survivalist. He didn't think the money would do any good in banks or stocks or anything. He offered to turn the place into a survivalist enclave if everyone could come up with a workable plan. They ended up with over forty containers, all with power and plumbing; limited, of course. You know, solar panels, composting toilets, and the like. They had a weapons cache and hydroponic gardens and, well, if someone thought of it, this guy could afford to buy it. So, they built all this stuff underground and then built worthless shacks on top of it all to fool the public."

"That's cool!" said Elaina. "How did *you* end up here?"

Patty crossed her arms. "My brother and I inherited it. That wealthy cousin of mine bought the land from the cement company and bequeathed it to one of my ancestors. By the time it got to my brother and I, it was trashed. Vandals had burned out a few of the containers; others weren't sealed properly and rotted away."

"It looks great now."

"Thanks. It took a lot of sweat to make that happen. We restored about a dozen, and I've added a few more since. Now it's this nostalgic yesteryear survival camp, and people pay a lot of credits to sort of hide out here."

"So, is your brother still involved?"

"Oh sure, he loves this place. But I'm the permanent caretaker," she said, pointing a thumb at her chest. "My husband helps during the winter months, but seven months out of the year, he works on a floating fish cannery in Alaska. And my brother, well, his job keeps him busy all the time. He comes up here when he can." She paused and then grinned. "You'll get to see him in a few days."

"We will?" asked Arcon.

"Sure you will," replied Patty. "His name is Ranger Dan Wilson."

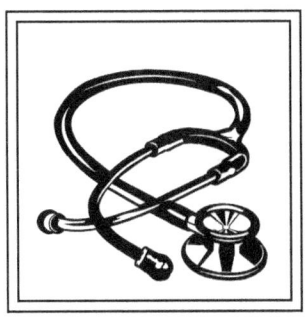

CHAPTER THIRTEEN

Noreena Chan had never sojourned into the catacombs of the High-Level Archives. Her training prepared her for what she might find, but she'd never had the need—or the desire—to enter this world of the past. But all her research had hit dead ends. The Archives was the only place left if she was going to locate relatives of Lee Franklin, Norman Ashford, Phillip Langston, or any of the other people whose names she found in the land documents.

Private records of the deceased—called Level One archives— were open only to family members, certain qualified personnel, and whoever the family trusted. Mid-level archives—those purged of sensitive information—were accessible by anyone. But both of these security levels were set apart from the High-Level Archives, which still used the various computer languages of the 21st century. No modern-day computers had ready access to that long-ago information or the ability to decipher it.

Noreena strode up the expansive concrete steps of the Central Library. She admired the ancient architecture and tried to discern the modern repairs. She'd watched a virtual tour of this venerated building—with archived footage of its former glory, its extensive damage during the Tribulation era, and then its restoration. She showed the receptionist her press credentials, then handed him the Information Request form and a signed Confidentiality Agreement. "What is the purpose of your examination of private records?" he asked.

Noreena was prepared for that question. "I am attempting to make an ancestral connection."

"Your own?"

"No, sir. I'm doing this for a young man who's from outside this geographical area."

"And you have no ancestral link to this person?"

"None, sir—unless you go back as far as Noah."

He shot a look at her and smiled. "Usually, I hear Adam or Eve." He perused her request form. "Why is this person not doing this research themselves?"

Noreena shifted her bag to her other shoulder. "He's unfamiliar with the resources. I also have reason to believe he may be uncomfortable with what can be discovered in the ancient archives."

He nodded. "Aren't we all?" Looking over her papers, he said, "I see you have more than one surname you're investigating. Do they have a familial relationship with this man?"

"Unknown." When he looked askance at her, she added, "Over time, this man's lineage has been lost. I have discovered these names in my research of what little past records can be found. I'm hoping a cross-reference will find a common connection to a particular family."

"Understood. Are you familiar with the procedure?"

Noreena breathed a sigh of relief. She'd begun to worry if she'd get past this guy. "This is my first time," she said, adding quickly, "But I've been trained in the protocol and have a lot of experience in Mid-level archive retrieval. I plan to start by inputting every name I have to see if I can get a hit."

"That's what I'd do. If you need assistance," he said, pointing at his lapel, "just ask anyone wearing a red badge like this. May God guide your efforts."

"Thank you, sir," she said, shaking his hand. "That's my goal here."

As Noreena entered the records room, she grabbed an English keyboard. She found a two meter wide monitor—the largest she could locate—and paired the two devices. She wanted as many documents in front of her face as possible. She furiously typed in every bit of information she had—people, places, businesses, timeframe—then watched as the screen filled with archived references.

All Noreena needed was a name—one that was a link between any of the Mojave People and those who are alive today. She had no desire to carry any of this information outside of these walls. *Just as well. I don't want that extra level of scrutiny.*

The reason for peering into someone's past had to be for praise and not condemnation. She could lose her press privilege in a heartbeat if she was dishonest or malevolent. Noreena had an excellent reputation because she consistently wrote praiseworthy articles for the Portal. She always looked for the good in people because that's what she sincerely hoped to find.

Once the Forgiveness Directive had been put into place, derogatory information was purged from society. Noreena was glad that only related individuals could do the purging unless the offensive information was flagged for scrutiny. The process minimized the wholesale destruction of past accomplishments, but she pitied those people who had to do the scrutinizing. Information deemed worthy of future consideration was translated into the new computer protocol—similar to determining which house items end up in a moving truck. Only in rare cases was the physical paper archived—in such a place as this library. Also, in this place were mountains of information no one has cared to deal with.

All of those facts left Noreena with very little to work with a hundred years later. *If the Mojave Forest People left society before any of this archiving, who would have kept—or purged—their information?*

It was like searching through a garbage heap for a lost wedding ring. But she scanned the monitor, quickly eliminating the irrelevant, until she found one important piece of data—Lee Franklin's home address in Los Angeles. She dug further and found an arrest record for him being a street evangelist in the early 21st Century. *Interesting. That could fit the cult theory some people have.* The arrest record gave her the piece she was missing: Leeland Augustus Franklin—his full legal name.

She did a search and screeched out loud when he was the only person with that name combination. She quickly made notes on her laptop. Parent's names, brother's name, home address, childhood address, schools he went to. She found an obituary for Constance Franklin—wife of Arnold, mother of Joshua and Leeland. *I should make a copy of that.* The obituary was archived by Joshua Franklin—Lee's brother. Now, all she needed to do was trace ancestry forward to the current time period. She jumped up from her chair and did a little dance.

Generation by generation, Noreena worked her way through the Franklin family tree. She made sure what she needed was in the Mid-level archives so she could use them without special permissions. By the time she finished, she had a list of thirty-six potential adult relatives who may still be alive. Now she had to hope she could find them, that they would talk to her, and that they might know something about the Mojave People. Then she hoped whatever news she found was praise-worthy. If it wasn't, she couldn't publish it, and she wouldn't want to. All she would have for her efforts was a satisfied curiosity.

It was still early morning when the three returned to Arcon's container. Patty set the cinnamon rolls on the table while Elaina fetched glasses for the milk. "By the way," he said to Patty, "thanks for letting me into the exercise room so I could run. I needed that." Exhausted, Arcon plopped himself on the sofa.

"Well, I figured I could close it down for you while everyone else was eating breakfast. I thought you could use some exercise after being cooped up for a couple days."

"And boy, you ran!" added Elaina. "I've never seen anyone turn a treadmill up that fast. Are you sure you'd never been on one before?"

"Been on one that didn't work. It was in the Room of Remembrance. There was no one left who'd ever used it, so no way to know what to expect with one that worked." Arcon shook his head and chuckled, "I don't normally fall when I run, but the gray strip of ground wouldn't stop."

Patty laughed. "That was the best entertainment I've had in years."

"I'm glad my pain could bring you amusement," said Arcon, grimacing. He pointed his thumb at them. "What does it mean when you point your thumb? I see that a lot out here."

Elaina turned his hand so his thumb pointed up, not out. "A 'thumbs up' means I approve of whatever just happened."

Patty got a call on her shoulder-phone. "Dr. Alicia Stone just arrived. I need to go lift the log for her. Elaina, you should go back to your own container while Dr. Stone is here."

"Sure, I understand," said Elaina, but stayed until Patty was gone. She touched Arcon's forearm and asked, "Are you all right with this?"

"All right with what?" he asked. "Seeing the doctor?"

"Doctors make some people nervous."

"I talked to the Medics all the time," said Arcon. "They're just people like you and me. Plus, they know some healing tricks."

"Then you don't mind if I leave you alone with this person?"

"No, I'm fine. Just make sure and come back later. I still haven't heard enough stories about you and Roberto."

"It's a deal. Just come knocking on my door when the doctor is through." She wrapped her arms around Arcon, giving him a big hug.

Arcon pulled her close and held her tight. He found it very easy to hold her, but it became more difficult to let go. This time, however, he gave her more of a quick, ArcPoint type hug. It seemed appropriate to end the hug before Patty returned with the doctor.

Arcon liked the lady doctor that showed up at his container. She reminded him a lot of the Medics at the Community, except for the gloves, mask, and face-shield. She wasn't in a hurry, didn't ask a lot of personal questions, and seemed to care about his well-being. She attached things to his chest, his head, his arms and fingers for awhile. She got a blood sample, a saliva sample, and others he'd never had to do at ArcPoint, and made him glad Elaina wasn't there.

Staring at a computer screen, she said, "You seem to be very healthy. Do you have any health issues that you're aware of?"

"I don't know of any," he replied.

"How about in the community where you lived? Were there any chronic problems among the other residents? You know, anything your doctors couldn't find a cure for?"

Arcon thought about that for a while. He raised a finger and said, "There's one thing I'd like to talk with you about, but I'd prefer you didn't say anything to Elaina. I need to talk to someone, and a doctor seems like a good place to start."

"I'll tell you what," said Doctor Stone. "I'll need to discuss whatever I find with the authorities. But I promise I'll discuss the test results with you first. I won't force you to tell me anything, but if I need to be looking for something, it'd be good to do so while I have all these samples."

"I know exactly what you mean," said Arcon. "I worked around a lot of lab technicians. I agree to your terms."

"Great," said Dr. Stone. "What's the problem?"

"For many years now, it's been difficult for women in the Community to have babies, especially girl babies. Our Medics can't figure out why."

Dr. Stone jotted notes into her comm-pad. "How many years has this been going on?"

"No one knows when it started because it was gradual. Across at least two generations, with some families, maybe four."

"How many years would that be?"

"At least forty," responded Arcon. "Maybe seventy."

"Whoa, okay. That sounds like a problem. The good news is, it's most likely not contagious, so it shouldn't affect your quarantine. But you're going to want to know what's causing it and whether it can be treated."

"Thank you so much," said Arcon. "I have a girlfriend, Elaina. She's the only girl I've ever cared about, and I know I can't hide this from her.

Dr. Stone nodded. "Well, it's up to you, of course, but I suggest waiting until we've investigated it for you."

"Thanks for understanding," said Arcon, ducking his head. "I'll be praying that God gives you insight and wisdom to find the problem. It's something our whole Community needs."

"I guarantee I'll do my best, and keep the results quiet until I've discussed them with you. We may need further testing, but we'll deal with that later. Right now, I'll rush these samples to the lab and see what we find." She stood and began gathering her things.

"It's been good meeting you, Dr. Stone," said Arcon, shaking her gloved hand.

"I've enjoyed meeting you as well, Arcon, and you can call me Alicia. I hope to see you on the other side of this quarantine."

"I agree to your terms," said Arcon, smiling.

CHAPTER FOURTEEN

The evidence Raymo found in the room of Ancient Evil couldn't be clearer. The outside world was a dangerous, wicked place. He felt privileged to be born in this cocoon of abundant peace. He literally knew every person who lived in the ArcPoint Community. Not a single one would rob you for your moccasins or knock you unconscious as some kind of sick game. There was no need to carry a gun or knife for protection and no reason to learn self-defense. *In this place, God taught you to care, not to kill.*

He scanned through the pages of books, magazines, and newspapers from the era of the Founders. He saw stories of murder and rape, disease and addiction. The ways in which people harmed children filled him with rage and tore at his soul. But it was what he didn't see that angered him the most. Nobody seemed to stop any of it. When roaming gangs went on the attack, the strong had fled, leaving the weak to suffer. Seemed to him that outsiders had turned into animals. If he'd been there, he would have laid down his life for the weak.

The more he read, the angrier he got at Arcon. What would motivate a person to leave this blessed place to live in a land of lunatics? Arcon had always challenged authority and questioned the traditions of the Community. It was good he was gone, but now it seemed only a matter of time before the outsiders might storm their place of seclusion. He just knew their violent world had become like Sodom, everyone lusting after new and different experiences. *The ArcPoint people would certainly be something unique to exploit.* Even if Arcon didn't return, they'd find out where he'd come from, and curiosity would lead them to this forest. Raymo planned to prepare for that moment, with as many faithful defenders as he could recruit.

Dr. Alicia Stone received Arcon's lab results early Thursday afternoon. By quitting time, she'd admitted she was stumped. Everything pointed to Arcon being perfectly healthy, except for higher than normal heavy metals in his blood. There were so many types of metals and rare earth elements she almost wanted to assume something had contaminated the samples.

The good news for Arcon was, none of the lab results would warrant continuing the quarantine. But she needed more information and more blood to determine where these metals were coming from. If others in his community had higher levels, it could lead to infertility. She'd call Ranger Dan Wilson in the morning to set up another meeting with Arcon. *At his young age, with this volume of metals in his system, what might the elderly of ArcPoint have?*

Elaina was glad Patty had allowed them to leave the containers at first light and hike in the hills surrounding the Camp. She thought she'd have a tough time keeping up with Arcon on the trail, given his height and muscle tone. But it was easy, since he stopped to marvel at all the different trees and flowers. He surprised her by knowing their scientific name. He told her the Botanical group at ArcPoint had many shelves full of books about plants.

"For years I studied what I might find outside the Forest. These flowers are far more impressive in real life."

At every high point in the trail, he seemed compelled to look around at the distant scenery. He'd see some interesting object in the distance and ask, "Can we drive to that place?"

At first, she told him, "If you'd like to." Occasionally she had to tell him, "If there are roads to that place," or "If we have time." Finally, she had to admit, "I don't know if we can get enough fuel to go to all those places."

"Why do you need fuel?" asked Arcon.

She chuckled. "That's what makes the engine in the car run."

"I know that," he snapped, "we had engines in the Community. But we had all the fuel we needed. If we needed more, we just made it."

"What do you mean, you just ... made it?"

"We'd go out in the orchard, pick the pods off the trees, and get the oil out of them. Then we have some people who turn it into fuel for the generators, oil for lamps, for a cook stove, or wherever else we need a flame." Arcon tipped his head. "Don't people out here make their own fuel?"

"We have companies that make fuel," replied Elaina. "But raw materials to make portable fuels are scarce. Most of it is used by vehicles that can't connect to the universal electric grid. Cars like mine that are driven far off that grid are considered a luxury, so fuel is rationed to us. I've been storing up fuel credits for a long time in order to do what we're doing. I'm not sure how much longer I can keep it up. Dad has been doing the same thing."

Arcon frowned. "You and Roberto have been saving up to help me?"

"Well, yeah, sure," she stammered. Then she gave him a sly smile. "So far, the entertainment has been worth it."

Arcon thought about that and replied, "So, as long as I fall off a treadmill every so often, you won't send me back?"

"We don't have a treadmill at home," she joked, "and I won't want to live *here* forever. You'll just have to put on the Tarzan suit once in a while."

Arcon stared at her. "So, when am I going to find out about this Tarzan and Jane thing?"

"Well, I planned to surprise you with it, but Patty says she's located an old Tarzan movie on disc. I thought we might watch it tonight in your container."

"So, is Tarzan a tree swinger like me?"

Elaina started walking again. "You'll just have to wait and see."

"How about Jane? Is she a tree swinger?"

She turned, hiking backwards. "Just wait and see," she repeated, pivoting and laughing.

"Well, someday I want to take you to where I came from, to the ArcPoint Forest."

She spun and said, "Really?"

Arcon gave her a big smile. "When we get there, I'm going to teach you how to swing through the trees like I do."

"I may surprise you," said Elaina, putting her hands on her hips. "I've spent a lot of time on ropes. My dad taught me how to rappel down cliffs. I even know how to tie a bowline." She showed him a smirk that let him know she could hold her own.

Arcon gave her his first 'thumbs up' and grinned.

Dr. Alicia Stone tapped her shoulder-phone and exited the elevator. "Call Ranger Wilson," she said as she walked toward her office. "Hi, Ranger Wilson? This is Dr. Stone. I have some good news for you."

"Hi, Dr. Stone, what's the news? Is our jungle boy free to go?"

"My admin is finishing up the paperwork as we speak. We found no reason to continue the quarantine. Except for a few scabs and bruises, that boy is as healthy as you or I."

"I'm excited to hear that. I was hoping Arcon wouldn't have to wait long. Will I get the paperwork in a few minutes then? I'd like to push this thing through the channels so it's official before the weekend. I'll be visiting him tomorrow. I'd like to break the news to him in person."

Dr. Stone walked to her administrative assistant's desk. "Is it about ready to go?" The admin held up two fingers. "The admin says you'll get it in two minutes. Is that quick enough?"

"That's perfect," said Dan.

"Speaking of visiting Arcon, I need to examine him again." Dr. Stone walked to her office to check her schedule. "If the Authorities lift the quarantine by this weekend, I could work Arcon into my schedule for Monday. Can you discuss that with him since I don't have access?"

"Again?" asked Dan, "I thought you said everything was okay."

Dr. Stone thought for a second. "It's a personal matter that doesn't relate to the quarantine issue. I told Arcon I'd talk with him privately first before I discussed it with you. I just need to take another blood sample and ask him a few questions."

"I understand," said Dan. "Doesn't sound like I'd need to know. Would I?"

"Technically, it's got nothing to do with the quarantine, so maybe not." Dr. Stone thought about the effects on the Mojave People. "Since you have authority over the Mojave, maybe it does. Let me talk it over with Arcon first. Right now, my tests are inconclusive, so I don't know how to focus the discussion, anyway. Just have Arcon contact me to make an appointment, and we'll go from there."

"Sounds good to me, doc." He chuckled. "I think you're going to make Tarzan and Jane very happy."

"That's my intent," she responded, privately hoping she could solve the infertility mystery. "Have a nice weekend."

Back at her hotel room, it took Noreena eleven phone calls to find someone home who remembered a Lee Franklin as a distant relative. Then it took more to find someone who might have some archived information about him. The name Dolores Reid came up a few times as being the family historian. If she didn't have the information, hopefully, she'd know who did. Noreena hadn't been able to reach her all day, so now she was trying during the dinner hour.

"Hello?" said a woman's voice.

"Hi, is this Dolores Reid?" Noreena asked.

"Yes," came the curt response.

"Hi, I hate to bother you at this hour, but it's important I talk to someone about one of your distant relatives."

"Who is this?" asked Dolores.

"Oh, sorry, this is Noreena Chan. Your cousin Jeff Franklin gave me your number. I'm a reporter for the San Bernardino Portal, an online news service." Noreena spoke as fast as she could to keep this woman on the phone. "I'm doing some research on a Mr. Lee Franklin who lived in Los Angeles over a hundred years ago. Would you have any information about him?"

"What kind of information?" asked Dolores, sounding like she wanted to hang up.

It was times like this that Noreena preferred a door she could stick her foot into. By phone, all she could do was be honest and hope for the best. "I'm investigating reports of a man walking out of the Mojave Forest last weekend, so I'm trying to find out anything I can about the people who moved there in the early 21st century. The name of Lee Franklin has come up often in my search. I would appreciate any information you might have about Mr. Franklin or the Mojave People in general."

A long silence elapsed. Eventually, Dolores asked, "Did you say you saw someone walk out of that place?"

"There were quite a few witnesses to the event, but unfortunately, I wasn't one of them. I'm trying to get permission to speak to the young man, but so far, he's been in the custody of the Mojave Park Authority." Noreena decided she needed to make her plea quickly. "Please understand. I don't want to violate your privacy at all. I have no intention of publishing anything without one hundred percent approval of all involved. I just have a passionate desire to reunite this man with any living relative he may have outside of the confines of that Forest." Noreena took a breath and slowed her pace, imploring, "Please allow me to talk with you if you think you might have any information at all."

"Do you think there's a possibility you could talk to this person?" asked Dolores.

"It's possible," said Noreena, "But I can't guarantee it."

Dolores was quiet again, then said, "All I can say is, I'm sure the family would very much like to meet someone from that area. We'll be willing to work with you if you'll work with us regarding what you publish, if that's what you're offering. But before I commit the family to anything, I'll need to discuss it with them."

"That's perfectly acceptable," said Noreena. "Thank you very much. I look forward to meeting you, and I'll continue to press the Authority to allow me an interview. Could I at least tell them I may have discovered descendants of that group? It might help."

"For right now, please say you are *looking* for descendants and *may* be getting close to finding some. If you give me your number, I'll let you know as soon as we decide as a family," said Dolores.

"Sure. Do you have something to write with?" Noreena Chan then gave Dolores all of her contact information, including her PID code. She could now turn her attention back to the Mojave man himself.

Arcon examined the cover of the disc, popped it open, then calmly walked over to the disc player. He inserted the disc as if he'd done it a thousand times. Elaina couldn't reconcile the vision of him arriving at the Rift in animal skins and the technical savvy she was witnessing now. A smile slid across her face as he deftly pressed a button on the remote and the disc tray slid into the machine. They cozied up on Arcon's couch as the television came to life.

It embarrassed Elaina that Patty had given them *Tarzan and His Mate* for them to watch. But Arcon seemed oblivious to the reference. All he could talk about was how his friend Jarden wanted him to know who Tarzan was. But the moment the movie showed Tarzan swinging through the trees, he blurted out, "How did he do that? The rope wasn't set." Throughout the movie it was, "He can't do that," and "That can't be real," or "Why did he yell like that?" But Arcon was on the edge of his seat once Tarzan started wrestling a lion or an alligator.

At first, Elaina was concerned, remembering how flippantly they'd called him Tarzan—maybe Arcon wouldn't take it as a compliment after watching the movie. They both blushed at the scanty clothes Tarzan and Jane wore, especially when Jane started swimming naked. She wasn't sure what to make of Arcon watching Jane's every move, following her actions in the water. Then he asked, "Can you teach me how to do that?"

"Do *what?*" Elaina asked.

"What they're doing in the water," he said, grabbing the remote. He pressed pause, and the movie froze on a frame of Tarzan and Jane in mid-stride as they raced away from an oncoming alligator. "That's called swimming, isn't it? I've seen pictures of it, but we didn't have any water deep enough to swim in. Can you swim like that?"

"I guarantee you I can't swim like *that*!" she said with a snort. "But yes, I can swim."

"Can we go up to that big lake so I can try it?"

"The answer to that would be no, on a lot of levels," she said, hitting him with one of the sofa's throw pillows.

"Why not?" he asked, grabbing the pillow from her.

"Three words—drowning, hypothermia, and swimsuit," she said, swiping it back.

"Explain those, one at a time. First, what is drowning?"

"That's when you go down in the water, and you don't come back up."

"Why?"

"Because you breathed water and died. Next, hypothermia," she blurted before he could ask a question.

"But…"

"Hypothermia is when your body gets too cold, and you die."

"Why?"

"Because the lake is made from melted snow."

"And that …"

"Number three is a swimsuit," she said, ignoring him. "That's what they don't have on, and you and I would need, or we're not going there."

"What do you mean?"

Elaina just pointed at the paused TV screen, where Jane was having an obviously naked moment, most of her backside on display. Arcon glanced at that, then back at Elaina. "Don't look at me like that," Elaina kidded. "How about if we just watch the rest of the movie and discuss it later?" Then she grabbed the remote and hit play. From that point on, Arcon was quiet.

CHAPTER FIFTEEN

Roberto showed up at the Junction Restaurant fifteen minutes early, but Ranger Dan's vehicle was already sitting in the parking lot. When he walked in, Dan was at the counter, talking to an attractive, dark-haired woman. Roberto walked up to them and gruffed, "Is this man bothering you, ma'am?"

Dan spun his stool around and threw out his hand. "Roberto, good to see you. You're early."

"And you're earlier," said Roberto, shaking his hand.

"Let's get a booth so we can talk. Marla, could you bring us some coffee? Oh, and no matter how much he protests, he's paying for breakfast."

"Sure thing, Dan," said Marla, the owner. "Do you want the usual?"

"Of course."

"That's good because I already ordered it for you." Then she looked at Roberto. "Are you ready to order?"

"If you have a Spanish omelet, I'll take that."

"Hash browns or toast with that?"

"I'll take the hash browns."

"Anything to drink besides coffee?"

"Just some water, thanks."

As they walked to their booth, Roberto said, "I take it you come here often."

119

"I came here with my parents when I was a kid. Marla was just a waitress then. Now she owns the place." Dan slid into a booth. "I stop here about twice a month when I go down to see my sister."

"She must live down here somewhere," said Roberto, sliding in the opposite side.

"Yes, at the Big Bear Lake Survival Camp. We own it."

"Oh, so that's how you found a place to hide Arcon so fast. I wondered how you managed it. Thanks again, by the way."

"Speaking of that young man, I have some good news for him, and probably you as well. They lifted the quarantine."

"Are you serious?" asked Roberto. "Is it official?"

Dan turned his coffee cup up and set it at the front of the table. "The official paperwork will come through at the first of the week. But from this point on, he won't be committing a crime by being in public." Dan leaned back and crossed his arms, glancing around for the waitress as he spoke. "He just won't have the needed papers to get his permanent identification and exchange account. But after we meet today and I give him the news, you can take him home. Congratulations, I think."

"Thanks, Dan. Elaina will be so excited." Roberto laughed, adding, "And I'll be excited to have Elaina cooking for me again." Marla set two glasses of water on the table.

Dan laughed too. "I know what you mean. My wife was in Oregon while I was trying to take care of myself and deal with all of this Arcon business. Glad to have her home again." Marla returned and poured the coffee. "Thanks," said Dan.

"Have you heard anything from a certain Portal reporter?" asked Roberto.

Dan sipped his coffee. "Almost every day. Usually, Becca gives her an official response for me. But as of late, I've had to be honest with Miss Chan and myself. Someday soon, the young man from the Mojave Forest will be free to make his own decisions about talking to reporters."

"Just so you know, I've decided to contact that reporter myself before that happens. I think it'll be easier to control the situation that way. She may not be the best person to break the news to the public, so I thought I should do some damage control on Arcon's behalf."

"I totally agree," said Dan. "I'll give you her contact information. For what it's worth, she's been good to work with so far. She's been tenacious but not overly aggressive."

"Good to know," said Roberto. "Plus, the Portal has a small audience. It'd be a good place to test the waters and see how the public reacts."

A different server, Jenny, showed up and settled a plate full of strawberry waffles, sausage, and a frothy glass of orange juice in front of Dan. Nodding at Roberto, she said, "Yours will be here in just a few minutes."

"That'll be fine." Roberto eyed Dan's breakfast. "You have that every time you come here?"

"It's one of my few indulgences. Plus, if Marla sees my car pull in, she orders my breakfast made before I step through the door. Saves me some time."

"How about if I pray so we don't waste more of it?" Dan nodded approval. Roberto said, "Father, we ask for your blessing on this food, our conversation, and our travel. Thank you for this stranger that has united us. Help us be faithful to your vision for his life and our participation in it. We give you the day, Lord. Amen." As he finished, Jenny handed him his breakfast. "Thanks, that looks like plenty."

The friends ate quietly for most of their meal. After a while, Dan leaned back and asked, "Did you say you have a vision for Arcon's future?"

"Well, no. I think God does, though. Elaina was compelled for years to communicate with him and then lately to work with him to get out of that forest. At first, I thought it was a childhood fascination, but I felt drawn to get involved too. I don't know what God has in mind for him, but I think whatever it is, it's important."

Dan was quiet again as he wiped up strawberry juice with his last bite of waffle. He pointed the forkful at Roberto and asked, "If I was to tell you something personal, could you keep it between us, at least for now?"

"Sure. What is it?"

"This whole thing with Arcon shook me up a lot more than I realized. I've listened to rumors about the Mojave People for a lot of years. I personally believed something tragic happened to all of them a long time ago. Then, last year, I became the authority over their land. You know how this authority thing works, right?" He poked the bite in his mouth as if his question was rhetorical.

"Not personally."

"Well, if two parties have a dispute about land in my jurisdiction, they come to me to get it resolved." He pushed his empty plate away. Jenny grabbed it as she walked by. "If it's a personal disagreement, that's governed by someone else. I only deal with land issues. In this case, I'm not allowed to set foot on *that* land. If someone makes a claim regarding the Mojave Forest—let's say they want to harvest the trees—I'm not allowed to approach any of the Mojave People to get their input."

"That'd make it difficult." Jenny filled their coffees and took Roberto's plate.

"I was afraid I'd have to investigate that place someday," said Dan. "I didn't even know if any of them were still alive. If they were, what were they like? Now I find out there could be hundreds of people out there, and their land is under my authority."

"Wow, I hadn't considered that. Have you thought about how you're going to deal with those people?" asked Roberto.

Dan turned and stared out the window. "I've been told what to do."

"You have?" asked Roberto.

"Yes. I don't know if you'll believe it, but Jesus appeared to me the other night. In my kitchen. I was lucky the place wasn't a total mess, with my wife away and all."

"Our Lord, Jesus? He appeared in the flesh?"

"He seemed as real to me as you are right now, only He appeared out of nowhere and left the same way. It was very strange. And very… peaceful."

"Did He speak to you?"

Dan nodded. "That night, after all the commotion with Arcon, I couldn't get to sleep. I was up having a midnight snack. When Jesus appeared, He asked to take my burden. It was as if a heavy weight was lifted off my shoulders. Then He asked who gave me dominion over the Mojave, and I told Him the County did. He corrected me and said they gave me authority, but He gave me dominion."

"Wait a minute. Does that mean you deal with both land and personal issues?"

Dan nodded. "He said I was to serve the Mojave People just as I serve Him. He also said He led Arcon to me as an ambassador for those people. I'd been so conflicted, and He gave me solace." Dan stared at his coffee mug.

"That's really powerful," remarked Roberto. He could see Dan was shaken up by the whole affair. He tried to imagine what it would be like. He considered his own actions in disobeying the law of the Restricted Area. "How do you think Arcon will take that?"

"I've had time to think long and hard about that. Somehow, God has to have prepared him for what he's done. I'm eager to talk with Arcon about it and see how our stories match."

Roberto crossed his arms and leaned forward on the table, interested. "I'd sure like to be there when you do. And I know you won't be able to keep Elaina out of it."

"To be honest, I don't think I could exclude Patty either," said Dan. "She's taken quite a liking to the boy. She had a lot of doubts about me getting involved in all this, but now I think she'll thrust herself in the middle of it. If she does, there'll be no stopping her."

"So far, everything I've heard about Patty makes me think she is… formidable," said Roberto.

Dan chuckled. "You assumed right on that one. How about if we head down the road so you can meet her?"

"Sounds good," said Roberto, sliding out of the booth. "I'll take care of the bill and meet you at the car."

"Hello. San Bernardino Portal. Noreena speaking." She may be eating toast and eggs at her kitchen table but liked to give the impression she was at her office desk.

The voice on the other end of the line said, "Hi, this is Dolores Reid. We talked yesterday about the Mojave People."

Noreena straightened. "Yes, Dolores," she said, surprised by the upbeat tenor of her voice. "Thanks for calling. I hope you have good news for me."

"What I can tell you is, I have a list of names of the original people who moved to the Mojave Desert. I'm sure it changed, but it was made by Lee Franklin and given to his brother. We wouldn't be comfortable turning that list over to the public, but if you give us the name of this person you spoke of, we could try to match it with the names on the list for you. Then maybe together we could track down relatives for this person."

Noreena felt deflated. "I don't have his name yet, and it's unlikely any of those people are alive after more than a century. If I had a copy of that list, I could ask this person if any of those names ring a bell."

"We may consider that if we have your word to keep it private," said Dolores.

"I can do that," said Noreena. "Do you have any other information in case we discover more people coming out in the future?"

"To be honest," replied Dolores, "I'm sort of an amateur historian, and I have a particular fascination with the ArcPoint Community, which is what the Mojave People called themselves. But I'd prefer you didn't make that information public either. There's still a lot of belief that the Mojave People are evil, but all my research has revealed the opposite. So, until we can sort through the truth with a living remnant of that group, we'd prefer to remain anonymous. I hope I can trust you with that."

"I completely understand. All I ask is, if I'm faithful to your requests, I'd like to have exclusive rights to the story, at least as far as the Portal is concerned. I'd like to be the one to break the news to the public, with the permission of all involved, of course."

"I think that's only fair," responded Dolores. "Are you any closer to interviewing this person?"

"I finally got a chance to talk to the man in authority, and he said this young man will soon be free to make his own decisions regarding interviews. That's about the best we can hope for so far. I'll let you know as soon as I hear more."

"Thanks, Noreena. You know, it's all kind of exciting. I know a lot of these families would like some closure on the subject. It'd be even greater if a number of people from that group survived."

"At least one has," remarked Noreena. "Thanks again for calling. Let's keep in touch."

"Let's do that. Goodbye."

Ranger Dan turned off Highway 18, angling up a steep gravel road until it leveled off. He stopped, then backed a little way up a narrow road that was blocked by a fallen tree. "Okay, we're getting close." As he typed away at his comm-pad, he said,

"I'll let Patty know we're here." They sat there with the engine idling, making small talk. Dan asked Roberto about his adventures in rescuing hikers, occasionally glancing in his rearview mirror at the dead tree.

Eventually, he grumbled, "I'm not sure what the holdup is. I'm going to drive down to where we need to meet her." Instead, he reversed, only looking in the rearview mirror as he raced up the hill backward, yelling wildly, "Whoa, whoa, whoa. What's happening?"

Roberto jumped to watch the road, the bank, and the road again until Ranger Dan cut loose with a huge barrel laugh. "I just love doing that!" he exclaimed.

"Very funny," said Roberto. "What happened to that tree in the road?"

"It's still there," said Dan, as he pointed down the road. Roberto blinked as he watched the tree drop back into place. "Now look up there," added Dan, pointing to the next driveway. There stood Patty, waving at them. Dan drove until he was alongside. "Hi Patty, this is Elaina's father, Roberto. Roberto, this is my sister, Patty Abrams."

"Pleased to meet you, Patty," said Roberto. "You two just about scared breakfast out of me."

"Would have been worth it," said Patty. "It's not my car."

"Enough of that talk," said Dan. "Patty, I think you have something that belongs to this fine gentleman."

"He can have the girl," said Patty. "I'm keeping the young man for some cheap labor. He knows how to fix the disc players."

"He knows how to do *what*?" asked Dan. "Where did he learn that?"

"Beats me," said Patty. "Why don't you go ask him? I'll see you at the office."

Dan drove off to park next to Elaina's car while Patty stopped by Arcon's container to let him and Elaina know they had visitors. Elaina didn't even wait for Arcon but scampered up the ladder and ran across the field to her dad. As she talked his ear off, Dan met Arcon and shook his hand. "Good to see you again, kid."

"Good to see you too, Ranger Dan, sir," responded Arcon, quickly adding, "I need to thank you for a lot of things, but especially for saving my life."

"What?" asked Dan. "When did I do that?"

"When you threw the rope around me at the Rift. Roberto showed me—my safety rope broke. I would've fallen and died if you wouldn't have roped me."

"Well, okay then," said Ranger Dan as Patty approached. "Patty, you're a witness. This kid owes me something important. I think he needs to repay me with friendship for life. What do you think?"

"That only sounds fair," said Patty.

Arcon smiled big. "I agree to your terms, Ranger Dan, sir."

Dan grinned. "Well, now, if we're friends, you never call me sir, just Dan."

Arcon put his hands on his hips. "And you can call me Arcon, never Tarzan."

Patty whispered in Dan's ear, "He watched a Tarzan movie last night."

Dan's eyebrows shot up. He nodded. "Arcon it is then, uh, I agree to your terms as well." He turned to Patty. "How would you like to give Roberto a tour of the place?" He looked back and saw Elaina hugging her dad. "Take Elaina with you. Looks like she'd like to spend some time with her dad."

Patty nodded, assuming Dan wanted a little private time with Arcon. "I'll keep 'em busy. You know I love to brag about this place." She walked to where the other two were standing.

"Arcon, let's go inside where we can talk."

"I'd like that," said Arcon, beaming.

In the door, Dan went straight to Patty's refrigerator and grabbed a bottle of water. "Need anything?"

Arcon grinned. "Does she have some of that green tea?"

"She sure does," Dan responded and grabbed a tea for him.

As they sat down facing each other, Dan said, "First of all, I have a personal message for you from Dr. Stone. She wants to meet with you on Monday to discuss a private issue. She said you can come to her office anytime, and she'll work her schedule around you."

"Would I be free to go there?" asked Arcon.

"That's the other news I have for you. Dr. Stone has recommended lifting the quarantine, so yes, you'd be able to go to her office."

Arcon's eyes got big. "Are you saying I'm free to go anywhere I want?"

Dan waved a hand at Arcon. "Now calm down, son. We still need the official paperwork in order for you to do all the things we do nowadays. That may take a week or two. What I'd like to do is discuss what needs to happen and how we can help you make it happen. Would you be okay with Roberto and Elaina sitting in on that, and maybe Patty too?"

Arcon didn't hesitate. "I've got no problem with that at all. I don't know how I would've survived here without every one of you. The only thing I feel strongly about is that God wants me here. I don't know if it's true or not, but it seems like God has put all of you in my life, even Patty. So yeah, if we're discussing my future, the more, the merrier."

That was exactly what Dan wanted to hear because it confirmed what Jesus had told him. There's already a plan in place for Arcon's life, and they all simply needed to step into their own particular roles in that plan. "Let me fetch the rest of them," said Dan. "It's time we got this show on the road!"

Dan walked out of Patty's container, spotted the three of them at the far end of the clearing, and gave a short, shrill whistle. When they looked his way, he beckoned Patty with his hand, and she acknowledged the signal, mimicking his gesture.

Back inside, Dan told Arcon, "I've got Patty herding the Gonzales duo in this direction. Follow me, kid. People have a saying here, 'Today is the first day of the rest of your life.' I think for you that's especially true."

Arcon's brow furrowed. "Isn't that true for everybody?"

Dan chuckled. "It certainly is, but most don't have their life take such a sharp turn." Inwardly, Dan decided now was not the right moment to tell Arcon it may be a U-turn.

CHAPTER SIXTEEN

When all five were in Patty's container, Dan addressed them. "Go ahead and get comfortable in the guest lounge. Get yourself something to drink if you need it. I'm buying."

"You are?" asked Patty, feigning shock.

"Put it on my tab," he responded. "I've got some big news for everyone. But I think everyone's already heard it, except Elaina."

"What did I miss?" asked Elaina.

Arcon said excitedly, "They lifted the quarantine!"

"Really? How come no one told me?"

"It was a secret," said Dan. "So, I only told one person at a time." They all laughed at that. Dan's tone turned serious. "With those of you I've talked to, I've been seeing a pattern of behavior that I'd like us all to discuss. We've all had a shift in our lifestyles by the appearance of the young man sitting here, and I think it's time we understood why. One by one, I'd like us to go around the room and tell what's been happening with each one of us. It's time we open up. Be honest. Patty, how about if we start with you?"

Patty mocked a look of disgust at Dan. "You want open and honest? How about this for a start? All our lives, you've picked on your little sister."

"You're not little," said Dan, feeling like he'd just poked a bear.

131

"Watch yourself now," Patty snapped back. She shrugged. "Anyway, I don't have much to say. I already told Arcon I didn't like you getting involved with him. I've read the diaries and stories of what happened in *this* place during the evil time. These people did not get along in close quarters, and before long, it was as crazy as the rest of the world. It became survival of the fittest. Steal, kill, or destroy, whatever it took to make it from one day to the next. I figured these Mojave People would be the same, only a hundred years worse." She winked at Arcon. "I got so worried for Dan that I had to talk to God about it. He gave me a peace that it'd be okay, but I didn't truly lose my doubts until I met Arcon and Elaina."

"That was great, Patty," said Dan. "But I'm big enough to take care of myself."

"Except against me," she countered.

"Uh, true," said Dan, glancing down. "Roberto, you're next. How has this adventure affected you?"

"Well, it's affected me pretty close to home. In fact, *in* my home. Not to steal too much of Elaina's story, but years ago, when she heard a strange Morse code signal on the radio as a child, it was like a treasure hunt or mystery for us. I enjoyed working with her to solve the puzzle. But like Patty here, when we figured out where the signal was coming from, I told Elaina to break it off, to stop communication with the stranger."

"And I did," added Elaina. "Quite a few times."

Roberto narrowed his eyes and said matter-of-factly, "And quite a few times, you started up again without asking me."

"You knew about that?" asked Elaina.

"I know more about you than you think," he confessed, softening his tone. "But I had a similar experience as Patty. God gave me a peace about letting you do it, but enough doubts to stay on top of it. Over the years, we learned enough about Arcon to believe he wasn't evil, and for some reason, he needed to escape that place. We both felt God compelling us to help him cross the Rift.

I'd quietly hoped our involvement would end there." He looked at Arcon. "Sorry, that's just the truth. But not how I think now."

"I never meant to cause any of you so much trouble," said Arcon in a sobering tone.

Dan interrupted. "Now, Arcon, it's not your turn. If you're through, Roberto, I'd like to hear what Elaina has to say."

"I'm through," said Roberto.

"Yes," said Arcon, "I'd like to hear what Elaina has to say."

Elaina blushed. "Are you sure Arcon can't go first?" She wasn't sure how much to say.

"No, Arcon is going last," said Dan. "Then me." They all gave Dan a pause, and he added, "You know what I mean. Go ahead, Elaina."

"I think everyone knows how I got started with this, by hearing that funny Morse code message on Dad's scanner." When Elaina got shrugs from everyone but her dad, she said, "Well, maybe you don't. Anyway, I guess Arcon was experimenting with a transmitter, sending Morse code messages, and I just happened to hear it."

"Just happened to?" asked Dan.

"Looking back now, I think God caused it to happen. But at the time, I was just bored, and that's what I used to do instead of playing video games. I was only fourteen. Anyway, what started out as a game and a mystery developed into a relationship of sorts. But I have to be honest. That Morse code drove me *crazy*. It was a fun riddle to solve at first, but it's no way to carry on a conversation."

"I looked forward to it every night," said Arcon.

"So did I," responded Elaina. "But I looked forward a lot more to talking with you face to face."

Arcon looked at her. "I couldn't agree more."

"Anyway, when Arcon first said he needed our help to escape that place, Dad and I weren't in agreement. He explained that the Mojave Forest was a restricted area, and no one was to enter or leave that place. It was Jesus himself who'd given that order, so the matter was settled. I started praying about it and told God if He wanted us to help Arcon, then He'd have to change Daddy's heart. He did."

"You did?" asked Roberto.

"See? You don't know *everything* about me," said Elaina.

"Evidently not."

Dan interrupted. "Did you have anything else to share, Elaina?"

"Not much, really," she replied. "Dad and I started working together with Arcon to come up with a plan to get him out. We never really thought about what would happen afterward."

Dan looked her in the eyes. "Is that the truth?"

"What do you mean?"

"Did you plan to get him to this side of the Rift and then just dump him into society?"

"Well, no, not really," said Elaina nervously. "We figured he'd stay with us until we found out how to get him established here."

"And then?" asked Dan.

Elaina stared at him. "What are you asking?"

"This will be a tough question," Dan responded, "But I think it's important to the discussion. Were you getting emotionally involved with Arcon? Maybe even romantically inclined? I'm sorry we didn't have this discussion privately, but I have my reasons for asking."

Elaina looked at Arcon, and he injected, "You don't have to answer that if you don't want to."

"I think I want to," said Elaina. "I've had some relationships with other boys, and they've all been very shallow. I've known no one like Arcon. He's open and honest. He's simple and straightforward, yet complex. I think life with him would be a constant adventure. Not that my life with Dad hasn't been, but it can't go on forever. I haven't discussed the matter with either of them, but I guess now is as bad of a time as any. I think spending my life with Arcon would be the best move I could make if he agrees with it." Then she considered her own words and added, "By the way, that's not a marriage proposal."

"Okay," said Dan. "I think you've said enough. Arcon, what about you? Start at the beginning, please, not where she left off."

It overwhelmed Arcon as he tried to think about what to say. "They lifted the quarantine, right?"

"That's right," said Dan.

"So, I'm free to leave?"

"Over my dead body," said Patty. "Remember, no one enters or leaves this place without my permission, and you're not leaving until I hear your story. Now start talking."

"Better listen to her, son," said Dan.

"Well, it was worth a try," said Arcon, with a grin. "Okay, I'll start at the beginning. In the beginning, God created the heavens and the earth—"

"Not that far back," said Dan, laughing. "We know about the ArcPoint Community being formed and how you all got trapped there. But none of you have ever tried to get out until now. Why?"

Arcon gave that question some thought. "We have a big building where we all meet and share our lives. We call it the Facility. In that place, we have a room we call the Room of Remembrance. That's where we put stuff to remind us what the outside world was like before the Founders moved there. No offense, but when we considered what this place was like, no one had the desire to leave the love and friendship we experience at ArcPoint."

"Until you came along," added Dan.

"Yeah, I don't know why I was different. But all the time I was growing up, people told me I was destined to lead the Community, because I was a descendant of the Great Founder, Lee Franklin. They forced me to study all the history of the Community and all of my Grandpa Lee's writings about the horrible state of the outside world."

"You told me you never read his journal," said Elaina.

"Grandma read that to me so often, I thought I'd heard it all. I never knew she skipped parts. Anyway, he was convinced God would take all of us in the Community to be with Him when the time was right; in an event he called the Rapture. That obviously didn't happen in his time. His writings were expected to inspire me to be their leader, but they only inspired me to see for myself what was out here in what we called the outside world. Once I started talking about leaving, they started saying I was different, in a bad way."

"Tell them what you told me," interjected Elaina, "About how you felt when we were communicating by Morse code."

"Well, it's kind of silly, but I felt like a baby bird inside of an egg, or a butterfly still inside of a cocoon. I felt I needed to break out of that place, to be set free. I wanted to be able to fly anywhere I wanted."

Patty added, "And now you're stuck in a container."

Everyone laughed at that, and Elaina asked, "Is that why when we're driving, you say we're flying?"

"Exactly," said Arcon. "I know humans can't fly, but driving is sort of the freedom I was looking for. To look out into the distance and then go there without the restriction of the needle brush."

"Speaking of those nasty sticker bushes," said Dan, "Why did you folks grow that stuff? It's a real nuisance."

"I'll agree with that," added Roberto. "I've had to dig through those briers to rescue people."

"They weren't grown intentionally," Arcon apologized. "What I've been told is they come from the genetically altered rootstock of our ArcPoint trees. With not enough personnel to maintain the pruning regimen, the rootstock took over. When the climate changed and brought more rain than expected, these vines started growing off the rootstock. The Community couldn't control them, so we learned to work around them. Ultimately, the needle-brush protected us from the evil outside world, and soon we were stuck there. Most of the Community was fine with that. I don't think any of us knew it was invading your area. What can I say?"

"What exactly are the ArcPoint trees?" asked Roberto.

"They were the main reason we were there, sort of. The original property owners developed the trees to produce oil for bio-fuel. That part of it works. We've always made our own fuel to run our generators."

"If I might interrupt," said Patty. "That's a long but interesting story that you might want to save for later."

"Oh, okay," said Arcon, his voice dropping.

"Was there something else you wanted to tell us about why you felt compelled to leave your community?" asked Dan.

"Not really. I sort of did what Elaina did. I told God that if I was supposed to leave, he needed to open up a way for me to do it. Getting Elaina's help was a big part of it. But it seemed like every time I was having difficulty knowing what to do, the understanding would come to me." Arcon fell silent for a moment. "I even abandoned my good friend, Jarden. I snuck away without saying goodbye because I thought he'd try to stop me. But instead, he not only found me escaping, he gave me his blessing, and he told me how to find Elaina."

"How'd he do that?" asked Elaina, surprised by this information.

"He showed me how the sun reflects off the windows in Calico. He said you'd probably be in Calico, so I should head toward those lights. He was right."

"So that's how you knew about Calico," said Roberto. Arcon just nodded.

Dan adjusted himself in his chair and said, "If you're through, I'd like to tell you what I've been through."

Roberto leaned over to Elaina and whispered, "You'll find this interesting."

"You've already heard this?"

"Just listen."

Dan continued, "I usually go down to the Rift parking area in the morning to make sure everything is ready for the day. The morning you arrived, I was late because I had a flat tire. I didn't know what to think when I crested a hill and saw the crowd that was watching you. When I asked what was going on, they told me some sort of rescue was happening. I think you all know what happened after that."

"You saved my life," said Arcon.

"I suppose I did. But what was so strange was, all of that seemed normal to me. To be honest, nothing seemed out of the ordinary until Ranger Dwight got out of my vehicle at a restaurant in Yermo."

They all laughed at that image and Roberto added, "I so wanted to be there for that."

Dan held up a hand and said, "I swear, when that happened, the weight of the situation hit me, and I panicked. According to the rulebook, I did everything wrong. Even Ranger Becca thought it was strange that I let you go like I did. I was so afraid the three of you would disappear, and I'd be left without my trousers."

They all laughed again, and Patty said, "I have your clothes, by the way. I had to confiscate them when they arrived. I washed them."

"Oh, good," he replied. "To continue my story, I was so troubled that night I couldn't sleep. I hadn't eaten my lunch, and my wife wasn't there to make me dinner. I got up in the middle of the night to eat the sandwich from my lunch. And then..." Dan paused to compose himself. "Then Jesus appeared next to me at the table."

"Jesus appeared?" asked Arcon. "In real life?"

Dan chuckled and cleared his throat. "He asked if he could share what I had, and I thought he meant my sandwich."

"Are you kidding?" asked Elaina.

"No, I'm not," said Dan in embarrassed chagrin. "But he said he wanted to share my burden, and then he lifted all the worries off of me. It's hard to explain, but I could feel it inside as well as outside."

"Wow," said Arcon. "Jesus Himself."

"I take it you know about Jesus?" asked Dan, gladdened by Arcon's response.

"About Him, but I've never met Him. That's amazing."

"Well, you'll find it interesting what He said next. He told me that I had not followed the manmade rules correctly in dealing with you, but I had followed His Spirit correctly." Dan put his hand on Arcon's shoulder as he delivered the Lord's message. "I was supposed to help you, and I'm to continue helping you."

Arcon's eyes went wide. "Really? He said that?" He looked at Elaina and she seemed as surprised as he was.

"Yes. And He said *you* were to help *me*."

"I'd be happy to help you, Ranger Dan. But how do I do that?"

"You need to understand how things work in our world, Arcon. Jesus is the ultimate authority over all of mankind. He rules from Jerusalem, and He's placed others in authority under Him."

"The First Resurrected," interjected Roberto, stunned at this turn of event.

"Correct. In chapter 20 of the book of Revelation, it tells us those who died during the Tribulation times would be the first ones resurrected from the dead. They would rule with Christ for a thousand years. Other Bible verses tell us Jerusalem will be the center of this ruling authority. Now we refer to these people as Central Authority. There are more people in authority over smaller areas under them, and so on. At the bottom are people who have authority over areas of land, while others are the authority over the people on the land. Do you understand it so far?"

"I think so," said Arcon. "We had something similar in the Community, but there weren't very many people."

"Okay. Around here, San Bernardino County has authority over the people in the County in general, outside of city limits, and they made me the authority over the land. That authority includes the Mojave Forest. Do you understand what that means?"

Arcon thought about that and said, "You are the authority over the ArcPoint Community?"

"No," said Dan. "I'm the authority over the *land*. Nobody had authority over the people because Jesus said that area is off-limits to everyone. So in reality, the only person to have authority over your people was Jesus himself."

"But I don't think anyone ever saw Jesus," Arcon stated.

Roberto and Elaina exchanged a knowing smile.

Dan smiled as well. "That probably means none of you ever needed governing, because you were properly governing yourselves. That's the way it works. Everyone is free to do whatever he or she desires until someone disputes what someone else is doing. Then the authorities step in to settle the disputes." Dan looked intently at Arcon and said, "There's something else Jesus told me."

"What's that?" asked Arcon.

"He said he's giving me dominion over the ArcPoint Community, land, and people," said Dan.

"What does it mean to have dominion?" asked Arcon. "Is that different from authority?"

"Yes, it's much deeper. As the authority, I'm like a judge. I scrutinize facts and evidence, and I work to settle disputes. At any time, I can walk away from the job, and someone else can be in authority. Having dominion means I'm more like a father. I can still settle disputes, but I'm to care for your Community as

140

if it were my child. I'm to provide for its every need and nurture its growth. And like a father, I can't just walk away." Dan saw Arcon staring at him with his mouth hanging open. "What are you thinking?"

Arcon was silent for a while, then said, "I think you'd be excellent for the job, but the Community may not accept your terms."

"I think that may be why Jesus also told me he wanted you to be my ambassador to those people. You are to help me serve them properly and care for their needs. Arcon, if I'm to fulfill his request—and I certainly intend to try—I'll need your help to approach them, get them to understand we want to help them. Jesus insists that your people remain free, but I feel they need our help somehow. I think that may be why you've come into our midst, to help us help them. Does any of that ring true to you?"

When Dan asked that question, Arcon looked the other way. "We do need help," he said softly. "There's only one generator still running, and it may not last long. The needle brush is encroaching more and more, and free-roaming area is getting smaller." He hung his head and studied his hands. "There's something I haven't told any of you. Remember that private matter I needed to discuss with the doctor?" he asked Dan. "I think I need to talk to all of you about it, especially you, Elaina."

This time, it was Dan who stood up for Arcon. "Son, you don't have to talk about it if it's too personal."

Arcon looked at Elaina. "I think I want to. Elaina, you're the only girl I've ever cared deeply for, and this problem could affect our relationship. I'm afraid to move forward without your knowing." He looked at the floor, then back at her. "And I want to move forward."

"Well then, spill the beans," said Patty, trying to change the mood.

Arcon looked down again. "For a long time, our women have had difficulty having children." He continued to tell the entire story about the infertility that plagued the Community. "Baby girls are rarely born in our community."

When he finished, Roberto asked, "Has the doctor found anything wrong with you?"

"She's found no diseases but said she needs to take more tests regarding this problem. I'm supposed to visit her on Monday, but I'll need somebody to take me there."

Elaina poked him so he'd look at her. "Would you mind if I took you?"

"Of course not. I'd like that very much," said Arcon, feeling relieved to be free of that secret.

"Then you need to understand something. Unless you're cruel or leave forever, you'll have a hard time getting rid of me. I'm willing to take you, no matter what that doctor says about you. I just want to be there when she says it."

Arcon turned to her, and they embraced. "Sorry I didn't tell you sooner."

"Oh, don't worry about her," said Patty. "She'll get over it. Now just stop getting all mushy, or you'll make Dan cry. And I don't like it when people make him cry."

They all had a good laugh and spent several more hours discussing Arcon's future, enjoying a lunch Patty had prepared, and discussing who would care to teach Arcon how to drive.

CONSTANCE
FRANKLIN

CHAPTER SEVENTEEN

Roberto leaned against Ranger Dan's vehicle as Dan and Patty discussed changes she wanted to make to one of the containers. Arcon and Elaina approached, having just finished packing the autocycle. "There's one last thing I'd like to discuss with all of you, before we go our separate ways," said Roberto. "There's a reporter for the Portal who's been trying to do a story about Arcon. It doesn't appear she'll drop it, so I think we should try to use it to our advantage."

"I tend to agree," said Dan. "Often with a reporter, if you don't steer the story, they'll make up their own. It only makes sense since that's their job, and it doesn't look good to put forth something that's incomplete. I'm familiar with Noreena Chan's work. She's a human-interest reporter. Does some good heart-warming stories. So far, she's been understanding and pleasant to work with. But she's also persistent, and I think she's getting impatient. We need to give her something to work with soon."

"What's she looking for?" asked Arcon. "How can we help her?"

"She wants to find out everything she can about you," responded Roberto. "She'll want to know where you came from and why you're here."

"Okay, I can tell her that," said Arcon, without hesitation.

Roberto shook his head. "Remember when we first drove up to the station? I warned you about the paparazzi? They're photographers who swarm celebrities to get pictures of them. I was kidding, but reporters can be the same way, Arcon. If reporters think there's a big story, they're on you like bees on a hive. Each one tries to be the first to get your story to the public. We'd rather pick one to tell your story to, hoping the others will leave you alone."

"Okay then," said Arcon. "Shall we go talk to her?"

"It's not that easy, son," said Dan. "As soon as that news comes out, most of us will be in some kind of trouble. And you'll probably have your freedom taken away again, either by the authorities or the public. If we have Noreena tell your story correctly, and honestly, and in a timely manner, then hopefully, we can appeal to the Grace and Forgiveness directive."

"What's that?" asked Arcon.

"Well, son, sometimes people make mistakes or poor judgments. Our society has laws and rules for punishment that are sometimes more severe than the infraction deserves. God is gracious and quick to forgive, but us humans, sometimes, are not. If a person thinks the human judgment is unfair, he or she can appeal to God to judge. Jesus has trained judges who are filled with God's Spirit. Their opinions supersede all others. The Grace and Forgiveness Directive is the set of rules Jesus laid out for us to follow to settle these types of disputes."

Arcon hung his head. "I didn't mean for anyone to get in trouble."

Dan gave Arcon's shoulder a shake and looked him squarely in the eyes. "Jesus told me his sheep make rules for other sheep to follow, but He put his laws in our heart. From his perspective, we've been doing things correctly, even if our human laws say otherwise.

"That's right, Arcon," said Elaina. "If we have to, we'll appeal to his judges. That's what the Directive is for."

"Don't worry about it; we're okay," added Dan. "We just need to move ahead cautiously. I agree with Roberto. I say he should set up a meeting with Noreena and probably include you. Oh, and Elaina too, of course."

"That's right," said Elaina. "Don't leave me out of the conversation *again.*"

"And don't forget about me," said Patty. "You're always welcome to hide here if what they told you doesn't work."

Arcon laughed. "Maybe I should hide here until it does."

There had been eleven responses so far on Noreena Chan's help wanted ad requesting information on the Rift crossing. So far, no one had witnessed the entire incident. But she was able to get the rights to some great shoulder-phone footage. A man in animal skins walking a tightrope across the Rift, and more of him getting into a vehicle. Although exciting to watch, that alone wouldn't prove he came from the Mojave Forest. He could've been performing a stunt for publicity or a thrill.

Someone claimed to have seen a man in animal skins moving through the trees on the other side of the Rift. Unfortunately, they didn't have any photos or video. But it was corroborating evidence that someone had broken the law by stepping foot in the restricted area. It also meant a criminal investigative reporter would take the story away from her.

Another saw the man in skins in a car with the Park Ranger, driving through Calico. But Noreena knew that was a hoax perpetrated by the Ranger himself. *The Park Rangers are definitely complicit regarding the Mojave man. But that still makes it a criminal story, not a human-interest story.* She had to find some way to get in touch with the Mojave man himself.

The Search and Rescue office had no record of the Rift rescue. They would be the key to unlocking the mystery and possibly getting an interview. She'd have to keep pressing the Rangers.

Having spent so much unfruitful time this past week on what her boss said was a marginally interesting story, she was now in the office on a Saturday evening, trying to catch up on regularly scheduled articles. She was about to leave when her office phone rang. She considered letting the machine get it, but thought otherwise. "Hello, San Bernardino Portal, this is Noreena."

"Hi, Noreena. I didn't expect to get you on a Saturday. This is Roberto Gonzales. I work for San Bernardino Search and Rescue. I may have some information for you."

Noreena almost dropped the receiver. She sat back down at her desk and looked for pen and paper to write his name down before she forgot it. "Would, uh, would this happen to be about a young man crossing the Rift last Sunday?"

"Will this conversation be off the record?"

To most reporters, taking information they could never use was a waste of time, especially on their day off. But Noreena's fascination with the subject made her want every fragment of information she could get. "I'll tell you what I tell others. I will publish nothing without one hundred percent approval of all parties involved. I just ask for exclusive rights for breaking the story."

"And if you don't get those rights?"

The question offended Noreena. "I will still maintain my integrity, sir."

"Then you'll get the information," said Roberto. "And the rights. Sorry, I had to ask. This is a sensitive situation. This young man has been through a traumatic experience, and he needs some time to heal before being thrust into the public arena. We feel if we break the news through one news source, there won't be much of a story left for the rest of them. We want that news to be accurate and complete right out of the gate. If you'll agree to work with us on that, you can have that first news release."

Noreena couldn't believe her luck. This was the type of story that could help her break into the big markets. Her job at the Portal paid the bills, but she always felt she was destined for something larger. Her love for what was good always seemed to be trumped by the public's love for the sensational. She needed a story that was both good in its nature and sensational in its occurrence, and this might be it. "I can agree to that wholeheartedly."

"We will expect you to withhold the information from your employer as well until it's complete and approved."

"That will be difficult to do, sir, and maintain my integrity."

"I understand," responded Roberto. "But less so if you do it on your days off. Would you be willing to give up some time tomorrow?"

"On Sunday? Absolutely." Roberto's logic made perfect sense. After all, her boss had told her to stop letting this story interfere with her other work. "Where can we meet?"

"I'm on call tomorrow. I can work from home or the office, but the SBS&R also has a remote site that will be unmanned on Sunday. It'll be a private place where we can talk freely. But we run the risk that I may get called away. Will that work for you, say around 9 AM?"

"If it works for you, I'm fine with it. Can I bring a recorder?"

"As long as I have your word that what you record remains private. We'll only approve the transcript after it's been redacted."

"I'm good with that," said Noreena. "Just not good at taking notes. I know that's kind of sad for a reporter."

Roberto laughed. "Integrity is more important to me than competence."

Noreena laughed too, "I suppose I can take that as a compliment."

"I meant it that way," said Roberto. "If you have something to write with, I'll give you the address."

"Believe it or not, I've been making notes as we speak. So far, I have your name."

"That's a start," said Roberto, giving her the address and directions to the Search and Rescue site near Silverwood Lake.

"That must be the reporter," said Roberto, peering out at the red autocycle pulling into the driveway of the Silverwood Lake SBS&R field station. "She has a car just like yours, baby girl."

Leaning against her dad's desk, Elaina said, "I like her already."

"I think I have to agree with Ranger Dan. I've never enjoyed talking to reporters, but I have a peace about her. She sounds like she'll be a good person to work with."

"Hope so. I still wish we could have just hidden Arcon away for a while."

Roberto looked at Arcon. "That would have been simpler, for sure. But after all we discussed yesterday, I wonder if she isn't part of God's plan as well. Why don't you two hide out in the back room while I try to find out where she's coming from."

"Why does it matter where she came from?" asked Arcon as he and Elaina hustled down the hall.

Roberto opened the door and stepped out to greet Noreena. As expected, she was indeed the same woman who'd questioned him at the Ranger station. There was no mistaking the wavy red hair framing a distinctively Chinese face. "Noreena Chan, I presume?"

Noreena noticed Roberto looking at her hair and said, "Before you ask, my father was Chinese and my mother was Irish."

"Well, before I apologize for staring, let me say I think it works well."

"Thank you," said Noreena. "It's always worked well as an icebreaker too."

"I can imagine. Come inside. Can I get you some coffee or ice water? That's about all we have here."

"No, I'm fine," she responded. "I just finished my coffee on the way up here." She glanced around. "What is this place?"

"It's a sheltered spot to gather if we have a rescue in the area. We have a few sleeping bunks, hiking gear, emergency supplies, that sort of thing." He walked into a large room with a fireplace and one wall covered with maps. Pointing to a large table surrounded by a few chairs and bar stools, he said, "Here we have a meeting area where we discuss tactics and share information. Why don't we sit here in this room? I'll be right with you." He walked away to reheat his coffee in the microwave oven. As he approached her again, he asked, "What is your understanding of the Mojave People?"

"Almost zero," she confessed. "A week ago, I didn't even know they existed. I've only been in this area a few months. I'm still not sure if the stories are facts or urban legends."

He looked her in the eyes. "Why are you so interested in this story?"

"Uh, do you mind if I turn on the recorder?"

"In a minute. I'd first like to know what motivates you to pursue this story so tenaciously."

Noreena bristled. "I know you think I'm just a reporter, prying into other people's affairs to make a living. But I assure you, I'm a human being first, and I care about family. So, let me take a minute and tell you *my* story. At the end of the 20th century, when the Communists were taking over Hong Kong, my ancestors and many others moved to Canada. Vancouver B.C., to be exact. There was an area of town where people spoke Mandarin, and mostly we kept to ourselves. Many families moved back to Hong Kong in the early 21st century, but some, like my family, lost too much in the first move and got trapped here. After more than a century and all the tribulation troubles, it was a laborious task to reunite with family in Hong Kong. You may not believe me, but my main goal is to help this young man, whoever he is, find any relatives that may exist on this side of that canyon."

"Wow. If that's the case," said Roberto, "then I believe we can work well together."

"So, will you at least trust me enough to let me turn on the recorder?"

"Sure, absolutely," said Roberto apologetically. He watched her set it up. "It's a video recorder, I presume."

"Yes. Standard practice. People prefer to watch rather than read."

"What would you like to know first?"

"Will this young man be available for an interview soon?"

"He should be here in a little while, and you'll be able to talk to him."

"Does he have a name?"

"Of course. His name is Arcon."

"Is that his first, last, or only name?"

"That's his first name. His last name is Franklin."

"Okay. Do you have any idea how many ... whoa, wait a minute. What did you say his last name was?" Noreena jerked her briefcase open as she waited for Roberto's answer.

"Franklin," he replied.

"You have got to be kidding," she said as she flipped through pages in a notebook. "Arcon Franklin?"

"That's right. What's the problem?"

"Just a second." She scanned through a few pages until she found what she was looking for. "Here, read this," she said, handing a sheet of paper to Roberto.

Roberto accepted the paper from her and realized he was reading an obituary. "Constance Franklin died of a sudden heart attack ..."

"Skip down to the survivors," said Noreena.

"Constance is survived by her husband Arnold and two sons, Leeland and Joshua Franklin."

"Do you see it?" asked Noreena excitedly. "Arnold and Constance Franklin? Ar-Con Franklin?" As Roberto continued to stare at the paper, Noreena asked, "Has this man ever mentioned a Mr. Lee Franklin?"

Roberto stared at Noreena, dumbfounded. "Arcon refers to him as Grandpa Lee."

"Mr. Gonzales, I believe I may have already located some of Arcon's family."

Roberto stared in disbelief. He glanced at some of Noreena's other notes and then back at the obituary. "Excuse me," he said, calling to his daughter. "Elaina! Come on out!" To Noreena, he said, "You can call me Roberto."

Elaina emerged from the back room. Roberto and Noreena stood up to greet her. "Noreena Chan, this is my daughter."

As they shook hands, Noreena said, "I've met you before."

"That's right," said Elaina. "At the Rift."

"Right, we never exchanged names."

"No. Hi. Mine's Elaina."

"That's what your dad told me."

Elaina smiled. "I've heard a lot about you."

"Uh-oh. Good, I hope."

"No comment," said Elaina. "Just kidding."

Roberto interrupted, handing Elaina a piece of paper. "You gotta read this."

"What is it?" Elaina asked.

"Just read it," he replied. "Silently."

Elaina looked it over first and saw it was a photocopy from an antique newspaper. "Oh my. Is this what I think it is?"

Roberto nodded, then pointed to the back room. Elaina handed the page back to her dad and scurried out of sight.

Noreena shook her head. "I'm shocked the one person I focused my investigation on would somehow be connected to this Mojave person."

"I'm sure this isn't the only time you'll be shocked," whispered Roberto. "He's not what we expected either."

Elaina emerged a few moments later with a young man at her side. Roberto turned to Noreena. "I'd like you to meet Arcon Franklin."

"Hi, my name is Noreena Chan."

"Arcon," said Elaina, nudging his arm with her elbow. "Look at this!" She took the paper from her dad and handed it to Arcon.

Arcon glanced at it, then looked closer. "I've got one of these; only mine is all yellow. It's from when my Grandma Connie died. Where did you get this?"

Elaina and Roberto both pointed at Noreena, who said, "I was doing some research on the Mojave People, and Mr. Lee Franklins' name came up a lot. So, I looked for information on him and found this. I hear you may know of Mr. Franklin."

"Oh, sure," said Arcon. "Everybody knows my Grandpa Lee where I come from. He was one of the Founders."

"Well, I have some important news for you," said Noreena. "I think I may have located some of your relatives."

Elaina put her hand to her mouth and gasped as Arcon stood there in stunned silence. "I … I didn't know I had relatives. I was told that I'm the last of the Franklins."

"That's hardly the case," said Noreena. "I have a list of three dozen people who might be related to you. One is named Dolores Reid, and she says she has a bunch of historical things from your family. Would you like to meet her?"

Roberto stepped in, saying, "I don't mean to speak for Arcon, but I've been given responsibility for his security and care until he's fully established here. It's important we take things slowly in accordance with the Authorities."

Getting defensive again, Noreena tensed and said, "Mr. Gonzales, I understand your concern, but I won't report on any of this until Arcon is ready, and you are ready, and his relatives are ready, and everything is properly authorized."

"I'm ready," responded Arcon.

"And your relatives are ready," said Noreena. "They've been wondering for decades whatever happened to Mr. Franklin and his family. They deserve some closure. Would you please consider meeting with them soon?"

"I'm ready to talk to them right now," said Arcon. Then he looked at Roberto, who was shaking his head. "But if you don't mind, I need to talk to Roberto and Elaina first."

"I think we should do it," said Roberto in a soothing tone. Just not this very moment. Noreena, there has to be a reason you were able to find all that information. This whole experience has God's fingerprints on it. If you'd be willing to coordinate a meeting with Arcon's family, we'll give you a list of acceptable dates as soon as we clear everything."

Noreena put her hands on her hips. "That'd be great, Mr., uh, Roberto. Would it be okay if I sat down with Arcon and just talked about his life in the Forest? I'll turn off the recorder."

"That sounds enjoyable, actually," said Roberto, and the others agreed. For the first time in a week, Roberto felt he could relax.

CHAPTER EIGHTEEN

When Arcon walked into Dr. Stones office, he was surprised to see her without face coverings. "Now you remind me of an ArcPoint medic," he joked.

"Now I know for sure you're safe," she replied. "In reality, you're more at risk from us. You probably haven't been exposed to a contagious disease in your entire life."

Arcon smiled at Elaina. "Maybe I should be wearing a mask when I kiss you."

Elaina swatted him on the arm with the back of her hand.

"Have a seat here," said Dr. Stone, pointing at a chair. "Rest your arm on the table and roll up your sleeve." Arcon obeyed, and she took his blood pressure. She inspected his lymph glands, listened to his chest, and checked his ears, nose, and throat. Then she picked up a syringe. "Sorry to have to do this again," said Dr. Stone, as she poked a needle into Arcon's arm to draw some blood. "We found heavy metals and rare earths in your previous blood samples. We've ruled out contamination of the samples, but we need to verify what we've found with another round of labs. This may also help us determine if an environmental change has had an impact on your condition."

Arcon couldn't fathom how he could have gotten metal and dirt in his blood. "What does that mean?"

Dr. Stone finished drawing the blood sample and handed it to her assistant, who left the room with it. "We believe you were exposed to something in that area. Some metals, like iron and zinc, are good for you. Heavy metals aren't, and they're microscopic, so you wouldn't know they're getting into you. Now that you've been away from there for a while, we're hoping to see a reduction of these products in your blood. But if we see too much, it may indicate a problem with our initial testing."

Arcon glanced over at Elaina. She was listening closely but didn't seem alarmed. "What if the tests were accurate?"

"I've been discussing your case with a Reproductive Endocrinology specialist," she said. "We've concluded that the metals could cause problems with the follicle-stimulating hormone and the luteinizing hormone, which both need to be at proper levels for pregnancy to happen. We'll be testing your blood and urine for those hormone levels, but it'd help if we could examine one of the females in your group."

Arcon knew that would never happen on this side of the Rift. "Is there any other way to find out?"

"It'd help if we knew how you ingested heavy metals—how they got into you. These elements would need to be in the air you breathe, water you drink, or food you eat. But you told me you came from the Mojave Forest. There's no industry in that area capable of contaminating the air. How do you get your drinking water?"

"We collect rainwater at the Facility," he answered. "Us hunters use a dew trap."

"Interesting. Where do you get your food?"

"We have aquaponic gardens that give us vegetables and fish," he said.

Elaina leaned forward. "I thought you called it hydroponics."

"We have both. Hydroponics doesn't have the fish."

"What else?" asked Dr. Stone, nodding and taking notes.

"We raise goats for milk and cull out the older males for meat. We also eat rabbits for protein. We have some vine foods like berries and grapes. And then there are the ArcPoint trees themselves. A lot gets harvested from them."

"What are ArcPoint trees?"

"That's the Mojave Forest," interjected Elaina.

"More or less," added Arcon. "They were supposed to be an oil-producing plant grafted onto a genetically engineered rootstock. But we used that rootstock to create other trees that produce olives, nuts, and fruit. Most of the trees you see from this side of the Rift are just the rootstock, which produces its own fruit. We eat that as well."

"Tell her about the briers," Elaina reminded him.

"Right. Well, there are two types of thorny things, actually. There are rhizomes that grow out of the rootstock—we eat the berries from them. But if you eat too much without eating a little protein with it, it can be… unpleasant. Don't ask me to explain."

"Understood," said the doctor, smiling. "What's the other type?"

"The rhizome berries have seeds, and when those get planted, they produce a really thorny vine that blooms and puts out big, delicious berries. When the rhizomes and berry vines get all tangled together, we call it needle-brush."

Elaina leaned forward. "My dad and I think the berry vines are what grows over here. We think birds eat the berries and, you know, drop the seeds on our side."

"Well then, we can examine that fruit for heavy metals," said Dr. Stone. "Are those berries similar to anything we have here?"

"They're like our wild blackberries, but bigger and lumpy … different in some ways than anything else. We think it has something to do with the genetic things done to their rootstock."

Dr. Stone looked at Arcon and asked, "How much of your people's diet would you say comes directly from that rootstock?"

"Boy, I hadn't thought about that," answered Arcon. "It'd probably depend on your job. The gardeners eat mostly vegetables from hydro, uh, the hydroponic gardens. Us hunters eat a lot of the tree fruit and berries because it's convenient for us in the forest. Sometimes we have to eat the rhizome berries. I'd say for us it could be as high as half of what we eat, the gardeners maybe twenty percent, other folks somewhere in-between."

"It just doesn't make sense the contamination would come from the air or rain water, so I'll have a discussion with Ranger Wilson about the soil. He'll contact you himself regarding what he wants to do about that. Meanwhile, we'll test these blood samples again and see what we can discover. I'll see if I can get some of those berries to test as well."

"They're not ripe yet," said Arcon.

"Well, we'll see what we can come up with. We'll do everything we can."

"Thanks, Dr. Stone. I appreciate your help."

"So do I," added Elaina, shaking Dr. Stones hand.

Dr. Stone walked them to the reception area. "It was good to see both of you. Hopefully, I'll have some good news the next time we meet."

Elaina awoke and rolled onto her back. She'd heard a noise downstairs. Probably her dad. She opened one eye and saw it was just starting to get light outside. She rolled towards the dark wall, determined to fall back to sleep. If her dad wanted to get up at the crack of dawn, that was his choice. This was the first day in weeks she could sleep in, and she was going to do it.

She heard another noise and tried to ignore it. Then she remembered—in the middle of the night, her dad woke her to say he had to leave. Something about a forest fire and needing to evacuate people and how he'd probably be gone for a couple of days.

She was suddenly wide awake. *Who's making noise downstairs?* She calmed down when she remembered their house guest. Now sleep was impossible, so she got up to see what Arcon was doing.

When she walked into the kitchen, he looked her way, shrugged his shoulders, and said, "Tweet, tweet."

Elaina laughed. "Always the early bird. I thought we agreed to sleep in this morning."

"You didn't have to get up."

"Yes, I did," she answered back. "I was awake anyway."

Elaina saw Arcon looking her up and down. She realized it was the first time he'd seen her without makeup. Her clothes were frumpy and her hair was probably lopsided and twice its normal size. Even at the Survival Camp, she'd been all made up by the time he'd seen her in the morning. "I must look like a mess," she confessed.

"No, I like the way you look."

"You're joking, right?"

"No, I mean it. It makes me feel comfortable, like worn-out skins."

"Is that supposed to be a compliment?"

"Where I come from, it is. New skins are clean and neat, but they're also stiff and uncomfortable. After a while, they soften, and you prefer to have them around you."

She stepped closer and put her arms around him. "And they stop rubbing you the wrong way?" she joked.

He pulled her close. "Eventually."

She noticed this hug felt different. It didn't come with anxiety or concern, or self-consciousness. It just seemed normal, unlike when she'd hugged other boys. She never would've considered spending an entire day alone with any of them for fear of what would be expected of her or might be said about her. Arcon was easy to be with.

Arcon interrupted her thoughts. "Could I try some of that coffee stuff again? The flavor is kind of strong, but I think I like it."

Elaina sighed and let go of him. "Sure. I'll even walk you through how to make it."

Ranger Dan was at his desk, working his way through his mail messages, when Ranger Becca yelled, "Dan, Dr. Alicia Stone on line one."

"Thanks, Becca," he said and pressed the button. "Hello, Dr. Stone. Any fresh news for me today?"

"Hi, Ranger Wilson. Sorry—I wish we had more to go on. Arcon's blood tests show both rare earths and heavy metals of various kinds. We're convinced this plays a role in the infertility issue. We're also concerned that long-term exposure could cause other health issues."

"Understood. Do you still think ingestion is the most likely source?"

"Affirmative. He's showing no respiratory issues, so we can rule out inhalation. At this point, we must hand it over to you to determine where those elements are coming from."

"Okay, thanks, doctor. I'll take it from here."

"Let me know what you find. We'll keep working on a way to purge it from his system."

"That's great, doctor. I'll keep you informed. Goodbye."

Ranger Dan pressed the call button. "Becca, could you set up a meeting for me with Jim Dixon, Jonathan Greywolf, and Tarzan... uhh... Arcon? I'd like to meet as soon as it works for all of us. Jim probably has transportation, but you'll need to set up taxis for the other two."

"You got it," came her reply.

"Thanks. Oh, and call Jonathan first. When you get him on the line, let me talk to him for a minute. Then I'll send him back to you."

"Sure thing."

Dan couldn't wait to talk to his favorite miner again. Since he'd mined the Mojave area for most of his hundred-plus years, no one would know more than his buddy about minerals in the area. He was just starting to go through his mail again when Becca yelled, "Mr. Greywolf, line one."

Dan tapped the button. "Jonathan, how's life been treating you?" He leaned back, the springs from his chair protesting.

"I'm talking to you again, so what does that tell you?"

"Tells me you're still on top of the dirt when you want to be," said Dan, with a laugh. "Praise God for that. I'm having a problem in the Mojave Forest area. I need your help with it."

"Another one?" chided Jonathan. "Does it involve a drone?"

"No. This time it concerns the minerals in the area."

"Can't help you. All joking aside, the area is restricted," said Jonathan.

"Jesus Himself gave me this task," Dan countered. "I'm supposed to help a man who lived there."

"He lived in the Mojave? Is he one of the Mojave People?"

"Yes, he is." Dan let that news sink in. "It's just as we expected—there's still a large group living there, and they need our help."

"I can only imagine. All my life, I've wanted to meet someone from there. My father told me stories; said they were good people."

"And he was right. They're having certain health issues. Their bodies are picking up trace minerals that are interfering with childbirth. Stands to reason the minerals are coming from the soil. Do you have any knowledge of there being heavy metals and rare earths in that area?"

"Companies have tried to mine the heavy metals around there. Some even gained permission to bore under the restricted area. But it's too expensive to extract the small amounts contained in the rocks. They're too deep underground."

"Could any of those metals be on the surface?" asked Dan, marveling at Jonathan's wealth of knowledge.

"Not in large quantities, unless there were mining spills. Some mining operations will process tons of ore to get ounces of wanted material. The crushing of the ore releases many metals, and water further dissolves it and concentrates it. If that water is spilled, the soil becomes saturated with the metals."

"Were there any spills that you know of?"

"Hmm. Not in my lifetime. But, before the evil days, a very large rare earth mining company went bankrupt because of a spill."

"That would be over a hundred years ago!"

"Yes, that would be."

Dan took notes. "Was it very close to where we flew the drone in?"

"Depends on what you mean by close. Went there once with my father as a teenager. There's an enormous pit there. It was an open-pit mine, you see. We walked down into it. You can't do that now because it's filled with water. Of course, you can't go there anyway, cause it's part of the restricted area. Although ... it's north of the old I-15, so it's just outside the line. But you'd have to hike into it because you can't drive on the highway."

Dan drummed his fingers. "Fantastic. How far away is it?"

"Oh. Hmm. About a hundred kilometers, I suppose. Too far to be a concern, I believe."

"Well, these people are ingesting these metals, so somehow they're getting into the food chain. How could that be possible unless the metals are getting to the surface?"

"Plants need water, and they could absorb the metals from a spill in small amounts," said Jonathan. "Some metals are good for health, some bad. Plants don't know the difference. If you think about it, the plants can be trees, which the Mojave has acres of. That's where I'd look first."

"Here's what Arcon—the man from Mojave—has told me. The rootstock they used for the trees was genetically engineered to produce oil for bio-fuel, so they never intended consumption of the fruit. It had a taproot that went deep into the soil to survive in the desert."

"Then a spill wouldn't be necessary," said Jonathan. "The roots would go to the metals."

"Arcon said that when the rains came, the trees took over the landscape."

Jonathan countered, "In those days, the water table rose. It flooded many mines."

"Would the metals rise with the water table?" asked Dan.

"No. The metals are heavier than water. But the water could dissolve the metals out of the surrounding rock. It would then be available for the roots to absorb. But then ..." Jonathan's voice went silent.

"What is it?" asked Dan. "What are you thinking?"

"When I was young, the water table receded, and many mines were once again accessible. Think about what that would do to the trees."

Dan imagined the roots reaching out for the water. "The taproots of all these trees would follow the water table down."

"And as the water level dropped, the dissolved metals would settle out into the surrounding rock, becoming more concentrated. As the roots went deeper, the risk of contamination would get greater. But you said they didn't consume the fruit of the trees."

"No, I said they didn't *intend* to consume it. They started grafting other edible varieties onto the same engineered rootstock. And they also started eating the fruit of the rootstock itself."

"My son, I believe you have solved the mystery on your own. But I still expect to get paid my normal consulting fee."

"On the contrary," said Dan. "I owe you twice. Once for what you told me, and once for what you taught me."

"If you buy me lunch, we'll be halfway to even."

"It's a deal," said Dan, although he knew he'd pay Jonathan more credits than he asked for, which was often nothing. And he knew he could justify his actions to anyone, even Jesus Himself. "I'll send you back to Becca. She wants to arrange a time for you to meet this Mojave man."

"Wow, I'd like that very much. And I'll see you as well?"

"Absolutely," said Dan. "Good talking with you, Jonathan. Here's Becca."

CHAPTER NINETEEN

Arcon fidgeted at the kitchen table, waiting for Elaina to finish washing the lunch dishes. Elaina was finally going to teach him how to use a comm-pad. There were so many things he wanted to search for on the info-net. "Can I try something while I wait?"

"Almost done," she yelled over the running faucet. "Just wiping down the sink." The water stopped. She walked over to him while drying her hands and peered over his shoulder. "Do you see all those little pictures?" She pointed at the icons on the screen. "Now, tap on this one to pull up a map. Okay, see? There's the Rift and the Mojave Forest."

"And there's Calico, right?"

"That's right. Now, watch what I do with my hand." She slid her finger and panned until Calico was in the center of the map. Then she spread all her fingers, and the map zoomed in on Calico. "Just like at the Ranger Station, only on the screen rather than beside it."

"How does it do that?" asked Arcon.

"No one really knows," said Elaina.

"What?" asked Arcon, taken aback.

Elaina chuckled. "Well, *I* don't know. Let's just leave it at that."

"Wow, if I had one of these maps, I'd be looking at it all the time!" said Arcon.

"I thought you were going to be driving all the time," said Elaina.

"I'm going to be driving *and* looking at this map!" Elaina turned and scrunched her face at him. "Just kidding," he said.

"I certainly hope so," said Elaina, "It's too dangerous. Now, want to see something even more impressive?"

"Sure. I want to see everything."

Elaina went away to one of the back rooms of the house and came back, carrying a rolled-up object.

"I remember that thing, Roberto said to be careful with it."

"That's right. It's called a roll-up screen." She rolled it out on the kitchen table, connected it to her comm-pad, and waited. "This is gonna blow your mind."

"Is that a good thing?" he asked. Suddenly, a picture of Arcon in the trees on the other side of the Rift flashed on the screen. He was wearing his skins and reaching for ArcPoint fruit. "Wow, is that me?"

"No, it's Ranger Dan." she mocked. "Of course, it's you. This is what we were watching you with. This, and a high-powered telescope connected to a laptop. I took a screen snap of you and then put it on the comm-pad as a background picture for the roll-up. How do you like it?"

"It's impressive," he answered, trying to follow her lingo.

"Well, it still makes me nervous."

"What? Screen snaps?"

"Seeing you hanging out on a limb like that. If you'd have fallen, we may not be having this conversation."

Arcon walked around the table as he looked closely at different parts of the screen. He'd walked out on branches many times and other things that were definitely more dangerous. "I don't agree," he said as memories flooded his mind. "I believe we were supposed to have this conversation. I think God wanted me right where I am, with you, with Roberto, with Ranger Dan. I feel favored, though I've no idea why."

He tried to hold back the tears but finally had to give in to an intense sobbing that came from deep within him. This had happened to him when he was alone in the container and again as he sat alone in his bedroom in the basement, but he didn't want it to happen in front of anyone, especially Elaina.

The sobbing ended as abruptly as it started, and Arcon wiped his eyes with his shirtsleeves. "Sorry about that. I guess I'm a bit overwhelmed with everything."

"I think it's deeper than that," Elaina responded. "Do you want to talk about it?"

He really did, but just the thought of it started the sobbing again, but this time only briefly. "I suppose I should," he said as he felt his face contort again. When it stopped, he laughed. "If I can." Then they both started laughing. "I just remembered something from my childhood. And somebody."

"What did you remember?"

"My grandma," said Arcon, in an emotional daze. "She lived in our home when I was growing up. She used to read the Bible to me every day, and she always had comments on whatever verse she was reading. One day she read Matthew twenty-four, verse forty-five. It asked the question: 'Who is a faithful servant, whom the Lord has made ruler over his household, to give them meat in due season?' ... that isn't word for word, but it's what I remember. After she read it, she told me the verse was for me, that someday I would rule over the ArcPoint Community, just as Joseph ruled over Egypt."

Arcon sat quietly while Elaina held his hand. "It was a very rebellious time for me. I still loved my grandma, but I wasn't getting along with my parents. I wanted to be a hunter, and they wanted me to join them in the chemistry lab. I didn't see things the way my grandma did. Instead, I just focused on providing meat in due season. I believed God was calling me to be a hunter. The next day I told them hunting would be my pursuit, and I went to Jarden to apprentice with him." Arcon struggled to get his words out, but he was determined to make his final confession. "In less than a year, my parents both died in an accident ... and I blamed God." Arcon's body convulsed as the tears flowed.

Elaina hugged him, and they wept on each other's shoulders for a while. "You *do* know He wasn't to blame?" she asked.

"I blamed myself more. I really thought God wanted me to be a hunter. I told Him to change the heart of my parents so I could. When they died, I thought He was answering my prayer in a horrible way."

"Do you still think that way?" asked Elaina.

"No. I've gotten to know God better since then. But it took time." Arcon sat quietly for a minute. "That's when my heart turned against the Community," he continued. "I didn't want to lead them, and I didn't want to feed them. I stopped going to see my grandma, except occasionally, and never to have her read to me. I told her I was old enough to read the Bible on my own."

"And did you read it?"

"Eventually. Contacting you helped a lot with that. It gave me a new purpose, a new direction to my life. I could finally function in the Community, even as I fought to leave it. I renewed a close relationship with my grandma before she died. More importantly, I could sense God guiding me again. I firmly believe He led me here. Especially after hearing what He's done with the rest of you."

Elaina squeezed his hand. "It's hard to know what happened with your parents. I agonized over losing my mom and still do once in a while. But in my job, I see accidents happen all the time. I just have to think God has His reasons, and He helps us through it."

Arcon held her at arm's length and looked her in the eyes. "And I believe He puts people in our path to help us as well."

Elaina smiled at him. "Amen to that." Then she remembered something. "What happened to those rocks you showed Patty?"

"In my pocket."

"Can I see them again? I only got a quick glimpse last time."

He reached in his pocket and pulled out one that was attached to a leather cord. "This is one that Jarden polished. He made this necklace for my mom, but she died before he could give it to her." He handed it to Elaina and asked, "Would you like to have it?"

"Oh, no. Jarden would want you to have it," said Elaina.

"You're right, he would," said Arcon. "And he'd want me to enjoy it." He smiled at her. "I'll enjoy it a lot more around your neck than in my pocket."

Elaina took it from him. "It's beautiful. The setting is so intricate. What's it made of?"

Arcon laughed. "You'll never guess. It's made from copper car wiring and the windings of an electric motor. That maroon color is the insulation on the wire." He pulled another rock out of his pocket and handed it to her. "Now look at this one."

"Wow, that's beautiful. What is it?"

"It's a plume agate. See the red plumes along the bottom? And how there are white plumes, black and gray plumes, then another layer of light blue and red? Not very many agates have all those layers."

"Where did you get it?"

"Jarden found it on the back side of Far Ridge."

"Where's that?"

"It's on the edge of what you folks call the Mojave Forest. If you look at old maps, it's called the Cady Mountains. Here. Take it and hold it up to the light."

"It's so lacy. It has a nice polish, too."

"I did that. It took a lot of rubbing on a piece of railroad track and a slurry of special sand. Jarden taught me." His voice cracked as he said, "I wanted Grandma to see the plumes better."

Elaina handed the stone back to him. "Do you keep this to remember her?"

"Yeah, and Jarden. I also use it to remind me of Jesus."

"How so?"

"Jesus is the rock of my salvation, the stone the builders rejected, and the one that crushed Nebuchadnezzar's statue. He's the rock we're to build our foundation on. Grandma had a lot of sayings about Jesus and rocks. That's why I made this and gave it to her. She always told me it was her favorite possession, although I think she really liked her cuckoo clock more. She got that from my Grandma Victoria."

"Okay, help me remember. Victoria was who?"

"She was my Grandpa Lee's wife. That'd make her my great-great-grandma."

"It's so confusing. Why do you call all of them your grandparents?"

Arcon laughed. "That's my Grandpa Lee's fault. The story goes that one day my dad was trying to figure out how many greats to use. Grandpa Lee told him not to worry about it. Nobody is that great. After that, we dropped the greats for everyone. Since he was the great Founder, the whole Community stopped using the term. Now the term *Great* only refers to my Grandpa Lee, the one person who didn't want to hear it. Ironic, isn't it?"

"It sure is. And it seems confusing."

"Not to us. Everyone in the Community has a unique first name. For instance, I'm named after my Grandpa Arnold and my Grandma Connie, uhh, Constance. Get it? Arnold? Connie? Ar-Con?"

"I figured that out when I saw the obituary," she said.

"Oh, right. Now Jarden is an exception. He was named James after his dad, James Arden-Merrick. To keep them straight, everybody called him little Jimmy, and he hated that.

So now he wants everyone to call him Jarden. Get it? J for James and ... "

"I get it. I get it. Arden-Merrick sounds interesting."

"His mom's last name was Arden; his dad's was Merrick. When they married, they kept them both."

"Hmmm. Jarden Arden-Merrick. It's got a ring to it."

"Officially, it's Jarden Merrick. To be safe, when you meet him, just call him Jarden."

"I'm going to meet him?"

"Someday."

CHAPTER TWENTY

Arcon enjoyed his newfound freedom. As Elaina drove through the countryside, he marveled at the things he recognized from books in the Room of Remembrance. For years, he'd dreamed of traveling. By car was great. By airplane would be the ultimate. But today, he might experience the most thrilling way to move about. Today he'd have a chance to touch a horse and maybe get on one. "Are horses dangerous?" he asked, seeing the fences and wondering why they were caged.

"No, not at all," replied Elaina. "Well, there are wild horses that could conceivably be dangerous, but there won't be any at this dude ranch."

Except for short grass, Arcon saw little vegetation inside the fenced areas. "Do they eat bushes?"

"No, I don't think so. Why do you ask?"

"We didn't have any horses, but we had goats," said Arcon. "They'd eat plants, so we had to keep them away from the gardens. We'd tie them to trees, so they'd eat the rhizomes."

"Okay, that makes sense."

"Why do people have horses?"

"They like to ride them," answered Elaina.

"But you said they don't use them for travel anymore."

"Horses aren't for long distances. Cars are better for that. But for recreation, they're still very popular."

"Oh." As they drove along, Arcon saw another bunch of grazing animals he recognized. Arcon thought about that and asked, "Why do people have cows?"

"Some of them are for milk, and some are raised for meat. The shoes we got you are made from their hides."

"Oh, okay. We used goats for all that." Arcon thought about riding a goat when he was a child and asked, "Do people ride cows?"

"Tell you what," said Elaina as she slowed down for the driveway. "I'll let Ranger Dan answer that." They pulled up and parked near a sign that said "Guest Registration." As they got out of the autocycle, Dan was waiting for them. He looked different in blue jeans and a flannel shirt.

"Welcome to the Apple Valley Dude Ranch, folks," barked Dan as he tipped his cowboy hat. "Come on in and revisit the Wild West days." He threw out his hand to Arcon.

As he grabbed Dan's hand and shook it, Arcon asked, "What is this place?"

Like a sideshow barker, Dan exclaimed, "The Wild West, son. Cowboys and horses. Roping steers and bucking broncos. Like it used to be in the 20th century. Leave your city life behind and get your behind in a saddle. You're about to go for a wild ride!"

Elaina gave Dan a big hug and said, "I like the cowboy look."

"Well, thank you, ma'am."

"I knew this place was here, but I didn't know you were part of it. How long have you been doing this?"

"Oh, off and on, since I was a youngster. I grew up near here and started out cleaning the stalls. I earned credits for college doing rodeo stunts like shooting balloons and lassoing strangers." He looked at Arcon, and they both started laughing, but Arcon was oblivious to the reference. Dan saw the confusion and said, "Lasso, son. I'd lasso strangers. Well, actually, I'd lasso young steers."

Arcon suddenly put it all together and said, "Oh, can we do that here? I want to learn how to lasso."

"We won't do that today, son. That takes some time to learn, and we have a lot to discuss. But I think we might have time for the first lesson." Dan stood tall, puffing his chest out as he said, "Come on in, folks. Let me give y'all a quick tour of the ranch." He held his elbow out for Elaina, and she wrapped her arm around it. Then she looked at Arcon, stuck her nose in the air, and strolled arm-in-arm with Dan like a debutant.

Flames raced past Roberto's position, so close the heat was painful, but his reflective fire blanket did its job. He struggled to hang onto the Australian Shepherd he was trying to protect. When he'd first run to retrieve the little girl's pet, he hadn't expected the winds to shift so suddenly. He hadn't planned on being a hero—now he was glad he wasn't a statistic. He believed God heard his cry to see Elaina again because the last time he'd looked, the flames were racing in his direction.

He'd been away barely a day and a half, but it seemed like weeks. *Baby girl, when will our lives return to normal?* The dog lurched away again, but he had a firm grip on its collar. He pulled it back, holding it close, completely enveloping the dog with his body as the flames raced past.

He knew by the sounds around him that he'd be alright, but didn't get out from under the blanket immediately. Instead, he held the dog until it calmed down and then Roberto quietly thanked God for another day. As he pondered his situation, he thought about Elaina. He'd been smothering her with protection, the same as he did with this dog. But now, he'd hand the dog over to another person, and he'd need to turn his beloved daughter over to Arcon. For the first time since all this had begun, he felt he could do it.

As the roar of the fire died down, so did the struggles of the dog. Prevailing winds moved the smoke away from their position, so he threw the silvery blanket off them. The storm that had produced the lightning was now providing a light rain. His job here would soon end, and he could return home. He'd do so with an entirely different outlook on the future.

Elaina glanced at her watch. This hour-long tour had already taken two hours because of Arcon's questions. Stories about cattle drives and bronco busting fascinated him, as did the Pony Express. Now Dan was introducing him to a fully saddled horse. It made Elaina nervous, watching Arcon scrutinize every part of the saddle.

Just as she'd feared, Arcon grabbed the horn of the saddle and stuck one foot in the stirrup. "Don't do that," she warned, but Dan smiled and stopped her. He nodded approval to Arcon, who then stood in the stirrup and threw his leg over the saddle.

He sat there, holding the horn with both hands. "Now, what do I do?"

"Nothing!" yelled Elaina. She looked at Dan. "I swear, he'd jump out of a plane with a parachute and *then* try to figure out how it works."

"Now, now, give the boy some credit," Dan scolded. "He's paying attention—he just doesn't seem to have any fear."

Dan's words stung a little, but she understood. Arcon had never seen someone bucked off a horse, so he didn't realize it was possible. Elaina had experienced it firsthand, and had spent weeks on crutches afterward. "I take it this is a pretty tame horse."

Dan confided, "I made sure of that," then chuckled and whispered, "I'm figuring this boy out."

"Well, you could have told *me*," she said.

"And spoil my fun?" he joked, to which Elaina punched him in the arm. Dan glanced at his watch. "Whoa, time's flying. I still want you to see the arena. Here, take the reins. I'll give you some lessons on the way." Dan clicked his tongue, nodded, then opened the gate and walked out. Red stayed at his side with Arcon in the saddle. "He does what you tell him, but you need to know *how* to tell him."

"Did you just tell him something?" asked Elaina.

"Uhh, yeah. I said, 'Follow me.'"

When they got to the arena, Dan said, "Here's your first lesson, Arcon. Have you ever watched any old Westerns?"

"I don't know what you mean."

"Good. You don't have to unlearn anything. Just remember that Red is a sensitive horse. Now, hold one of the reins in each hand."

"Like this?"

"Not that high. Just relax. That's it. Now, if you want Red to go right, just hold the rein against the left side of his neck, and press his side with your left foot." Arcon held the left rein against Red's neck. "You don't have to pull it tight. Just hold it there. That's better. Left foot—good. If you hold your right foot away from him a little, it'll encourage him that direction, too."

Arcon did as Dan told him. Then he reversed all the moves. "Is this how I turn left?"

"Hey, that's it. You're a quick learner. Now, if you want to stop, lightly pull the reins straight back."

"Like this?"

"Exactly."

"How do I make him go?"

"Loosen the reins, press both feet against him, and do this." Dan made a clicking sound. "But before you do that, when you ride around the arena, you want the horse to think he's doing everything on his own and not like you're controlling him. Do you understand?"

Arcon stared at him. "Not really."

"Don't worry about it. Red does everything on his own, anyway. Now, see if you can walk him around the arena. Okay, go!"

Arcon loosened the reins, squeezed his legs, and made a strange sound that made Elaina laugh. Red began plodding away from them. "Whoo-hoo," yelled Arcon.

Elaina commented, "That horse is huge!"

"He sure is," said Dan. "Imperial Red is gentle as they come. He was a national champion halter horse in his day, both here and in Canada. He's been retired for a few years now. The kids love him, and he's constantly hungry for their attention."

Red slowly walked around the arena, zigging and zagging as Arcon practiced guiding him with the reins. When they got close to Dan again, he pulled back on both reins, and Red stopped. "Hey, it worked," he said.

"Now, one last trick. Pull both reins as if you're stopping him. Then press both of your feet against his side." Red began walking backward.

"Now that's impressive," said Elaina. "I never rode a horse that could do that."

"Would you like to?"

"Very funny, big guy. I'll never reach the stirrups."

"We'll boost you up. Right, Arcon?"

"Sure we will." Arcon climbed down off the horse.

After a few minutes of coaxing and lifting, Elaina was in the saddle and headed around the arena. When she got to the other end, she turned Red and did a figure-eight in the middle of the arena. "Show-off!" yelled Arcon. She raised one arm in the air and waved it around.

When she got back, they helped her out of the saddle. Dan said, "It's lunchtime. How about if we all get some grub up at the chuck wagon?"

"Grub, I understand," said Arcon. "That's like bug larvae. But what's a chuck wagon?"

Elaina shuddered. "Ranger Dan, if we have to eat bug larvae, I'm going to *need* a chuck wagon."

Dan laughed. "I never thought of it like that. Arcon, let me put it this way. We're going to get something to eat at the food vendor's cart."

"Good, I was getting hungry. I've eaten grubs before. They're not too bad if you get the right kind and roast 'em. What kind are these?"

"Mexican," said Dan, glancing at Elaina with a grin. She punched him again, and he said, "Okay, I'm just kidding. No grubs, just a variety of sandwiches. Then we can go up to the lodge. But first, we need to get Red back to his stall. Would you like to do that, Arcon?"

"Sure."

"Okay, get in the saddle." After Arcon had swung up, Dan said, "Now, loosen the reins, slump over, and close your eyes."

"What?"

"Just do it. Act like you're sound asleep." Arcon shook his head, then did as he was told. "Okay, now, start snoring."

"You're kidding, right?"

"Just try it."

Arcon gave a loud snort. Red began walking back toward the barn.

Dan smiled at Elaina. "I taught him that myself. I call it, 'Asleep at the Wheel.' Red thinks the ride is over, so he knows to go back to the barn."

Arcon marveled at the large wooden supports and ceiling beams in the main Lodge. He ran a hand over one of the supports. He could see they were made from smaller pieces of wood stuck together and wondered how and why they were crafted like that. He turned and saw Ranger Dan and Elaina approaching.

"If you're through looking around," said Dan, "I found a small room where we can talk."

"Sure, I'm ready."

Dan led them to a private room and turned the conversation toward the topic of the day. "Arcon, I've been talking to some folks about the situation with your people in the Mojave. I think we're getting closer to finding a cure for the infertility problem."

"Really? What is it?"

"Well, son, it's a tad complicated. There seems to be three parts to the problem, and it takes all three working together to cause the issue. First, is the location. That area has a large concentration of heavy metals and rare earths in the soil. Most of it lies buried deep in the ground where humans wouldn't normally come in contact with it.

"The second part is the ArcPoint trees. You told us the rootstock was genetically altered. Well, whatever it was those folks did, the trees are very efficient at sucking up those heavy metals. We don't know for sure, but we think whatever grows out of that rootstock will have those metals in the fruit.

"Lastly is the climate change that happened in the 21st century. When the rains came, you said the trees multiplied on their own and made the forest we see now. Well, that rain also washed the metals loose from the soil. When the rain backed off in the 22nd century, that rootstock worked overtime to find more water, and with there being more metals in that water, it was a perfect storm of environmental hazard. You folks have been living in the middle of it. Good news is, all they need to do is stop eating the fruit from those trees."

"That's it?" asked Arcon. "It's that easy?"

"Well, there's more to it than that, but to keep it from affecting anyone else, yeah, it's that simple. Now, for those folks loaded up with this stuff, we'll have to figure out how to purge it from their system. Dr. Stone has people working on that. The problem is, you're their only test subject. It'd help if we could test more people from your community."

Arcon recalled how adamantly the ArcPoint people were against the outside world. They wouldn't allow strangers in if they could help it. He could try to persuade them, but he didn't know if they'd let *him* back in, much less the outsiders. As hard as it had been to leave, going back in could be a disaster. "Would that include the nuts and the olive oil? And what about the goats? They eat the rhizomes from the rootstock."

"It'd all have to be tested," said Dan. "But I wouldn't trust the milk or the meat. The fish are probably okay because you said they're grown in rainwater. If the rabbits eat ground cover, they may be okay. But I see your point. It's going to severely limit their food choices."

The more Arcon thought about the dangers, the more dire the circumstances seemed for his ArcPoint friends, and the more determined he was to do something about it. *But how*? Softly, and with little conviction, he said, "I need to tell them."

"I've come to the same conclusion," said Dan. "I can provide you with resources, but you need to be the one to get us there. You're the only one they'd trust."

Arcon hated to think about going back. He wanted to learn to drive, swim, and ride a horse. Most of all, he was eager to begin the courtship dance with Elaina, if he could just figure out what the courtship rules were.

In the Community, he'd ask Jarden about courtship. But he didn't have a Jarden in his life here. He didn't want to approach Roberto about it. He would have to consult with Ranger Dan. "Elaina, can I ask you to do something difficult?"

"I, uh, I suppose so. As long as it's not eating grubs."

Arcon appreciated the humor, but it only made the question more difficult to ask. "Can I talk to Ranger Dan ... in private?"

"Sure, Arcon. No problem. I saw a little museum at the other end of the lodge. I'll go check that out."

"Thanks. I'll come find you when I'm done." Arcon watched as she got up and left the room. His heart ached to have asked her to leave. When she was gone, he turned to Dan. "I'm sensing God drawing me back to the Community. But I have to be honest. I don't want to leave Elaina, but I don't think I could take her to ArcPoint. I'll need more time."

"No problem," said Dan. "This health issue isn't urgent."

Arcon leaned forward in his chair. He glanced toward the door. "Can I ask you a personal question?"

"Sure, what is it?"

"Did you ever have a difficult time starting a romantic relationship with a girl?"

"Oh sure," said Dan with a chuckle. "My first one. But in my case, it never would have worked, anyway."

"Why not?" asked Arcon innocently.

"Well, in all honesty, she was an untamed filly, and I was more of a free-range chicken." Dan laughed, but Arcon made no response. "That went right over your head, didn't it? Okay, sorry. So, what's troubling you?"

Arcon sat back in his chair. "I want to court Elaina, but I don't know what the rules are."

"What do you mean?"

"In the Community, we have rules for courting. They were originally put in place because of our limited resources."

"Are you talking about food or the gene pool?"

"What? Oh." Arcon blushed and ran a hand through his hair. "Uhh, both, I guess."

"Sorry. Didn't mean to throw you off the trail. What are the rules?"

Arcon collected his thoughts. "Young men and women can't be alone together for long periods without an official Request for the Daughter's Hand."

"In marriage?"

"Uhh, no, not exactly. But yes, eventually. I mean… The way we look at it is, as she's growing up, the daughter holds her father's hand for security. In this case, I'd be telling Roberto that I'd like to assume that role—to take Elaina's hand, be at her side, and keep her safe. I'd be requesting that he trust me to that extent. But I'm also saying I intend to fill that role permanently by someday marrying her. Otherwise, there's no point in him giving her up."

"Sounds a bit formal, but it makes sense. What if the girl doesn't like you?"

Arcon grinned. "It's a lot less embarrassing if it's discussed with her before making the request to the father."

Dan nodded. "I bet it is. What happens if they agree to the request?"

"There are two lines to sign. The father signs the first one, and the courtship begins. Even so, men can't marry until they're thirty years old."

"Is that so? How old does the girl need to be?"

"That's up to her parents, but usually in her twenties, at least. Anyway, the man has to have his own apartment to prove he can maintain a dwelling. During the courtship time, the young couple needs to spend a lot of time together in the company of adults, especially their parents. The whole Community needs to approve of the couple's behavior together. Meanwhile, this couple collects the names of ten life guarantors—people who commit to helping the couple stay together and thrive. Once all those things are in place—and the father thinks his daughter is ready—he signs the bottom line on the original request. Then the leaders of the Community announce it to everyone, and they're married."

"Whoa, just like that?" Dan's eye got big. "No ceremony or anything?"

"Oh, there's a big celebration all right," exclaimed Arcon.

Dan sat in stunned silence. Eventually, he remarked, "It sounds like you have this all figured out already."

Arcon hung his head. "Well, I do know a lot about it. There was a girl. We played together as children. But when we got to a certain age, everyone expected me to start courting her." He looked up. "Dan, she was like my sister. Neither one of us felt comfortable with courting. Besides, I knew someday I'd leave that place, and there's no way she'd go with me. Anyway, I know it seems kind of sudden, but Elaina is the type of person I had in my heart to marry. But out here—How am I supposed to get my own place? Who will be our life guarantors? I have no way to prove to Roberto that I can take care of Elaina."

Dan leaned back in his chair. "It's not as complicated as all that. But then, maybe it should be. Your people probably didn't have any divorce."

"What's that?"

"I *think* you just answered my question. Divorce is when people become, uh, unmarried."

"Oh, okay," said Arcon, a little lost in thought. "My grandma read to me about how God hates divorce, but she never explained it to me. I never bothered to ask. So no, when people got married, they stayed that way, as far as I know."

"Well, to answer your question, we don't have official rules. Roberto may have a few of his own, just to protect Elaina. But typically, here, if a girl is over eighteen, she can make her own decisions, regardless of what her parents or anyone else think. I doubt Elaina would ever cross her dad, of course, but she's free to make up her own mind."

"And I would never cross Elaina's father," responded Arcon. "I like Roberto, and I want him to like me."

"You know what I'd do?" asked Dan. "I'd make up one of those Requests for the Daughter's Hand and give it to your future father-in-law. And I'll want to be the first of your Life Guarantors. Patty will probably want to sign as well." He crossed his arms. "Actually, she'll want to be signer number one, but that's not happening. Believe me, with the two of us, you won't need ten."

Arcon beamed. "Thanks, Ranger Dan," he said, shaking his head as if holding back a surge of emotion. "I don't want to go back to the Community before I establish some kind of understanding with Elaina. I've found her worthy of being my life partner. I hope she feels the same. I can't even consider going back unless I know for sure. I hope you understand."

"Perfectly," said Dan. "Take your time. It's not like your community is going anywhere. Now go find her before she worries that we're talking about her."

"But we are," said Arcon, tipping his head.

Dan shook his head and laughed. "Tell you what I'll do. Based on what you just told me, I think I can write up a Request for the Daughter's Hand for you. I'll sign it, get Patty to sign it, and you can give it to Roberto. How does that sound?"

"That sounds great. I didn't know how to do it without Elaina's help, and it really shouldn't be done that way. Thanks."

"Consider it done," said Dan. "Now go get things squared up with your lady friend. And don't be surprised if I spring another meeting on you soon, if you get my drift."

There was an undertone in that statement Arcon didn't fully understand, but he trusted Dan. "I will plan to not be surprised." He stood and shook Dan's hand. "Thank you. I'm going to Elaina now."

CHAPTER TWENTY-ONE

Elaina watched Arcon and her dad talk. She tried to put a finger on what was different. It hit her. *This is backwards.* She was used to Arcon asking questions about every new thing he saw. But ever since Arcon talked with Ranger Dan, he's been quiet—almost moody. *Now Daddy is the chatty one. This last rescue trip changed him somehow. Did he and Arcon have some altercation I don't know about?*

Now her dad peppers Arcon nonstop with questions about his life, his people, and his plans for the future. *That's not a surprise— not after that meeting with the reporter—but Dad is relentless.* She'd witnessed this kind of change in him once before when she was young, right after her mom died. At that time, *she* was the one getting all that attention.

Arcon is different, too. Normally, he's excited to share himself with anyone who asks, especially her dad. She can tell he's enamored with her dad—jumping at any chance to converse with him. Now he's short with his answers, rarely giving her dad anything to continue the conversation with. *Yup, these two are acting backward.* The juxtaposition between the two altered personalities was getting under her skin. Both men seemed intent on hiding their difficulties from her, and she couldn't understand why.

In a couple of hours, she'd deal with at least one part of this problem. Ranger Dan had arranged for a driverless taxi to take Arcon to a meeting with a plant expert. *As soon as he's gone, I'll pounce on Dad and find out what's going on with him. If I have to, I'll pull out the mama card.* She and her dad promised to honor her memory by being open and honest with each other, no matter how painful. Her dad had pulled that trick on her quite a few times. Now it might be her turn to force him to open up.

"It looks like your one o'clock just drove up," yelled Ranger Becca, from her office to Dan's.

"Would that be Greywolf, Dixon, or Tarzan?"

Becca watched a young man get out of a taxi wearing blue jeans and a tie-died tee shirt. *A definite improvement over baggy Ranger clothes.* "Trust me, that isn't Tarzan anymore. That young lady has turned him into a handsome young gentleman."

Dan walked into the reception area. "Now, now, Becca. I think he's taken."

"So am I, unfortunately," Becca quipped. "Just kidding, of course."

"Your secret's safe with me," said Dan, going to the door. He opened it just as Arcon was reaching for the knob. "Arcon, come on in. Say hi to Becca while I authorize the delivery charge." He walked toward the taxi, then turned, adding, "She's delighted to see you." He glanced at Becca, who shook her finger at him before Arcon looked her way.

"Hi, Arcon," said Becca. "How're you doing? I missed you the last time you were here."

"Hi, Ranger Becca. I'm doing very well, considering I hardly ever know what I'm doing. What about you?"

"Just Becca, please, and I always know what I'm doing, but I have to do it anyway," she responded, laughing. As Dan came back through the door, she said, "Working for Ranger Dan is always a mundane adventure. Oh, excuse me. I meant a *wonderful* adventure."

"Don't believe much of what she tells you, Arcon," said Dan. With big eyes, he asked, "Why not?"

"Yes," snapped Becca. "Tell him why not."

"Point taken," said Dan, emphasizing the word *taken*. "Becca, the other two should be here any minute. When they show up, just bring them back to my office. Arcon and I have a few things to discuss." He turned to Arcon and said, "Follow me, young man," and started down the hall.

Arcon turned to Becca. "Nice seeing you again. I need to go now."

"You certainly do," said Becca. "But I'll see you again before you leave. Now, get moving before Dan says something."

Arcon darted down the hall and into Dan's office. Glancing at the map on the wall, he noticed something. The words 'Mojave Restricted Area' had a line drawn through them. Underneath, someone had written 'ARCPOINT.' He sat in a chair facing Dan, who asked how his trip was.

Arcon's eyes got big. "That car ride was strange. I've never had machinery control where I was going."

"Yeah, those driverless cars aren't for everybody. They're hard to reprogram on the fly, like if you forget your briefcase or want to stop for a donut. Most folks prefer to have control of their own vehicles. But in a case like yours, where you don't have a car or a license, they're perfect." He handed Arcon a piece of paper. "Here ya go."

"Is this it?" Arcon asked, holding the document out with both hands.

"That's it," said Dan. "An Official Request for the Daughter's Hand."

Arcon smiled and read the wording carefully, taking his time. It impressed him that Dan had remembered his instructions. Aspects of the traditions were mentioned fairly well, considering. Its wording wasn't quite like the document the Community used—in fact, it was a bit verbose and technical—but that didn't matter. When he read the signatures of the life guarantors, he found more than he'd expected. "Ranger Becca and Dr. Stone signed it too," he remarked.

"Yeah, sorry about that. Patty let it slip. But they insisted on signing it."

"Do they know what it means?" asked Arcon.

"I believe so. They're to take responsibility to keep you two married for the rest of your lives or theirs. Did I get that right?"

Arcon stared at the paper. "That's right, but they're supposed to watch how we are together, see if we're compatible. So they know if we're right for each other before signing."

Dan recalled the way they acted at the Dude Ranch and Patty's comments about their time at the Survival Camp. "Trust me, we've all seen enough already," he said, jokingly. "So, have you had your talk with Elaina yet?"

Arcon hung his head. "No. I haven't had any time alone with her. Roberto has been asking me question after question. He wants to know what my plans are. I can't make plans until I've talked to Elaina. I don't know how to respectfully get him to go away and leave us alone. I'm hoping he'll go to his office soon and let us spend the day together."

"Well," said Dan, leaning back in his chair, "I think he may just be nervous. After all, that girl has been his life for quite a few years. But I don't think he'd mind if you asked to have time alone with her. I think he'd understand."

Becca interrupted, yelling from the reception desk. "Dixon's here!"

Dan shook his head. "I really need to get that intercom fixed." He lifted one eyebrow. "Can you fix phone systems?"

"I ... I could try," said Arcon.

Dan laughed. "I'm just kidding. By the way, thanks for agreeing to meet with this guy. He's excited to talk with you about the ArcPoint trees. Many years ago, they tasked his grandfather with finding some way to kill those sticker bushes. Jim has wanted to study the trees they came from, but there haven't been any on this side of the Rift."

"I hope he won't be disappointed. I didn't study the trees much, except to make swings."

"You might be surprised. You may know far more than he does." As Becca ushered Jim into the office Dan said, "Jim Dixon, I'd like you to meet Arcon Franklin, of the Mojave People."

"ArcPoint Community Endeavor!" corrected Becca as she walked away down the hall.

"Right," said Dan. "What she said."

Jim thrust out his hand. "Arcon, it's a pleasure to meet you. You're quite a celebrity around here!"

Arcon's brow furrowed as he grabbed Jim's hand, so Dan injected, "That means you're popular, son."

"Oh, thanks," said Arcon. "I don't mean to be."

Dan turned to Jim. "That means he hasn't had a moment's peace since he got here. Have a seat, Jim."

Jim sat down and shook his head. "I can imagine. I appreciate you taking the time. I have a few questions about those trees of yours over there. What can you tell me about them?"

Arcon started rattling off the story about how the trees came to be. Dan interrupted. "He already knows what you told us about how the trees got started. Jim, how about if you ask him some questions, and he can try to answer them?"

Arcon nodded in agreement, so Jim said, "Works for me." He pulled a comm-pad from his briefcase. "You say the trees were originally for a portable fuel source. Were they ever able to produce well for that?"

"Sort of," said Arcon, eyeing the comm-pad as Jim wrote on it with a stick of plastic. "We're able to make a high-quality fuel for our diesel generators, but not the gas ones. I don't know why, but we have records."

"Fantastic," said Jim. "We've a problem coming up with enough portable fuel here. That's why most transportation is land connected, or what we call grid-dependent. If what you have works, your people are sitting on a precious resource. You say you use a small refinery? Is that right?"

"I don't know what you mean by small," answered Arcon. "But we don't need much fuel. We only have one generator left that works. We also make lamp oil and cooking oil, and fuel for burners and welders. But most of our technology happened generations ago. Now we just follow old notes and try to keep everything working."

"But you still have all the research that's been done over the years?"

"Oh sure, we have a complete technical library. We all read a lot. There's not much else to do but learn things. Unfortunately, I studied electronic stuff, not botanical."

"That's okay," said Jim. "Chemistry is actually my strong suit, but my dad is more into trees, so I ended up in that field."

Just then, Becca leaned into the room. "Excuse me—room for one more?"

"Jonathan, come on in," interrupted Dan. "Arcon, I'd like you to meet Jonathan Greywolf. His father knew your Grandpa Lee."

Arcon shot to his feet, his eyes big as saucers. "He did? How is that possible?"

Jonathan smiled as he shook Arcon's hand. "Your people came to our land."

Arcon stared at the gray braids hanging past Jonathan's shoulders, his dark, wrinkled face perfectly framing a broad smile, and blurted out, "You're an Indian."

Jonathan smiled and nodded. "And you're a white man."

"I'm sorry … I didn't mean …" Arcon stammered as the others chuckled. "I've never seen one of your kind before, except in books."

"Then we are equal," said Jonathan.

Dan interrupted, asking, "Do you know Jim Dixon?"

Jonathan looked at Jim. "If his father is Christopher Dixon, then yes, I have met him, but as a much smaller person."

Jim stuck out his hand. "It's an honor to meet you again, Mr. Greywolf. My father spoke with you often, but I only saw you once when I was eleven."

"How is your father?" asked Jonathan, shaking his hand.

"He's working in forestry up in Canada."

"Speaking of forestry," said Dan, "We were just talking about the Mojave Forest and what a valuable resource it is."

"Oh, yes," said Jim, turning to Dan. "Can I ask him?"

Dan looked sheepish and said to Arcon, "I hope you don't mind. When we discovered the heavy metals were coming from the trees, we brought Jim in for his expertise in both trees *and* chemistry. He's part of the team we put together to help your people with the, uhh, infertility problem. Jonathan here helped us understand the mineral side of things."

"It's kind of embarrassing, but I realize you're all trying to help." Arcon turned to Jim and said, "What's your question?"

"Let me first say that I find your trees fascinating. We have nothing like them." Jim looked intently at Arcon and asked, "Do you think your people would be willing to share their technology with us?"

Arcon shrugged his shoulders. "I don't know how to answer that. The ArcPoint people share everything, but I don't know how they'll react to outsiders. I never thought about us having anything *to* share. At this point, I just don't know."

"Sorry," said Jim. "That was an unfair question. Let me tell you where I'm going with it. There are two things our world desperately needs. One is a portable, safe, and reliable fuel source that can be easily and inexpensively produced. The other is rare earths and heavy metals—" He held up his comm-pad. "Which these things need in order to work. Your trees are a source for both. I can't tell you that we know how to best extract what we need, but it'd be worth trying to discover it. And it's very possible your people already know how to do that. They'd at least be able to reduce the research effort required. Would you be willing to ask them?"

"Whoa, whoa, whoa," said Dan. "Rein in the horse and stop the cart. Arcon, I know you have some personal details to work through, so you don't have to answer that. Jim, let's give Arcon some time to mull it over. He's hardly had time to think since he got here."

"I completely understand," said Jim. "It's a lot to take in all at once. I just wanted ... "

Arcon held up his hand so he could get a word in. "Can I say something?"

"Sure," said Dan. "By the way, everyone, take a seat."

"I may not know much about the trees," said Arcon as he sat down. "But I know my people. We have some needs as well." He started getting emotional as he said, "One thing we need desperately, is purpose. Our people are very intelligent, but we have no resources to work with and no reason to work with them."

He leaned forward in his chair. "The ArcPoint people worry about what lies beyond the confinement of that forest. But I know now that their fears are unwarranted. I feel a strong need to let them know that you're all good people and that Jesus is ruling in Jerusalem. That's all they'll need to hear, and I know they'll want to share anything they have that'll help you. All I ask is that I can tell them in my way and in my time. Please. That's all I ask."

Dan could hear the desperation in Arcon's voice. The situation was difficult for this young man, but Dan believed it was what Jesus wanted. *Arcon is advocating for his people.* He turned to Jim and said, "I think you got your answer. If I can speak for Arcon, I'd say he'll take your offer to the ArcPoint people sometime in the future." He looked at Arcon, who nodded, so Dan asked him, "Is there anything you need from Jim? Anything you think your people might need?"

Arcon brightened. "Yes, technical information. My people love to study and learn. It doesn't matter how technical or complicated it is. If you can explain your point in detail and write it down, it'll save me from having to learn it. When I go back to them, I'll give it to them, and let them decide. But if they reject your proposal, please understand that I'll want their decision respected."

Jim stuck out his hand again. "Deal. I couldn't ask for anything better. I have another idea I'm working on too, but I'll need to talk with Mr. Greywolf about it."

"How can I help?" asked Jonathan.

"Well, I think it's agreed that nobody likes the briars, including the Mojave People. If there is a possibility that the briars contain heavy metals, we could design a machine that chews them up in a way that facilitates extraction. But even if the metals aren't there, it would still eliminate the nuisance while preserving the trees for oil harvest."

"Interesting," Jonathan mumbled, eyeing the ceiling.

"What are you thinking?" asked Dan.

"I am seeing something strange in my mind," he said. "A machine like a gold dredge—only instead of digging up dirt and spitting out gold, it grabs the briar vines, grinds them up, and removes the heavy metals."

"There are a lot of unknowns to deal with," said Dan. He turned to Arcon. "If it could work, do you think your people would be interested?"

"Right now, I can't tell you what they'll agree to, but I know that in all things, they are interested."

"Jim, I think it's up to you and Jonathan to draft up a bunch of information for Arcon to take back to his people."

"I like Jonathan's concept. I'll get my people to work with him to draw up an agreeable proposal and all the technical information they can muster."

"And I'll get the medical people to write up an explanation of the health issues and how the heavy metals cause the problems," said Dan.

Then Arcon said, "I'll work on giving you a time when I can return to my people. I just need to work out a few details first."

"Nothing trivial, I'm sure," said Dan, as he slapped him on the shoulder. "Take your time. Tell you what, mind if I drive you home?"

"I'd like that very much," said Arcon, remembering the driverless taxi. "I enjoyed watching the scenery go by, but I didn't have anyone to talk to. If you drive me, I can talk to you."

"That you can, son. That you can. Meanwhile, how about the four of us discuss this dredge idea? Would that be like a weed-eater slash chipper? Or would it be more like ..."

"Daaad, how could you even think about hiding that from me?" Elaina buried her head in her father's shoulder and held him tight as she sobbed.

At a break in his own sobbing, he said, "I wasn't trying to hide it from you. I was just waiting for the right time."

She pushed him at arm's length and stared into his eyes. "The right time is always the first moment we see each other, okay? That's what we agreed on." She hugged him hard again. "What were you thinking?"

"I don't know, girl. I guess I just didn't think it was a good time with Arcon around. This is the first we've been alone since the fire."

Elaina was glad she'd confronted her dad about his strange behavior. She hadn't known she'd nearly lost him to a wildfire. When he first confessed it to her, there'd been almost no consoling her. Memories of losing her mom came rushing back, for both of them she was sure. They wept and held each other for quite a while. It was the closest they'd been since Arcon had arrived.

Roberto kissed the top of her head. "We could've lost each other, but we didn't. I really think God helped with that because it sure looked like the flames were coming right at me. I told him I wanted to see you again, but I honestly didn't think it would be without burns. He's a good God, and we should rejoice about that, not cry."

They broke their embrace as she said, "These are tears of joy, Dad, see?" She smiled a big smile at him, but her chin was still quivering.

"I'll take your word for that," he joked. "Hold that thought because I've got something else to discuss with you. But can we sit down?"

"As long as you don't make me cry. I need to be holding you when I do that."

He smiled and moved toward his recliner. "This may make me cry, but I think you'll be okay."

She kept one eye on him as she backed toward the sofa and sat down. "Does this have to do with Arcon?"

Roberto leaned forward on his forearms. "Why do you ask?"

"You've been acting strange around him, and he's been acting strange around you. Did you two have a disagreement I don't know about?"

"No, not at all. I agree *he's* been acting differently. I didn't know *I* was."

"Well, never mind. What did you want to talk about?"

"The fire," said Roberto. "It's funny what goes through your head at a time like that. I'll tell you, that dog I was holding desperately wanted to get away from me. He must've thought I was stupid to lie down in front of a fire. I had to bury him under me so he wouldn't bite."

Elaina watched her father as he spoke. The way in which his lips moved, the waver in his voice, and his lowered gaze told her he was still emotional. "What is it, Dad?"

"God showed me some things about myself that day."

"I suppose that happens at a time like that."

"Yeah, I suppose. But this concerned the two of us. I understood it better when it was all over, and I handed the dog to its owner." He hesitated, staring off at nothing for a moment, then looked at her. "God showed me I've been smothering you with protection, but I know I might someday have to hand you over to Arcon. I think he was preparing me to let you go."

"But Dad, it's different with us. That dog belonged to someone else first. I've always belonged to you and always will. It'll just be different when I'm out on my own. Besides, who knows if that'll be with Arcon or not?"

"What do you mean? Haven't you two discussed all that?"

"How could we? We've hardly had any time together since he got here."

"What about those days at the Survival Camp?"

"We only had a few waking hours that Patty wasn't with us. Certainly not enough time to talk about anything serious. Plus, it didn't seem like Arcon wanted to talk about anything, you know, romantic. Maybe that was because of the infertility thing."

"That shouldn't be a problem now."

"It's not," said Elaina. "Now we're back to not having time alone together."

Roberto laughed and said, "I guess God was right."

"About what?"

"That I've been smothering you. I've been keeping the flames of passion away from you."

Elaina could feel her face flushing. "Now you're just getting weird."

"I'm in a weird position," Roberto replied. "But I'll try to stay out of the picture for a while. I know how hard it is to get up the nerve to talk seriously with someone. It took me six months to ask your mom to marry me, even after God told me I should."

"Okay, that was more information than I needed. It better not take Arcon that long to figure out if I'm part of this new world he's in. I couldn't stand six months of you two acting strange around me."

"Tell you what," said Roberto. "If he takes over six weeks, I'll have a man-to-man talk with him—find out what he's thinking."

"That's probably a good idea," said Elaina. "I don't want to start this Morse code process all over again with some other stranger." They both looked at each other and burst out laughing.

CHAPTER TWENTY-TWO

"What's troubling you, son?" asked Dan as he drove Arcon home. "You've been quiet for quite a few miles."

"I don't know how to get Elaina alone," he answered.

Dan thought about that. "You know what people do out here when they start dating? They go out to eat." He patted his belly. "That's how all this gets started."

Arcon chuckled, then turned serious. "How can I take her to dinner? I can't drive, and I can't buy anything. I suppose we could take a driverless taxi, but I don't know how to do that." He stared out the window and continued, sounding frustrated. "I wouldn't know where to go, and I couldn't pay for it."

Dan thought some more and was quiet for a while. Then he said, "I have a plan. When you get home, you tell Elaina you're taking her out to dinner. Don't take no for an answer, and don't let Roberto join you. Elaina will have to drive, but you tell her where to go. I have this great restaurant in Lucerne Valley you can take her to. I'll write down the address, and you hand it to her. You can put the dinners on my tab, but you don't have to tell her that. You just tell her you're taking care of it."

"But how?"

"Hold your horses, I'm getting to that," said Dan, chuckling. "When you get there, ask for Marla. Tell her you want the quietest booth in the place. She'll ask if you're Mr. Franklin. When you say yes, she'll know what to do. I guarantee it."

Arcon stared at Dan in disbelief. "Are you sure? You don't have to do all that."

"Of course, I don't," Dan replied. "But I'm going to, anyway." His tone grew serious. "You would honor me to accept this gesture and dishonor me if you don't. Which will it be?" Dan stared at the road, clearly unwilling to take no for an answer.

Arcon looked intently at him. "It will be an honor to honor you, sir."

"Fine then, it's settled. Now let's make sure you have the plan straight. And order a good dinner. Don't worry about the cost. Agreed?"

When Arcon agreed, Dan called the restaurant and talked to Marla. When he finished, he gave Arcon a few lessons about dining at a fancy restaurant.

When Elaina saw Ranger Dan's vehicle pull into the driveway, she burst through the front door and ran to meet them. Arcon crawled out, and she hugged him. "I was expecting a driverless taxi."

Arcon didn't hesitate a moment to hug her back. "Ranger Dan gave me a ride."

Roberto joined them. "Dan, what brings you to our humble home?"

"Oh, there was a store I wanted to get to in Victorville before it closed, so I gave the boy a lift. It turned out my meeting was really short, so I had plenty of time. Hey, it's only four o'clock. Mind if I come in for a cup of coffee?"

"Sure, absolutely," said Roberto. "Follow me. I was just going to make a pot. You kids want coffee?"

"No thanks for me," said Arcon, still hugging Elaina.

She looked at Arcon and loosened her embrace, but he only held on tighter. "I'm fine too, Dad. None for me."

"I hope I'm not intruding," said Dan, as he followed Roberto into the house.

As soon as they were alone, Arcon kissed Elaina lightly and said, "I have a surprise. I'd like to take you out to dinner."

"Well, that would be fun," said Elaina, "But I'm getting low on—"

"I'm not taking no for an answer. Don't worry about anything. I'll take care of it."

"Yeah, right," retorted Elaina. "How do you plan to do that?"

"I told you not to worry about it. I only need you to drive us there." He handed her a slip of paper with the address. "Here's where we're going."

"Where is this ... wait. The junction of highway 247 and 18? That's all you have?"

Arcon's smile faded. "Isn't that enough?"

"It's enough if there happens to be a restaurant there."

"Okay, then it's enough. Let's go."

"Wait. I should get Dad's account card in case you can't ..."

"Nope. Roberto can't go, and you can't worry. Just trust me."

Elaina felt like someone was playing a trick on her or Arcon. But she realized it must be important to him, so she said, "Okay, just you and me? Sounds fun. Just let me tell Dad we're going." She looked at what she was wearing. *Gosh, he looks nice.* "I should probably change clothes."

"What did I just tell you?" asked Arcon, softly. "Don't worry about it. You look great to me. Just tell your dad we're going and come back, okay?"

"Okay." Elaina trotted back into the house and heard Dan telling her dad a story about something. As she approached them, he stopped, so she said, "Dad, I'm going out to eat with Arcon."

"That's great, girl. Have a good time. Don't stay out too late."

"What?" asked Elaina.

"You heard me. Have a good time. Hurry up; he's probably waiting for you."

Elaina walked away in a daze as Dan continued telling his story. Now she felt *certain* she was being set up for something, and Dan was probably behind it. *Well, two could play at that game*, she thought. Whatever was about to happen, she'd be prepared and would turn it back on their heads if she needed to. *For now, I'll just play along and at least get a free meal.*

She stopped in her tracks. *Those two highways don't even connect.* She saw Arcon with his arms folded, waiting for her. She grinned and began walking again. *I'll let him worry about that.*

Elaina was happy about one thing. Located on a short road connecting highway 247 with highway 18, they found a place called The Junction Restaurant. As they walked through the parking lot, Elaina hesitantly slipped her hand through Arcon's extended elbow. *Is he emulating Dan's actions at the dude ranch? Are they walking into one of Dan's practical jokes?* She didn't know. But she did know Arcon wasn't being himself.

She was wary when he asked to talk to someone named Marla.

"That's me," she said. "Can I help you?"

"I'd like the quietest booth in the place," said Arcon, smiling big.

"Are you Mr. Franklin?" asked Marla.

"Yes, I am," he said, rolling his shoulders with an air of confidence.

"Then follow me; we have your table already set up." Elaina glanced around at the other patrons as Arcon strutted behind Marla to the far corner of the restaurant. "Here you are," she said. "Jenny will be your waitress. She'll be with you shortly."

Elaina was shocked to see the table covered in a beautiful tablecloth, and set with fine china, silverware, and two champagne glasses. A bottle of sparkling cider was half buried in a bucket of ice. Elaina wondered if she should search for hidden cameras, but Arcon seemed as surprised as she was.

Elaina slid into the booth and grabbed her menu. As she opened it, she noticed Arcon mimicking her actions. He'd probably never seen a menu before. Jenny the waitress showed up and asked, "Would you like anything else to drink?"

"No, I'm fine with this," said Elaina.

"Me too," said Arcon.

"Fine, let me pour this for you." Jenny opened the seal on the bottle and carefully poured each of them a glass of sparkling cider. They were getting stares from the other patrons, since they were in more of a truck stop than a high-class restaurant. "Are you ready to order?"

Arcon spoke first. "I'm a bit undecided between the filay mig-nown and the lobster. Do you have a suggestion?"

"Today, the lobster is very fresh," said Jenny.

"Then I'll have lobster."

Elaina stifled a snicker at Arcon's order. She was pretty sure he didn't know what either of those things was. It was clear Dan had been coaching him. But it was so cute there was no way she'd let on that she knew.

She perused the menu a little to be sure of her choice, then flipped back and forth through it. Lobster wasn't even on the menu. She looked at the waitress and said sheepishly, "I'll have the Fettuccine Alfredo."

"Excellent choice," said Arcon.

Elaina was tempted to ask if he knew what Fettuccine was, but she didn't want to embarrass him.

The waitress just smiled, collected their menus, and walked away. Arcon took a big swallow of the cider and grimaced a little at the fizz. "Excellent year," he finally said.

Elaina tried desperately, but couldn't keep from giggling. As soon as she started laughing, so did Arcon. Soon they were both laughing so hard, half the room was too. "This was Dan's idea, wasn't it?" she accused.

"I tried to tell him it wouldn't work."

"Well, you know what? He'd want us to enjoy it. Here's to Ranger Dan." She held up her glass and stared at Arcon. He stared back. "You're supposed to hold up your glass; we're making a toast."

"Toast?"

Elaina just stared at him and pointed at her glass. When Arcon lifted his, she said, "To Ranger Dan! Now drink it. Not so fast."

After they drank their cider and poured more, Arcon fell silent. "What are you thinking?" asked Elaina.

"I'm thinking about Dan," he replied. "He did all this so I could be alone with you."

"Oh, that's so sweet of him. We have to make sure and thank him."

Arcon was quiet again. "He did it for a reason. He did it so I could have time to tell you something."

Elaina felt nervous, but it was a *good* nervous. She watched the bubbles in her glass. "What do you want to tell me?"

More than once Arcon opened his mouth to speak but couldn't seem to get the words out. Then he reached for his shirt pocket, and Elaina's heart jumped. She didn't know what to think when he pulled out a piece of paper and handed it to her.

"What's this?" she asked.

"Just read it," he responded. "Then I'll explain it."

When she read, Official Request for the Daughter's Hand, it made little sense to her. Then she read, I, Arcon Franklin, ask you, Roberto Gonzales, for the hand of your beloved daughter Elaina Gonzales.

The letter became too difficult to read. She wiped her eyes and said, "Please tell me this isn't a joke." When he hung his head, she realized the question hurt him.

He answered, "Ranger Dan tells jokes. I'm not much good at it."

Elaina read some more. "Were you seriously planning on giving this to Dad?"

With what looked like a regretful nod, he responded, "I'm sorry if it's not the right thing to do. I don't know what to do. I want to court you and to marry you. This is how we do it at ArcPoint. Ranger Dan thought this would work for you and Roberto."

"There's that Ranger Dan again!" Elaina exclaimed. "Well, you tell Ranger Dan something for me the next time you see him. You tell him…" she paused for a moment as she tried to regain her composure. "You tell him … it's perfect!"

"What?"

"It's perfect. Daddy will love this. Of course, at some point, you should actually ask *me* to marry you. But I suppose that can wait."

Arcon looked up at her and blinked. "Would you?"

"Would I what?"

"Would you marry me if I asked you?"

"Are you asking me?"

"Well … yeah … I mean … I think we should do some courting first, but… yes, when the time is right, I really do want to marry you."

"I should probably take some time to think about it," she responded, swirling the cider in her glass.

"Of course. As long as you need to."

"Is this long enough?"

This time, she could see Arcon's eyes welling up with tears as he asked, "Are you saying yes?"

Elaina nodded her head. "Yes, Arcon. I'm saying yes."

He leaned forward in his seat. "Well, before you do, I need to tell you something."

At that moment, Jenny arrived with their meals, and Arcon sat back in his seat as she put the plates down.

Whatever it was Arcon needed to tell her, he didn't seem to want to do it in front of a waitress. The moment the waitress walked away from the table, Elaina leaned in and whisper-shouted, "What is it you need to tell me?"

"I need to go back to the ArcPoint Community."

Elaina said, "Oh," and leaned back. "Permanently or temporarily?"

"You mean you don't care if I go back?"

"If it's for a visit, of course not, as long as I can go with you. I'd love to see where you grew up. But if you're thinking permanently—"

"It would certainly only be a visit," he said, interrupting. "Just so I can report on what I've seen here. They need to know the outside world is a good place. But here's the thing ... I don't know if I can take you with me."

"Why not? Won't they like me?"

"No, it's not that. It'd be too dangerous. You'd have to run the tree branches and fight through needle brush."

Elaina gave him a goofy look and started laughing at the thought of trying to keep up with him. "We wouldn't have to fight through needle brush to get in there, silly. A pilot could just drop us in with a helicopter."

"A what?"

"A helicopter. Remember the drone that brought you the survival supplies? A helicopter is like a huge drone, and we'd be the package. We'd just need official approval, but Ranger Dan or my dad could get that. So, when do we go? And when are you going to try your lobster?"

Arcon scrutinized his dinner as if seeing it for the first time. "It looks like a big scorpion."

"Trust me; it'll taste better than a scorpion."

"I sure hope so." He picked the whole lobster up, looked at the claws, and with a crooked smile asked, "How do you eat it?"

Elaina twisted off a claw and handed it to him. "Now crack it open."

Arcon tried bending it and twisting it, but the shell wouldn't crack. Then he placed it between his palms and squeezed hard. It burst open, showering both of them with bits of lobster meat. "Oops."

"Yeah, oops," said Elaina, picking lobster out of her hair. She picked up the nutcracker. "Try using this next time."

Arcon looked at the device in her hand. "We had those. We used them for nuts."

"Look around you, Arcon. The only nut at this table is you."

He saw her smiling and shaking it at him. He smiled back and said, "You really crack me up."

Elaina laughed. "Very punny, Tarzan."

"You're the only one who gets to call me that."

For the rest of the evening, they discussed the trip to ArcPoint, their plans for the future, and how perfect this crazy idea was that Ranger Dan had. Except for the lobster.

As they pulled into the driveway, Arcon commented on how Ranger Dan's vehicle was still there. "I wonder what that means," he asked.

"I wouldn't worry about it," said Elaina. "You know what we agreed to. If Daddy is still awake, you said you'd show him the request thing."

"Can I wait till Ranger Dan leaves?"

"Let's just go in and play it by ear."

"What?"

"You told me Ranger Dan helped you write it. Maybe he stayed to see if you went through with showing me. If he did, he won't leave until you hand it to Daddy. Let's go."

Arcon watched Elaina get out of the three-wheeler, then crawled out himself. Elaina reached toward him. "Here, take my hand. You said you wanted it."

He stared at her. "Shouldn't I wait till your dad says it's okay?"

"Arcon, I have two hands. You can both hold one."

He smiled, then grabbed her hand. "I agree to your terms."

They walked hand in hand until stepping through the door. Searching through the house, they found Roberto and Dan in the home office, staring at the big roll-up screen. "What are you two looking at?" Elaina asked them.

"You're home!" exclaimed Roberto.

"Are those pictures of the fire?"asked Elaina, biting her bottom lip.

"Not the one we talked about," said Roberto. "This is the Camp Creek fire."

"Oh, yeah, that was a big one."

"It sure was baby girl. Do you remember…"

"How was the dinner?" interrupted Dan. "Anything good on the menu?" Dan winked at them and nodded.

"I had the scorpion," said Arcon.

Elaina poked him in the arm. "He had lobster, and it *wasn't* on the menu. I checked."

"Way to go, Marla. I didn't think she could make it happen." Dan furrowed his brow. "Anything else interesting?"

"The drink was fizzy," said Arcon, but when Dan rolled his eyes at him, he glanced at Elaina and stammered, "I… I've got something I need to share with you, Roberto."

"What's that?"

"Here's a clue, Dad." Elaina held up one hand.

"I don't get it."

"And you're about to lose it," mumbled Dan.

Roberto looked back and forth at Elaina and Dan, then turned to Arcon. With a crooked smile, Arcon handed him the folded piece of paper he held.

"What's this?" Roberto asked, unfolding the paper. "Official… You want to marry my daughter?"

Elaina poked him. "Daddy, read it all before you say anything."

"Okay." He pulled glasses out of his shirt pocket and put them on. "It reads…"

OFFICIAL REQUEST
for the DAUGHTER'S HAND

I, ARCON FRANKLIN, REQUEST THE HAND OF YOUR BELOVED DAUGHTER, ELAINA GONZALES. I DESIRE TO ASSUME YOUR ROLE IN CARING FOR HER, PROTECTING HER, GUIDING HER, AND LOVING HER. AS YOU HAVE HELD HER HAND THROUGH LIFE'S TRIALS AND TRIBULATIONS, THROUGH ITS JOYS AND SORROWS, AND ALL ITS UPS AND DOWNS, I NOW WANT TO START THE NEXT ADVENTURE OF MY LIFE HOLDING THAT HAND.

WITH YOUR PERMISSION AND SIGNATURE ON THE APPROPRIATE LINE BELOW, WE WOULD LIKE TO BEGIN THE COURTSHIP PHASE OF OUR RELATIONSHIP. TO THE BEST OF MY ABILITY, I WILL BEGIN PREPARING A DWELLING PLACE FOR THE TWO OF US, I WILL PURSUE GAINFUL EMPLOYMENT, AND I WILL SEEK TO IDENTIFY HER WANTS AND NEEDS IN ORDER TO PROVIDE THEM.

MY INTENTION IS NOT TO REMOVE HER FROM YOUR CARE, YOUR WATCHFUL EYE, OR YOUR LOVE. I SIMPLY WANT THE CHANCE TO PROVE TO YOU THAT I CAN SUPPLY THOSE ATTRIBUTES MYSELF. I ALSO INTEND TO DO THESE THINGS

ON A PERMANENT BASIS, EVENTUALLY CULMINATING THIS COURTSHIP PERIOD WITH A MARRIAGE OF PROPER CEREMONY APPROVED BY BOTH YOU AND ELAINA, AND THE AUTHORITIES AND CULTURE IN WHICH THE ABOVE-SAID CEREMONY WILL COMMENCE.

IF AT ANY TIME THIS COURTSHIP PROVES TO BE UNWORKABLE, THE HAND OF ELAINA GONZALES WILL BE RETURNED TO YOU INTACT. IF, HOWEVER, IT CAN BE PROVEN TO YOUR SATISFACTION THAT I AM CAPABLE OF ASSUMING THE ROLE OF HER LIFE PARTNER, THEN YOUR SIGNATURE IS REQUESTED ON THE LINE PROVIDED AT THE BOTTOM OF THIS REQUEST.

TO ENSURE WE WILL FOREVER MAINTAIN OUR MARRIAGE VOWS, I WILL GATHER THE SIGNATURES OF TEN INDIVIDUALS WHO WILL MAINTAIN VIGILANT OVERSIGHT OF OUR RELATIONSHIP WITH EACH OTHER. THEY WILL BE LIFE GUARANTORS, HELPING US WHEN NECESSARY TO NAVIGATE LIFE'S TRIALS. I REQUEST YOUR OVERSIGHT AS WELL, AND I ASK ALL PARTIES TO ASK GOD FOR HIS.

IF YOU FIND THIS OFFICIAL REQUEST FOR THE DAUGHTER'S HAND ACCEPTABLE, PLEASE GIVE YOUR ACKNOWLEDGMENT BY SIGNING HERE:

_____

LIFE GUARANTORS:

_____, _____,

_____, _____,

_____,

_____, _____,

_____,

_____, _____.

I, ROBERTO GONZALES, DO HEREBY CERTIFY THAT ARCON FRANKLIN HAS FULLY AND SUCCESSFULLY ACCOMPLISHED THE TASK OF PROVIDING FOR THE DESIRES AND NEEDS OF MY DAUGHTER, ELAINA GONZALES. I HEREBY GRANT TO ARCON FRANKLIN THE HAND OF MY DAUGHTER ELAINA GONZALES IN MARRIAGE. MAY GOD BLESS THEIR UNION. HERETOFORE WITNESS MY SIGNATURE:

The room was dead silent when Roberto finished reading the Request, which made Arcon even more nervous than he already was. He suspected Dan had already talked to him about this whole process, because at one point in the reading, Arcon had heard Roberto chuckle, and a couple of times, had seen him wipe away a tear.

Roberto slowly raised his head and looked Arcon in the eyes. "Am I supposed to sign this now?"

"Oh no, sir. You should sign it when you agree with it. It's probably too soon for you to know if it's right. I should have waited, but ..."

"Girl, find me a pen."

Family Tree

CHAPTER TWENTY-THREE

Noreena walked into the Sierra Room of the Burbank Cultural Center. "How's it going, Simpson?"

The bespectacled man looked up from the video console. "Doing the final checks, Noreena. We've tied into twenty BCC surveillance cameras for walk-by footage. We have three controllable cameras pointed at the chairs and three at the stage, and only two carried, just as you requested. Tell me again why you want so few cameras on the floor."

"I don't want the families to feel intimidated. They know they're being filmed, but I'd rather have a lot of cameras that aren't right in their faces."

"Makes sense. Anyway, all of the cameras feed to this console. I'll do a rolling edit, as if it's a live broadcast. Later, we'll check the other footage to see if I missed anything juicy. If the crew and I do a good job, we won't need to edit much."

"Let's see, if I want to check all the footage myself, that's only three hours of video times, what was it, twenty-eight cameras? I'll have Dolores Reid do it," she said with a chuckle. "You've met Dolores, haven't you?"

"Yes. Nice lady. Actually, the BCC cameras are motion-activated, so they won't be likely to have a full three hours on them. Speaking of Mrs. Reid." Simpson pointed at one of the monitors. "She just passed the stage door walk-by."

"Thanks. I'll go get her."

Noreena met Dolores as she entered the main meeting room. "Are you ready for this, Mrs. Reid?"

"I'm not sure yet. Ask me again later. I've never done this sort of thing before."

"And you think I have? Just kidding, but I am more of a one-on-one reporter. By the way, thanks again for letting us film this multi-family reunion of yours. I hope the cameras aren't too intrusive."

"Well, you were pretty convincing about it being important. But so you know, everyone in the family agreed with you, including Arcon. Although it does make some nervous about being linked to those *evil* Mojave People."

Noreena looked at Dolores, and they both laughed. "They're certainly evil, all right," Noreena joked. "Especially that Arcon fellow."

"Isn't he just the sweetest?" asked Dolores.

"He sure is. I love the way he listens so intently—makes me wish I had more to say. Can't wait to meet more of his people."

"Do you think you'll get to?"

Noreena shook her head, making her red dangle earrings rattle. "Not soon. Right now, the plan is just to send Arcon and Elaina in someday. If that happens, we hope to have a lot of cameras on them, so we'll at least get to see those people on video. And then I have to hope they let us use the images."

"So, you're still planning on doing a documentary about the Mojave People?"

"You bet. The Portal is helping me put it together. They finally realized what an important story this is. The difficult thing now is to keep it under wraps until we can finish it. Oh, and before you say anything, yes, we will let the families approve it before we release it."

Dolores held up her hand and said, "No problem. We trust you. Will we get to see the footage of the Mojave as soon as you have it?"

"You don't know what you're asking for," said Noreena, smiling. "Have I got a job for you."

As they looked around the meeting room, Noreena pointed at the hundreds of chairs. "Can you believe we found this many relatives of the Mojave People?"

"Oh, I firmly believe it," responded Dolores. "I had to track down these people, and then contact them, and then convince them I was serious, and verify who they were, and find out if they were coming, and…"

"Okay, I get it, I get it. But I helped a little."

"Yeah, you helped a lot, really, with your press credentials. It would have taken me forever to get into the archives or even know how to do it, for that matter."

"I don't think I could have done it without all the permissions that Ranger Dan Wilson got for us," said Noreena. "He must have had some connections high up the chain."

"So, what do you plan to call the documentary?" asked Dolores.

"I think you'll like it. There have been documentaries about other remote people who missed out on all the tribulation chaos. But I didn't want to call it *The Lost Mojave People*. That seemed too ordinary. I'll call it "*Lost in America—Before America was Lost!*""

Arcon crossed and uncrossed his legs, fidgeting in a recliner in the Gonzales' living room. He was excited to meet more people from the outside world. But he wasn't comfortable being the center of attention. That's how it had been when he was young, and that hadn't turned out well.

All his life, people had pressured him to live up to their goals and their needs, not his own. But so far, in this world, everyone seemed to be working hard to help him fulfill his *own* desires.

He didn't want to reject that, but now he'd rather give back, somehow.

Right now, waiting to go to the Center, he especially longed to be anonymous, to be high up in the branches where he could marvel at it all, with no one the wiser. His thoughts landed back in the chair when Elaina walked into the room. "Ready to go?" she asked, picking up her jacket.

"I don't know," he answered. "I really am looking forward to meeting these people. I'm just afraid I won't live up to what they expect."

"Do you *know* what they expect of you?"

"I really don't," he answered. "That's what makes it so hard to know what to do."

She took his hands, pulled him to his feet, and got right up to his face. "No, that's what makes it *impossible* for you to live up to their expectations. You can't know, because you haven't met them yet. But there's one thing they all expect, and that's you, showing up. You've only been away from your people for a couple of weeks. They've been away for generations. They probably have almost nothing left to remember by now. They'll appreciate anything you can give them. Anything."

Arcon looked at Elaina's stern expression, saw the sincerity in her eyes, and considered her words. He kissed her forehead. "I agree to your terms. Let's go." Then he smiled. "You know, you sounded a little like Jarden with that lecture. I'm sorry for only thinking about myself. Now I can handle questions."

"Good, but just remember one thing. If we go back to see your people, we can take unanswered questions with us. But don't tell the crowd. We don't know for sure when, how, or even if we'll be able to do that."

"I know, don't get their hopes up."

"Maybe tell them you hope to go back someday, that you just don't know when."

"And it'll be the truth," said Arcon.

"Yes, it will," said Elaina. "And I'll be at your side. Now let's get in the car; we're late."

They saw Roberto standing by the back door of the Center when they drove up. Suddenly he disappeared inside, then reappeared, opening the door again just as they got to it.

"I just let them know you've arrived. Go straight through that next door and down the hall."

Rounding the corner, they could hear Noreena prepping the crowd. Arcon felt somewhat embarrassed by the nice things she was saying, calling him intelligent, warm, easy to talk to, and delightful to be around. In the Community, he was considered aloof, challenged, and difficult. He could feel Elaina's pep talk wearing off and squeezed her hand for courage. She squeezed his hand back. It reminded him she was there for him.

Elaina bumped him with her shoulder and said, "You're on! Just go up and stand by Noreena and Dolores and smile at the crowd. The rest will just happen." He'd started to go when Elaina tugged on his hand and said, "Love you!"

Arcon turned and looked at her. "I love you too. I'm going now," and stepped out from behind the stage curtains.

He heard Noreena say, "And here he is everybody, our visitor from the Mojave Forest, Mr. Arcon Franklin!"

The crowd thundered with applause, followed quickly by a standing ovation. People were talking and pointing, and some were whistling. Arcon fought an enormous urge to cringe and forced a smile, but he was too humbled by it all. He'd done nothing to deserve such an enthusiastic response by so many strangers. *God put the desire in my heart to leave the Forest and laid out the path for accomplishing it.* As that thought entered his mind, he hung his head and slowly pointed upward. The applause surged once more.

Noreena, seated on stage next to Dolores, leaned over to whisper, "That's a great response."

"I think he deserves it, but look at him. He's three shades of pale. I think he's overwhelmed."

"I better help him," said Noreena, waving her arms to quiet the crowd. "And here's the father, daughter duo that helped him get here—Roberto and Elaina Gonzales!"

Elaina scurried onto the stage to be with Arcon. She stopped halfway to motion to her dad to hurry and join her. The crowd continued to applaud as Elaina hugged Arcon, and Roberto waved to everyone.

Noreena motioned to the crowd to sit down. As the roar turned to a soft rumble, she walked up to Arcon and whispered, "Here's something so they can hear you better." She pinned a wireless microphone to his shirt collar. "Just talk normal, and they'll hear you."

"Will I be able to hear them?"

"We'll have them come up to a microphone so you can," she said. She turned and gave a signal to the soundman and said in her own microphone, "We should also thank Dolores Reid for all her hard work to track you folks down. Dolores, would you like to be the first to ask Arcon a question?"

Dolores started to speak, even as the crowd was applauding her. "Thanks, everyone. I would like to ask…" She tamped the air with both hands. "Okay, that's enough, you guys. I'd like to ask Arcon what most of you probably want to know ... Arcon, what prompted you to want to leave the Mojave Forest? Oh, before you answer that, I should say that my maiden name is Franklin, and I'm a descendant of Mr. Lee Franklin, the Founder of the ArcPoint Community Endeavor. I guess that would make you and I cousins somehow." Dolores addressed the audience. "Anyway, whenever one of you asks Arcon a question, let him know whom in that group you think you're related to. Now, back to you, Arcon."

Arcon looked at Dolores and started to say, "As far as being motivated ..." but stopped when he heard his voice over the speakers. He looked at the crowd and said, "Sorry, I'm not used to that." He waited for the laughter to die down and began again. "Lee Franklin was a Founder and my great-great-grandfather, but I call him Grandpa Lee. Anyway, maybe it sounds strange, but I believe it was God who motivated me to leave. Ever since I found out about the outside world, I've wanted to discover what was out here. I was told I shouldn't *want* to because it was evil. But I could never escape thinking about it." He turned to Elaina. "Now I'm glad I couldn't'." the crowd gave a light applause.

"What made you think we were evil?" asked Dolores.

"Now, now," interrupted Noreena. "Remember the other rule. No follow-up questions."

"Oh, that's right," Dolores responded. "Just a reminder to everyone. Try to limit it to one question per family if you can, to give everyone a chance. In fact, how about if the first ten people who have questions come on up to the microphone?"

There was a gradual assembly of guests lining up, and the buzz of mumbling and chair movement. When the room settled down again, Dolores waved at the older gentleman in a tweed brown suit at the microphone. "Hi David. I thought you'd want to go first. Tell Arcon who you are."

He leaned into the mic and said, "Hello!" His voice reverberated around the hall, so he leaned back. "Hi, Arcon. My name is David Bryzinski. I'm related to Dr. Norman Ashford."

"Norm is one of the Founders," interrupted Arcon. "He was a close friend of my Grandpa Lee."

"So, you know about him?" David sent an imploring glance at Dolores. "Wait. That's not my question."

When everyone laughed, Noreena said, "Don't worry. We won't be that strict. Except with Dolores because it was her rule."

"Okay, good," he said. "My question is, what happened to the research Dr. Ashford was doing? The story from our ancestors was that he thought the work he was doing would change the world because he was developing some kind of alternative fuel. Was he able to develop it, and did it actually work?"

Arcon looked at Noreena, who just smiled. "Well, that was three questions," said Arcon. "But I think I can give you one response. For over a hundred and thirty years, we've been surviving off the fuel that Dr. Ashford helped develop. His work also gave us a lot of food plants that produced abundantly in the desert. If it wasn't for his research and God's help, we wouldn't have survived. Dr. Ashford is one of the Community's most honored men."

"Thanks for that news," said David, stepping away from the microphone to let the next person speak.

"Hi, I'm Jake Harvey. I'm related to Randy and Janice Harvey. We have some papers that Randy wrote about Lee Franklin. They explain a little about why the group moved out there, but not much. Does the name ring a bell with you, and are there any Harveys left?"

"There certainly are," said Arcon. "Some are mechanics, and some work with the hydroponics. But Randy must not have been one of the Founders because I don't know his name specifically. As kids, they taught us to memorize the names of the Founders, but I apologize; I didn't concern myself with any of the others."

"But you think I may have relatives still living there?" Jake pressed.

"I can't guarantee that, but I sure think so," said Arcon. "There are over thirty Harvey's that I know of. But our first names aren't what they used to be. People are sort of creative naming their kids. So, I don't know of any current Randy's in the bunch or Janice's. Sorry."

"Oh, don't be sorry," said Jake. "We appreciate knowing there's hope."

Arcon didn't expect to be so moved by these people. He realized it wasn't about him or his discomfort in front of these people. He was becoming more and more eager to return to the Community with news about family in the outside world. He was tempted to announce that he'd try to return, but stayed with the plan.

One by one, for the next two hours, people came forward to find out if they had family members that may still be isolated in the Mojave Forest. Some were brief as if they'd been coached to keep it short. Others rambled on and needed some prompting to let others speak. But everyone Arcon spoke with seemed happy to know that the Mojave People were good, God-fearing folks.

As the line of people at the mic dwindled, someone approached who looked somewhat familiar. He was a young man, with a short and stocky build, and black hair. He said, "Hi, my name is Victor Merrick. I'm related to …"

"Wait a minute," said Arcon. "What did you say your last name was?"

"It's Merrick, sir," the man said, clearing his throat.

Arcon fought back his emotions. *There might be a connection.* "My very best friend in the world is Jarden Merrick. He took care of me when my parents died, and he taught me how to hunt and swing. He's eighty years old and is one of the most important people in the Community. And to be honest, I sort of see a resemblance. He has to be one of your relatives. His father was a Merrick, and his mother's last name was Arden. Are there any Ardens here?"

There was a rustling as everyone looked around the room, but no one raised their hand. Then Dolores spoke up. "Sorry, Arcon. That wasn't one of the names you gave us. But we'll start going through more archives and try to find one."

"Thanks," he said. "I'd appreciate that. He'd like to know."

Then Victor asked, "Does that mean you'll be going back there?"

Arcon stammered, "Well … I … someday, I suppose …" He wasn't sure how to answer or whether he should. He turned to see what Elaina and Roberto might say, but they just shrugged their shoulders.

A booming voice from the back of the crowd said, "Could I say something about that?" A very large man in a Ranger uniform slowly stood up.

As soon as Arcon heard the voice, he recognized it. and the uniform. "Everyone, I'd like you to meet the man who saved my life by roping me like a cow, Ranger Dan Wilson!"

Noreena added, "Ranger Wilson, would you come up and say a few words? At least explain to us how you roped Arcon."

Elaina and Roberto started clapping for Dan, and the crowd joined in as Dan made his way to the microphone. "No, come on up here on the stage," said Noreena. Dan turned to the side of the stage and up the stairs. He shook hands with Elaina and Roberto as he passed, and Arcon walked up and hugged him while Noreena fit Dan with her lapel mic.

"Hello, testing," said Dan. "Yeah, you'll want to turn it down ... that's better. Hi everyone. My name is Dan Wilson. I'm the head Ranger for the Mojave area and the Authority in charge of trying to keep this kid under wraps, if you know what I mean. I'd like to give you folks some news that'll make you happy, but I need you to do something for me. Especially you, Noreena. I need you all to keep quiet about what I'm about to tell you, at least for a while. So can the news people please shut down their recorders and erase what I've said so far?" He turned and looked at Noreena, who nodded and motioned to her crew to cut the recording.

When he was officially off the record, he said, "I've been working with the authorities and with Arcon to devise a way for him to return to the Forest." A rumble went through the crowd. Dan turned to Arcon and whispered, "I hope you don't mind if I tell them."

"Please do," said Arcon.

Dan turned his attention back to the crowd and cleared his throat to get their attention. "It will still take time because of the restrictions on that area, but everyone realizes this is a unique situation and an important opportunity for us all. We don't want this turning into a media circus, so for everyone's sake, please don't talk about this to anyone. Except ..." Dan stopped to build a little anticipation. "We would like to send Arcon back with as much family information as we can give him. So, we'd appreciate all of you organizing all the family history you can muster. We'll enlist all the government resources we can to facilitate archival recovery for you. Can we count on your help with that?"

The thundering applause moved Arcon. He knew those in the Community would love to find out about relatives on the outside, and even more, that they all seemed to be good people. An idea struck him. He whispered to Dan, "Can I talk with you a minute?"

"Sure, just a second." He turned to Noreena and told her to kill their mics, and she motioned to the soundman. Then he said, "Hello?" in the mic, but heard nothing. "Okay, what is it?"

"Right now, the most influential person in the Community is Jarden. I'd like to take Victor Merrick with me when I return, if he'll do it. It'll mean a lot as Jarden has no family left at all in ArcPoint."

"I see," said Dan. "The decision is not solely mine since it'll depend quite a lot on logistics, primarily if there's room in the helicopter for him. I'm assuming you still want Elaina to join you."

"Absolutely. She has to go."

"Okay, I'll take care of it." Dan motioned to Noreena again. When his mic was active, he said, "Excuse me, everyone. I think I've interrupted enough of the festivities. I'll turn the stage back over to our guest of honor here, so you can pepper him with more questions. But any of you that want to discuss family info, talk to Noreena or Dolores. I'll hang around a while afterward to talk with you as well. Thanks, everyone."

Ranger Dan walked off the stage to a loud applause while Dolores stepped into his former location next to Arcon. "Can I have your attention?" she said, quieting them down. "Let's have just five or six more questions, and then we can grab something to eat. Then you can talk to Arcon one-on-one, but please, don't hog his time. Share him with everyone. Oh, and please let him eat something."

Arcon smiled. "I agree with her terms. Now, who is next with a question?" He was getting comfortable in this situation, just like Elaina had said he would. As the next person was stepping up to the mic, he could see Dan working his way through the crowd to Victor.

"Hi, Arcon," said a middle-aged woman. "My name is Maria Sanchez. My relative was one of the workers at your facility when the Rift happened. He got trapped there with his family but was able to send word that they were staying of their own accord. We never heard from them again and feared the worst, but there was no way for us to find out what happened. Their name was Garcia, and I'd like to know if there are any by that name in your group, but I would also like to hear the story about you getting roped like a cow."

The entire crowd cheered that request since they'd been waiting for Dan to tell them about it. Arcon laughed and said, "To begin with, yes, there are Garcia's in the Community. As far as getting roped, I suppose I'd better tell you all, or I'll have to tell every one of you the story one at a time later." So, he did just that, starting at the Mojave side of the Rift and ending with the 'tweet, tweet' on the other side. They all cheered when they heard how Dan lassoed him, and gasped when he told them about slipping off the super-rope.

It was late in the evening by the time Arcon was willing to stop meeting people and swapping stories with them. He couldn't recall a day he'd enjoyed so much. He couldn't wait to tell the Community about these people.

CHAPTER TWENTY-FOUR

Once again, Raymo noticed the bunny birds flying over the Facility. He ran to the Lookout tree and climbed up to the observatory platform. He watched as the flock of birds continued straight toward the northeast. He looked all around to see what was chasing them but saw nothing. It confused him.

A single bird flying straight meant nothing. But as a group, they usually flew in wide circles unless ravens were in pursuit. There were no ravens or any other reason for these hawks to be fleeing. He wondered if they were being attracted to something towards the northeast. As far as he could see, there was nothing there, but the birds never stopped heading in that direction. He watched them till they disappeared.

He climbed back down the tree and saw Jarden talking to a gardener. When he could get a word in, Raymo asked, "Jarden, I just saw something strange with the bunny birds and wondered if you could help me understand it."

"Sure, Raymo. What about 'em?" asked Jarden.

"Just a few minutes ago, I saw a flock of them flying in a straight line."

"Did you spot any ravens?"

"That was my first thought," said Raymo, "so I climbed Lookout tree and didn't see a single raven. I never heard one either."

"You're sure it was a *straight* line? Some circles can get pretty big when they're searching for a thermal." Jarden crossed his arms. "Maybe they just got bored with where they were."

"But it was weird, Jarden" said Raymo, tracing a line in the air with his finger. "It was straight as an arrow. They eventually disappeared out of sight."

"Which direction were they headed?"

"Northeast. I suppose they could be migrating?" asked Raymo, scratching his head.

"No," said Jarden, "It's too late in the year for that. It could mean a severe storm is coming from the southwest, but something like that rarely chases them. I don't know what to tell you." He started to walk away. "I need to get to the greenhouse."

"There's one other thing," said Raymo. "This is the third time I've seen it happen, and they were flying in the same direction."

Jarden stopped in his tracks. "The third time today?"

"No. It happened twice about a week ago. This is the first I've noticed it since then."

"Well, I can't tell you what those birds are up to. Let me know if it happens again."

"Will do, Jarden. I'll have the other security members keep an eye open too."

"Sounds good, Raymo. Now, I need to get back to this gardening issue."

Over a dozen people filled the small meeting room at the Calneva Rift Ranger Station. This would be the final gathering of those involved with Arcon's return to the Forest. After welcoming the last arrival, Ranger Dan said, "Hi everyone. Do you all have seats? Dwight, are you okay? You need a chair?"

"I can stand," said Dwight.

"Okay then. I'll go once around the room and see if we're ready. First, Rangers Becca and Dwight, you'll be covering for me while I'm dealing with this. Any questions for these folks?"

"We're good, Dan," said Becca, while Dwight nodded his agreement.

Dan turned to the rappelling expert for San Bernardino Search and Rescue. "Dave, I know Elaina is good to go. Did Arcon learn anything about rappelling?"

"He learned pretty quick. Dropping was a new concept for him, but he sure knows how to hang on."

"I'll bet he does," said Dan, laughing. "How about Mr. Merrick here?"

"He's ... he's doing okay."

"Not much conviction in that," said Dan. "Victor, are you okay with rappelling?"

"Well, I'm no expert, but I want to do it."

"He'll be fine," said Dave. "We all have jitters the first time."

"Then we'll keep him in the lineup," said Dan. "Now, Noreena, is your crew ready to go?"

"We're scrambling, but the cinematographer has a handle on it. The producer keeps asking for changes, but we can accommodate. The main thing is to get as much video recorded as possible, and we'll edit later. Sound is important too, so we'll have quite a few people wired. The director found a nifty platform we can drop the folks in on. It's got a great camera array on the bottom and lots of room to stand. Victor will love it."

"Does that mean he won't need to rappel?"

"If this works, he'll only need to hang on. The same with Arcon. We expect we'll still have Elaina rappel in, just for effect."

"That's great. Keep me informed. Now, the stars of the show, Arcon and Elaina. You're going to *drive* to the base camp in Baker? I'd still feel more comfortable if we could shuttle you there in a chopper. We got the road fixed, sort of, but that little car of yours will take a beating if you drive there."

"We'll make it," said Elaina. "Tell them, dad."

After a bit of radio silence, Dan said, "Roberto is in Baker. He's on the line, or at least he was earlier. Roberto, you there?"

They heard a crackling noise on the speaker and then a scratchy, "I'm here. Sorry, folks. I was giving you two thumbs up, but you couldn't see me because I was on mute."

They all laughed, and he said, "I just drove the road, and she can make it in the autocycle. Just take it slow in spots. Leave soon, and let Arcon see some of our world."

"Okay, thanks, Roberto. Arcon's giving you two thumbs up, by the way. Okay, who's next? The helicopter pilots. Are the choppers ready?"

"Hi, Roberto here again. Everything's good to go. Fuel, maintenance. Just waiting for D-Day and the packages."

"Sounds good. Speaking of packages, three are here with me: Elaina, Arcon, and Victor. How about the medical supplies and other goodies, such as the reams of information?"

"We have all the info on the medical issue here at base camp," said Roberto. "You'll need to get the family stuff from Dolores and bring that with you."

"Understood. Unless anyone has anything to add, we'll meet again at base camp in four days." Dan scanned the room, admiring the team and their professionalism. "Thanks, everyone. This meeting is adjourned."

Raymo walked straight through the Room of Remembrance to the door marked Ancient Evil. He knew the combination to its padlocked door and didn't hesitate to use it. He was again reminding himself of the importance of keeping this evil Arcon had unleashed *out* of the Community.

It was no wonder the Community chose to remove these items from the Room of Remembrance and lock them away.

Scattered around the room were pictures, posters, and news articles portraying the evils that the world had refused to give up. And on one wall, in large letters, was the Bible verse that foretold of that happening. Once again, he read Revelation 9:20 as the Founders had translated it: "They would not give up taking innocent life, consuming pharmaceuticals, viewing pornography, and stealing from each other."

He moved to another area that focused on political corruption. The elite of the nations used their power to suppress and control the godly and the poor, and gave favors to evil men to maintain that power. Judges no longer convicted the guilty but instead subjugated the righteous. Raymo recalled reading in the book of Jasher how corruption had destroyed Sodom. As he thumbed through the stacks of articles, he saw evidence of the same behavior, only more widespread. He thanked God for rescuing the ArcPoint people from that evil, just as Lot was from Sodom.

Then he went to the area that turned his stomach. It was labeled, The Great Falling Away. It listed all the ways in which God's people had turned away from His truth. They worshipped manmade objects, embraced those who were sexually immoral, and gave themselves over to doctrines of demons. There were books that listed the flawed philosophies of many worldwide religions and cults. The stories from the Founders said that the true believers had gone underground like the ArcPoint people had. *How could they walk away from such blatant evil without giving their lives to try to stop it?*

In another area, in very large blood-red letters, hung the title WAR, and below, the statistics for death from all the major wars. The Founders had said World War three was just beginning when they moved to the Mojave. There was a Bible verse mounted on the wall that read, "Isaiah 2:4 And he shall judge among the nations, and shall rebuke many people: and they shall beat their swords into plowshares, and their spears into pruning hooks:

nation shall not lift up sword against nation, neither shall they learn war any more." There was a rumor among the Community that this may have taken place already. He didn't believe it. *If Jesus was on earth, somehow, they would know.*

On one end of a table in this area were the few guns the Community owned and what remained of the ammunition. It had all been put there long before he was born, with the understanding they would never use them again. As part of the Security team, Raymo was allowed to use anything required to defend the Community, including these guns and ammo. But condemnation would be swift and powerful if they were used unnecessarily. He picked up one of the guns, loaded a shell, aimed it at a picture of a terrorist, and then put everything back the way he'd found it. Then he walked out of the room.

As he left the Room of Remembrance, a thought came to him. He went back into the room of Ancient Evil to look more closely at the ammunition. The bullets that remained were .22 caliber. He looked the guns over and found two .22 caliber rifles with identical ammo clips. He looked around just to be sure he was alone, then filled one clip with birdshot and the other with bullets. He put the clips back in the rifles and the boxes of ammo back where he'd found them. He locked up and left, feeling better prepared for the future.

Raymo's only concern now was the bunny birds. He told the other members of Security to alert him whenever they saw these birds over the Facility, or if they were ever flying in a straight line. If so, he planned to grab the pair of binoculars that Security possessed and race to the top of Lookout Tree. He knew they were curious birds, and he hoped to find out what they were curious about. What he envisioned was an invasion force just beyond the ridge of mountains to the northeast. If so, maybe he could spot smoke from a campfire or something.

He'd just talked with his small group of defenders, and they all agreed to be on high alert. And not just for bunny birds.

CHAPTER TWENTY-FIVE

A helicopter flight from the Ranger station to the base camp in Baker would take less than an hour. But because of the Rift, it would take someone over twelve hours to drive. Elaina and Arcon decided to do a road trip and spend three days getting there in the autocycle. Arcon wanted to see as much as he could of Elaina's world before he landed back in the Mojave Forest. He needed to try driving and swimming before he saw Jarden again. More than anything, he wanted to spend time alone with Elaina.

Their first stop was the end of the Rift at Twenty-Nine Palms. They agreed it wasn't as impressive as when they first saw it with Patty. This end would have been his alternate escape route. He looked at the hills. Not much likelihood for water in this direction, and no ArcPoint trees for food. He never would have met Ranger Dan. He chuckled to himself as he thought, *It was well worth tightroping across the Rift.*

Before they got to the city of Parker, Elaina turned up the abandoned Highway 95 so she could give Arcon a driving lesson. Stopping in the middle of the road, she asked, "Are you ready for this?"

"I've been ready for over twenty years," he said with a grin.

"Well, we'll see about that." She hopped out of the autocycle and waited for Arcon to crawl out of the back seat. "I bet you'll be glad to sit up front with more leg room."

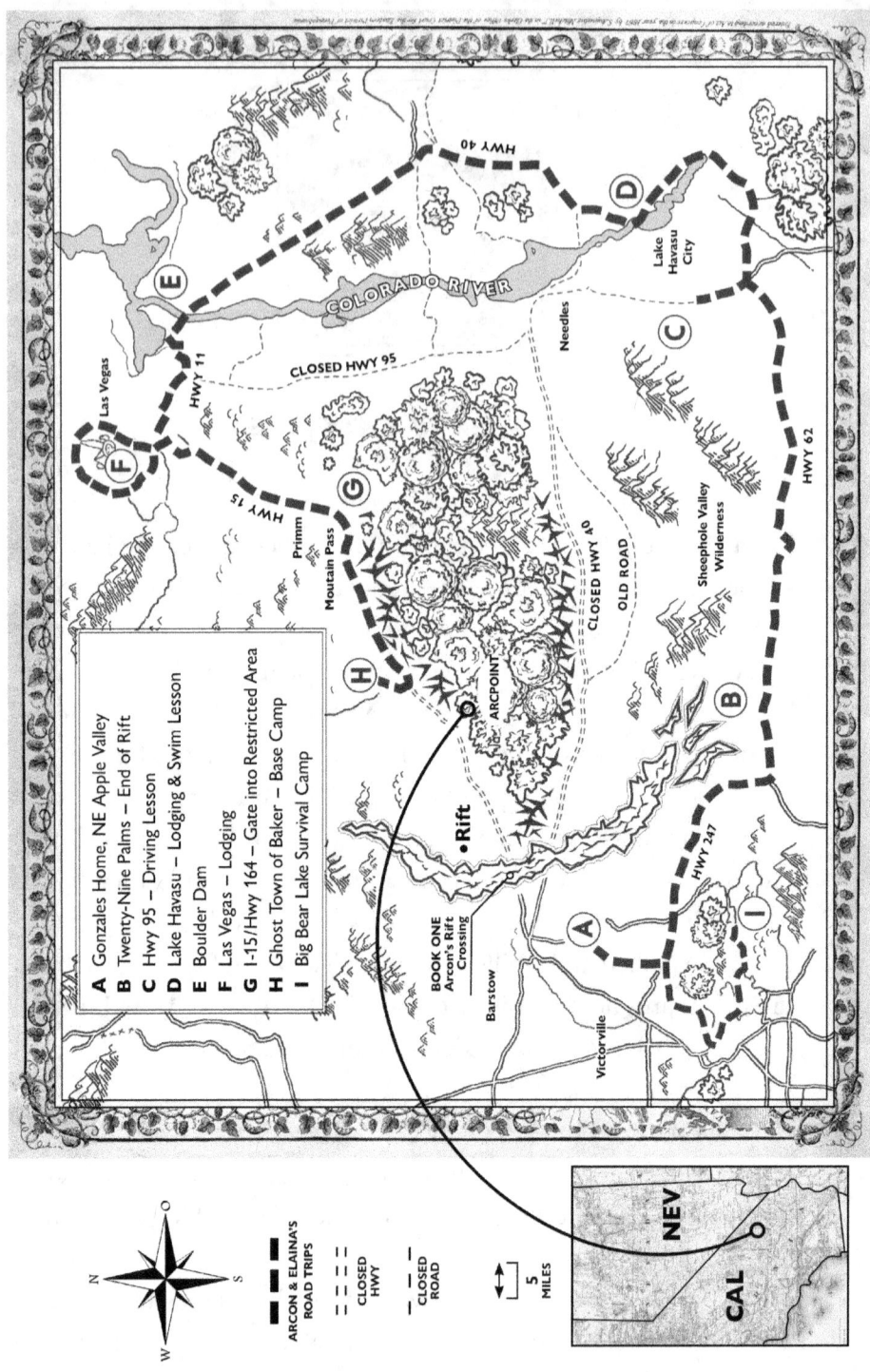

A Gonzales Home, NE Apple Valley
B Twenty-Nine Palms – End of Rift
C Hwy 95 – Driving Lesson
D Lake Havasu – Lodging & Swim Lesson
E Boulder Dam
F Las Vegas – Lodging
G I-15/Hwy 164 – Gate into Restricted Area
H Ghost Town of Baker – Base Camp
I Big Bear Lake Survival Camp

BOOK ONE
Arcon's Rift
Crossing

ARCPOINT

• Rift

COLORADO RIVER

Las Vegas

HWY 11

HWY 40

Lake Havasu City

Needles

CLOSED HWY 95

HWY 62

Sheephole Valley Wilderness

CLOSED HWY 40

OLD ROAD

HWY 15

Primm

Mountain Pass

HWY 247

Barstow

Victorville

NEV

CAL

ARCON & ELAINA'S ROAD TRIPS

CLOSED HWY

CLOSED ROAD

5 MILES

N
S
E
W

234

"I'll be glad to be in control."

"You sound like Patty," said Elaina as she crawled in the back. "Wow, this is a first for me. I've never ridden back here before."

Arcon squeezed into the front seat, but had to fold his legs to fit. "How do you move the seat back?" he asked.

"Oh, sorry. Just under the front of the seat is a lever. In the middle. Slide it to the left." Just as she said that, the seat slammed toward her. "Whoa, I think you found it."

"Sorry. Are you okay?"

"Yeah, no problem. I wasn't using my legs anyway."

"Oh, no. Do you need more room?"

"I was kidding, Arcon. No, just make sure you're comfortable." She instructed him how to tilt the seat, adjust the mirrors, and find other controls. "I think you're ready. Let's start with the easy one."

"What's that?"

"Electric only. Press that big button with the letter 'E' on it. Okay, now put the manual transmission into neutral."

Arcon grabbed the gearshift knob, pulled it, then wiggled it back and forth. "Got it."

"Yes, you did. I'm impressed."

"In our shop, we have a trainer set up. The Founders didn't want us to forget how to drive a stick shift."

"Well, that won't help for this lesson, but it will later. Okay, now, put your foot on the brake. That's right. Rest your foot on the accelerator, but don't press it down. Okay. Now, turn that key two clicks clockwise. Perfect. Are you ready?"

"Ready!"

"Press the accelerator slowly."

Arcon pushed down with his right foot and the car started moving. He pressed harder and it moved faster with just a faint whine from behind him. "Whoo-hoo," he yelled. "Giddy-up."

"It's not a horse," said Elaina, with a laugh. "Now try stopping."

Arcon stepped on the brake pedal and nearly hit the windshield with his head. "Oops."

"Classic amateur maneuver," joked Elaina. "Try it again."

Arcon sped the car up and slowed it down a couple more times, and drove it around a few corners. When he stopped, he asked, "Can I do the stick shift now?"

"Let's do it," said Elaina. "Turn the key off."

"Okay. Wait—don't tell me. Uhh, do I press the 'S' for stick-shift."

"No. Remember? That's for the starter. Press 'M' for manual."

"Oh, right, got it. Step on the clutch, tranny in neutral, turn the key two clicks, press 'S' to start it." Arcon did that and heard a light rumble. "Can I put it in gear?"

"Not yet. A safety instruction first. Press on the gas a little." The engine sped up. "Now some more. A little more. More. Still more."

Arcon could hear the engine screaming. "Isn't that too much?"

"It's more than you need, but it's not hurting anything. Okay, take your foot off the gas." The engine slowed to an idle. "Let's say you're sitting at a stop sign, about to cross a busy highway. If you're in gear and let out the clutch, what will happen?"

"We'll move through the intersection."

"If the engine is running like this, you'll go about two meters and stop. Then you'll get hit by a truck and the trip is over. If the engine was revved up like it was, you'd cross the intersection fast with the tires smoking. You want to run the engine between those two extremes, but it's better to rev too high than too low. Understand?"

"I think so." Arcon revved the engine a little. "How about this?"

"Won't hurt to try. Step on the clutch and put it in gear."

"Clutch is in." He put it in first gear.

"Wrong!" said Elaina. "Remember, on this car, first is granny low. For normal driving, you start in second."

"Right, right." Arcon shifted to second, took a deep breath, and let out the clutch. The car lurched and died. "Hmm. Should I have revved it higher?"

"Either that or let the clutch out slower. Try again."

He did it without killing the engine, so he sped up. "Can I try shifting?"

"If you're careful."

Arcon tried what he'd practiced over and over in the ArcPoint shop. It was different with a moving machine, but he learned fast—only grinding the gears twice. Elaina even let him drive off-road through the brush. She showed him how to raise the vehicle higher and use granny low gear to crawl over the berm on the edge of the highway. He was grinning ear-to-ear by the time they switched drivers again.

Next, Elaina drove him over the Parker Dam and up to Lake Havasu City, where they spent the night. The authorities had given Elaina a lot of per diem credits, so Elaina got Arcon a room with a king-sized bed. He'd never slept on anything so large and soft.

The next morning, they donned swimsuits and went down to the lake. Arcon tried swimming like he saw Tarzan doing, but every time he looked at Elaina, she was laughing. The closest he'd come to this was floating in a newly filled aquaponic fish tank. At only two hundred gallons, it just wasn't the same.

At one point, Elaina dove off the boat dock and Arcon jumped in after her. He panicked when he couldn't touch bottom, but was able to dog-paddle back to the dock.

"Let me show you what my dad taught me," said Elaina. "First, get in the deep water and hold on to the dock."

Arcon climbed down the dock ladder and moved away from it, keeping one hand on the dock. "Now what?"

"Take a few deep breaths, hold the last one, then let go of the dock. Don't paddle or anything—just be still. Count to twenty, then feel the top of your head. After that, reach up and grab the dock again."

Arcon thought about it. He was sure he'd sink to the bottom if he didn't paddle to stay up. If he had to, he figured he could climb up the pier. He did what Elaina told him. When he was done, he looked at her and said, "My head never went underwater."

"Interesting, isn't it? As long as you take a deep breath, you'll float. Then all you have to do is push down with your hands and your head will come up high enough to get a breath. You can last for hours like that and you won't drown, as long as you don't panic. But if you dog-paddle like you were, you'll wear yourself out. Now, try moving away from the dock. Don't worry, I'll be here if you need me—but you won't."

Arcon pushed himself away from the dock. He found out that with very little effort he could keep his nose out of the water and breathe normally. He slowly paddled further away, then turned around. "I can swim!" he yelled.

"You'll be like Tarzan before you know it," Elaina yelled back. When he got close, she said, "You've got more to learn, so don't get cocky and drown. I'll teach you other tricks later. Right now, we need to get back on the road."

"I agree to your terms, reluctantly," said Arcon, with a smile. "But at least I can tell Jarden I went swimming."

From there they went to Davis Dam, then up to Boulder Dam. He'd read a book about hydroelectric power and seen pictures, but now everything looked different. Still visible was the crack that crippled Boulder Dam not long after his people hid in the Mojave. "How deep is the lake now?" asked Arcon.

"Do you see that watermark on the dam near the water's edge?"

"Yeah."

"That's the deepest they let the water get now because of the crack. At the bottom of the dam, it's about seven hundred feet in elevation. At the top, it's just over twelve hundred feet. That mark is at a thousand."

"Hmm. So, the lake is about three hundred feet deep?"

"Wrong, Mr. calculator. It's about fifty feet."

"I don't get it."

"The lake is full of sediment. It washes down from the hills and settles out here. But we're lucky there's a lake at all. When the earthquake happened, there'd been a drought. The water level was down to about a thousand feet. They were able to lower it quickly to nine hundred by opening the floodgates. If the water level had been at the top, the whole thing might have collapsed. That would've sent a wall of water downstream, maybe all the way to the ocean."

"Really?"

"No one knows. The dams we crossed downstream may have stopped it, but it still would've been catastrophic. Want to know an interesting fact?"

"Sure."

"The river here is the same one we saw at Lake Havasu."

"The Colorado."

"Right. This river didn't use to flow to the ocean as it does now. But it did for a few weeks after they opened the floodgates here. When we have some time, I'll show you an article on the info-net about the history of the river." Arcon was so intrigued with what he saw, Elaina suggested they take the Boulder Dam guided tour.

"So, what did you think?" asked Elaina.

"About the dam?"

"Yeah, that, and all the changes that happened when it broke."

Arcon shook his head. "Wow. It completely changed my ideas about Las Vegas."

"What do you mean?"

"Well, we all knew someday we'd have to leave ArcPoint. From there, it was about the same distance to Los Angeles, Las Vegas, or Needles. Nobody wanted to go to Las Vegas. They said it was called Sin City."

Elaina's eyebrows shot up. "I've never heard it called that."

"In our Room of Remembrance is another room called Ancient Evil. That's where we store things to remember that we want to forget. In there we had a poster with a picture of Las Vegas, and it was titled Sin City."

"Wow, that's a new one on me. That must've been before the dam went out. When they lost all that electricity, it became a ghost town."

"Can we go there? I've never been to a ghost town."

"Sure you have. Calico was once a ghost town, when the silver mine shut down. Of course, it's not that way anymore, and neither is Las Vegas. In fact, not long after Las Vegas was given the title of the Largest Ghost Town in the World, there was a massive influx of people. It went from nearly a half million residents down to a thousand in two years, then back up to a hundred thousand in two more."

"What brought them back?"

"Nothing."

"What do you mean?"

"The people who moved to Vegas weren't the ones who'd left it. For years, immigrants had been coming into America illegally—escaping crime and poverty in the countries they came from. They were abused and robbed on their journey here, and had no way to legally establish themselves. When they heard about an abandoned city, they saw a way to rebuild their lives."

Arcon shook his head. "They just moved in?"

"Nobody tried to stop them. They were considered the good immigrants—farmers, laborers, even professionals. Undesirable characters, like drug dealers and gang members, had no business there. The immigrants had nothing for thieves to steal. But they knew how to farm, and the soil was fertile. They did little more than survive, but it was enough. And only a few years later, Jesus returned and gave them official recognition."

Arcon stared at her. "It sounded like you were reading that out of a textbook."

"It wasn't a textbook," said Elaina, getting emotional. "I read it in my great-great-grandmother's diary."

Arcon's mouth dropped open. "Your family is from Las Vegas?"

"On my mom's side. I'm the fifth woman to own the diary."

"But you said you've never been there."

"This is the first time I've been on this side of the Mojave. Mom always wanted to visit the family, but she died before she got to. It's a sore subject with Daddy, so don't ask him about it." Elaina started walking away from the viewpoint, heading for the autocycle.

"Understood," said Arcon, following after her. "Would you like to look for your family while we're here?"

"We don't have time, but I'd like to someday. I'd really like to see my grandmother, who used to have this diary."

"I'd like to read the diary myself," said Arcon, as he opened the car door. "It sort of sounds like my Grandpa Lee's journal."

"And I'd like to read more of that journal."

"I say we at least stay in Las Vegas tonight."

"That's good because there isn't anywhere else to stay between here and the base camp in Baker. We're not going to spend the night in *this* vehicle."

241

They drove around the streets of Las Vegas the next morning, comparing what they saw with archived pictures they found on the info-net. The massive destruction from the earthquakes and fires had all been cleaned up, leaving vast tracts of empty land. Gone were the multi-story hotels and casinos. As they were driving out of town, Elaina told him they were on the Interstate 15 freeway.

"This is the I-15?" he asked.

"It sure is," she responded. "We should see Daddy in about an hour and a half."

Arcon was silent as his mind recalled the history of ArcPoint. Founders called the I-15 the umbilical cord of ArcPoint, and Los Angeles was the womb. When the Rift severed the cord, ArcPoint was on its own. For years, he'd plotted how to get to the I-15. When he finally had, it got him to Elaina. He remarked, "People used to drive down this road and go right to the Facility."

"Maybe they will again someday," said Elaina. "For as long as I can remember, people have talked about rebuilding the freeway from Los Angeles to Las Vegas. But the I-15 and the I-40 have always been off-limits because of your people. It looks like that's about to change."

Arcon thought about that, then sighed. "I believe you're right, but I think the decision is still up to my people."

"So, you still consider them your people?"

"That seems strange, doesn't it?" he answered. "I don't know if they accept me anymore. I guess we'll find out soon." Then he thought about what he'd said. "Elaina, you and Roberto are my people now."

Elaina smiled. "Spoken like a true ambassador. It's easy to see why Jesus chose you."

Arcon didn't laugh. "I don't know what an ambassador is supposed to do. How can I be a good one?"

"To start with, you have the right temperament. You ask questions, and you listen; you try to help others where you can. You're the perfect person to speak for the Mojave people because you know them, and you weren't afraid to come into our world to represent them. You're also well qualified to represent us *to* them, although you might need Ranger Dan to help you with that. The big question—which will get answered on Tuesday—is whether your people will accept you in either position. They really need to accept you in both. But I think they will. I think Jesus would have known if they wouldn't. We just need to step out in faith with that."

"I think once I step out of that helicopter," said Arcon, "It'll all be downhill from there."

Elaina laughed and said, "I'm sure glad you're going first."

The road was smooth until they got to the junction with Highway 164. A gate blocked them at this point. To continue, Elaina had to enter a code her dad gave her. She reached out, pressed the numbers onto the keypad, and the gate opened. She drove through it, and it closed behind her. "We are now entering the restricted zone," she told Arcon. "I've always wondered what this area was like."

"It doesn't look any different so far."

From that point on, the road became the topic of conversation. The earthquakes had so buckled it that Elaina almost had to come to a stop in some areas. She raised the suspension on her car to its highest setting. They could see where minor earth cracks had been repaired, but mostly it hadn't been maintained at all. The pavement would often disappear under the soil, and only reflectors on poles would let them know where the road went.

When Arcon and Elaina drove into base camp on Sunday, they got quite a reception, especially from Roberto. He'd been there two weeks already and missed his baby girl. He gave her a big hug and asked, "How was the trip?"

"It was great," said Elaina. "I taught Arcon how to drive on the old 95, and he drove the rest of the way. I just slept." She watched for his response, and when his eyes went wide, she spared him. "Just kidding. The last few miles were rough, but we made it in one piece, as you can see."

"A bit of an obstacle course, I'm sure. But I bet you liked it."

"Loved it. I don't know about Arcon, though. He smacked his head on the roof a few times. After his driving lesson, he no longer pesters me about how to drive. Now he tells me."

"Sounds like a girl I used to know. Where did he go, anyway? I need to talk to him."

"He went to find Victor."

As Roberto glanced around for them, he said, "Those two seem to be hitting it off."

"I think Victor reminds him a lot of his friend, Jarden. I'm sure he'll love telling Victor stories about him."

"I can't wait to meet this Jarden character. I'll go see if I can track them down. Why don't you check in at headquarters—just down the street on your right—and find out where your rooms are. If I don't see you before, we'll meet for dinner. Okay?"

"Sounds great, Dad."

CHAPTER TWENTY-SIX

Arcon stared at the massive lake in the distance. He'd never seen it from this perspective. He looked at his watch. In less than two hours, he'd fly over the lake in a helicopter. Less than an hour after that, he'd be standing next to Jarden. *This is all happening so fast.* He heard the door of the converted fire hall open beside him.

"Quite the view," said Elaina.

"The lake looks different from here."

"I thought you said ArcPoint had no place to swim."

Arcon furrowed his brow. "Soda Lake? You can't swim there. Jarden says you'd have to walk a mile into it just to get the water up to your waist, and the mud would be up to your knees."

"He was exaggerating, right?"

Arcon stood up from the bench. "Probably. I tried to talk him into hiking to it, but he said it was too far. I planned to do it by myself someday. I made it as far as Lakeview Mountain, just so I could see it."

Elaina slipped her arm around him. "Where's that?"

Arcon thought about it. "About three kilometers this side of the Easter Outpost."

"Oh, that helps. I know exactly where that is." She shook her head. "At least you converted it to kilometers for me."

"Sorry." He pointed. "It's on the other side of those hills. I'll show you when we fly by it." Arcon stared at the lake. "I've never seen the whole lake before. Those hills blocked the view, so we

245

could only see the far edge of it. I had no idea it was this large and beautiful. Look at how it reflects the clouds."

"And the blue sky," said Elaina.

They sat back down on the bench, and Arcon pulled her close. "In the Bible, in Isaiah, it talks about a lake like this. It says the dry ground will become a lake, and springs of water will satisfy the thirsty land. A marsh will flourish where coyotes once lived."

"Looking at it now, it's hard to believe this was ever a desert."

"Sure is." Arcon scanned the horizon. "It's going to be strange."

"What is?"

"Seeing this land from the sky. This summer—after the lake dries up—us hunters were supposed to help the salt gatherers get to Soda Lake. We clear a trail through the forest for them to get to those hills."

"You'd clear a trail all the way from your Facility?"

"Oh, no. there was just… Okay. First, us five hunters hike about a mile, then we swing to the Easter Outpost. That's another five miles, and it sits on the railroad tracks."

"On the tracks, huh?"

"Well, we tore up all the tracks between the Outpost and the Facility. We needed the steel and the ties and the gravel. But coming this direction the tracks are there, so we have a wheeled cart we ride on for another three miles. Then we have to hack the needle-brush off the trail for another three miles. When we're done, the salt-gatherers arrive."

"How many people are you talking about?"

"There's about a dozen people who hike to some abandoned buildings on the edge of the lake. They stay for a week or so and gather salt and baking soda, and other minerals we need. Then they carry it back to the other side of those hills. Our job as hunters is to shuttle supplies back and forth for them."

"But you've never been to the lake?"

"Naah. I was too good at swinging. Other people would pack the supplies, and I'd swing it from one end of the Easter swingway to the other. Another group would carry the stuff back to the Facility. It was a big event for the Community." Arcon hung his head. "Maybe we'll never do it again."

"Are you disappointed?"

"Oh, no," said Arcon. "It was a lot of work for such a small amount of minerals. What we're bringing with us today will last ArcPoint for a year. It's just, well, it'll sure be different."

"Just remember what Ranger Dan said. Your people can change or not change whatever they want. The rest of us are just here to help."

Arcon looked at his watch again, tapping its face with his fingernail. "I don't think I like this thing."

"Why not?"

"It doesn't move fast enough."

"Well, you're the one who said we should wait until ten o'clock, or what did you call it, mid-morning break?"

"I still think that's the best time for us to drop in, literally. People start leaving their work stations about nine-thirty. By ten o'clock, many in ArcPoint are around the Facility. The sun will be high enough for them to see me, but it won't be in their eyes. They need to know it's me coming."

"Arcon, you're wearing your hunter skins and that bright yellow vest. Who else would fly in to see them dressed like that?"

"I guess you're right," said Arcon. "We probably should have worked harder to make you some hunter clothes." He smiled at her and added, "Jane."

Elaina smacked him on the arm just as Ranger Dan came through the firehouse door. "Uh-oh," said Dan. "Now's not the time to have a lover's spat. Should I leave you two alone to kiss and make up?"

Arcon said nervously, "We weren't having ..."

"I'm just kidding," said Dan. "Everyone is accounted for, so we're having a pre-launch meeting at nine o'clock in the mess hall. I expect you'll want to be there."

"The way Arcon is acting, we'll probably be early."

"Perfect," said Dan. "Gotta go."

As Dan walked back into the firehouse, Arcon looked at his watch again. "I sure wish we could go driving," he said.

"Why do you say that?"

"This watch goes really fast when we're driving."

"That's because you stop looking at it," she responded. "Why don't you try just *thinking* about driving? Maybe that'll work."

Arcon grinned. "It depends. Is it me driving, or you?"

Elaina stood and pulled Arcon up from the bench. "Tell you what, let's go find Victor. He's kind of lost here."

"I like that idea. The last time I saw him, he was talking with Ranger Dan. He's obviously not doing that now."

They walked in the main door of the long-abandoned County Fire Station that now housed Base Camp. They turned left into the large meeting room. Having once held two firetrucks, it was the best place in Baker for everyone to gather. At one end was the mess hall. Here they found Victor, slowly gnawing on a chocolate chip muffin and sipping some coffee. When they got to him, Arcon said, "That chocolate chip stuff is good."

"What?" asked Victor. "Oh, yeah. It goes well with coffee, too."

Elaina asked, "Are you doing okay?"

"Oh, I'm doing fine. I'm about to step out of a helicopter a hundred meters off the ground. I've done that many times."

"Have you really?" asked Arcon.

"Yeah. They made me do it six times, so I'd be comfortable with it."

"Are you?" asked Elaina.

"I'll let you know when my knees stop knocking."

"You know what I do to calm myself?" asked Elaina. "I remind myself that others went before me and survived. As long as I'm not the first, or the heaviest, or the clumsiest, I figure I'll make it through."

Victor looked back and forth between her and Arcon and said, "Uh-oh."

"What's the problem?" asked Elaina.

"I think I may be the clumsiest," said Victor, adding, "I'm not really worried about surviving. I'm sure there are plenty of safety measures in place." He bit into the muffin. Before he finished chewing, he said, "I think maybe it's the whole thing that's overwhelming. But it's exciting, and I want to do it. It's just tough having to wait around for it to happen."

"Well, that's what we're here for," said Elaina. "We need you to help Arcon wait it out. He's just like you, counting down the minutes, and it's driving me crazy. So can we talk about something else?"

"Yeah," said Arcon. "Let's talk about driving."

Roberto scanned the people gathered in the mess hall, letting them carry on their conversations as he put tick marks next to their names. He'd planned on doing an official roll call, but there was no need. He knew them all. He'd be aware if someone was missing. As he made his last mark, he yelled, "Can I have your attention?"

The din of conversations quieted down. Some people wandered around to find a seat while Ranger Dan got out of his and walked over to Roberto. He eyed the list on Roberto's comm-pad. "Are they all here?"

"The last one just showed up," said Roberto.

"I want to thank you all for being here," boomed Ranger Dan. "It's not every day we get to help people who've never asked for our help and surely don't even know we're about to let them have it, whether they like it or not." The room erupted with laughter while Dan looked at Arcon, who was sitting front and center with Elaina and her father. "Just kidding, son."

Dan saw Elaina shaking her finger at him as he continued. "You all know that we'll be filming this entire escapade, so I want everyone on their best behavior. Please, let's all be professional about our duties and not play for the cameras. However, be aware and do what you can to facilitate filming. Don't block shots, for instance. But our primary aim is to make contact with the Mojave, excuse me, the ArcPoint Community. As we have all learned these past few weeks, these are good people, God's people. In all of our behavior, we need them to know that we are, too. Arcon will explain that to them, but we have to safely get him in there. Roberto here would appreciate you getting his daughter in there safely as well. We won't worry about Victor."

When he said that, Victor got up and feigned walking toward the door. "Now, now, now," said Ranger Dan. "Don't worry, Victor. By the time you get on that platform, we'll know if it actually works. We'll have tested it with Arcon."

Elaina stood up and threw her hands in the air. "Oh, and Elaina here will have rappelled down," Dan continued, "So there's nothing to worry about … for you."

Ripples of laughter moved through the crowd as Victor returned to his seat. "Seriously, all of you, we need to be safe, but you know how well we've tested everything. We're good to go. What's unknown is how the ArcPoint people will react. Arcon has informed us they have firearms, but he doesn't think anyone would think to use them. He's so confident of that fact; he's going in first to talk with them. Elaina will go next, and you know Roberto here won't let her go in if it's dangerous."

"That's for sure," said Roberto. "But I'll be here at base camp monitoring the operation. I'll trust Elaina not to shimmy down that rope until she gets the okay from Arcon and me. And

I'll have to trust you folks in the helicopter to get them all in there safely and to stop *her* if she gets anywhere near that rope before it's time."

"You can count on that," yelled one man from the back of the mess hall.

"Glad to hear that," Roberto continued. "Just remember, we won't have anyone from the cinematic crew in the helicopters. No matter what happens, try to keep an ear tuned to their direction so we can get some good video. We'll also be able to use those cameras to monitor the situation from here, so if we spot any danger, we can let you know. In other words, your ears are probably more important than your eyes on this mission. Understood?"

Shouts of acknowledgment came to him from around the room. Arcon yelled, "We shouldn't lose our earpiece!"

Roberto pointed at him and said, "You know about that, don't you, son?" He saw Arcon nod and he continued. "Just as a reminder, here's the timeframe. By nine-thirty, I want everyone in the choppers. By nine forty-five, you should be through with the operational safety checks. At nine-fifty, both choppers lift off, provided everything checks out. Stop and hover a half kilometer from the drop zone to do a final readiness check. When ready, chopper one will continue to the drop zone, while chopper two keeps its distance, partly for filming purposes, but mostly so we don't frighten the ArcPoint people any more than we have to."

He swiped his finger across his comm-pad. "When chopper one is in position, we'll do a security and readiness check, and then Arcon will mount the platform. Once he's hit the ground, he'll assess the mood of the ArcPoint people. When he's comfortable with the situation, he'll signal for package two to drop. Elaina will then mount the rappel rope while they raise the platform to optimum camera height."

"Soon after she lands, we'll hoist her rope and attach package three, the crate containing supplies for the Community. They'll lower the camera platform to a better filming elevation. We'll also want Arcon and Elaina to work the crowd to get reactions as they receive the supplies."

"When we think we have adequate footage, we'll retract the platform and prepare to drop package four. That would be you, Victor. We'll carefully lower Victor to the ground. Please don't drop him. Once he's securely on terra firma, we'll react as the situation develops. All three vital packages need to keep alert to their communications."

Roberto went over his notes one more time. "Just remember— the helicopter will not be landing at this time. It's important to the mission that as few individuals as possible interact with these people. Once these three are safe, we will leave the area."

"Does anyone have questions regarding their particular role in this?" asked Ranger Dan. Seeing no response, he added, "Are we ready to go?" Hearing a lot of positive responses to that question, he said, "Let's pray." A hush fell over the room. "Arcon, they're your people. Would you do the honors?"

Arcon stood to his feet and said, "Gladly." He waited a moment for the room to be completely quiet, then said, "Father, first of all, I want to thank you for all of these people who have given their time to help my family, the ArcPoint Community. Please pour out a blessing on them for me. Guide us by your one Holy Spirit and give us that same singular spirit as we perform our tasks today. Grant us the skills we need and allow your peace to descend on the ArcPoint Community now. You have said in your Word that we are to be as one. Help us now to make ArcPoint one with the rest of your creation. Amen."

CHAPTER TWENTY-SEVEN

Raymo stumbled down the stairs from the sleeping loft, still groggy from his morning snooze. Now he understood why his shift had the name, graveyard. It was a killer. He wanted eight hours sleep, not three. But the noise of mid-morning break always woke him up. Weeks ago, he'd begun a new sleep regimen. He'd sleep from first sun—when he was relieved of guard duty—until the break. Then again, from sunset until his shift began. So far, it worked well. He was able to visit with his buddies—the Separatists—and occasionally Brina.

He was just entering the main room when one of the other security guards called his name. He turned to see the man point two fingers to his eyes, then point up and shake them toward the northeast. *Bunny birds.* Raymo sprinted to the security office and grabbed the binoculars. He raced to get out the south man-door. The other guard was already climbing Lookout Tree. As he got up to the platform, the guard pointed to other bunny birds that were joining the first ones they'd seen. They were headed northeast.

Raymo scanned the horizon with the nocs, looking for anything out of the ordinary. Not seeing anything, he handed the nocs to the other guard. Before long, the guard said, "I see something! Look in that direction." He handed the nocs back to Raymo.

"I see it," said Raymo. "There's a dark spot rising over those hills. Now it stopped ... and it's just sitting there, in mid-air. That's not a bird. Wait. Now there's a second one rising up. Here, take a look."

"Yeah, you're right. Two of them, just sitting there. How do they do that?" He handed the nocs back. "What do we do about it?"

"Go tell the boss," said Raymo. "I'll keep watch to see if they come this way."

As the guard climbed down the tree, Raymo looked toward the horizon but couldn't make out the spots with his naked eye. He put the nocs to his eyes, located the two shapes, and scanned for more but didn't see any.

When he looked back, he thought they looked different. They did. They looked larger. *They're coming toward the Facility*. Down at the ground the guard was walking toward the building. Raymo let out a whistle to get his attention. When the guard looked up, Raymo yelled, "THEY'RE COMING!" He watched the guard turn and run toward the building. Raymo set down the binoculars and climbed down the tree himself. He knew what he had to do.

Jarden was talking with one of the mechanics when he heard a door slam. A guard ran into the Facility, out of breath and gesturing toward the outdoors. "What's going on?" barked Jarden.

"We have some trouble. There's something flying toward us from the northeast. Raymo is watching them from Lookout and says they're getting closer."

"Flying toward us?" asked Jarden. "Like birds?"

"They're certainly not birds," said the guard. "They're a lot bigger." His head swiveled, his eyes searching the room. "Have you seen Keenan?"

"I think he's helping in the shop," said Jarden.

"Yeah," said the mechanic. "I just saw him there."

The guard ran for the machine shop. Jarden said to the mechanic, "I probably need to check this out."

"Sure thing. I'll go to the shop and see if Keenan needs me to do anything."

Jarden jogged across the Facility to the east exit. He had two troubling scenarios churning in his head. Either this was the outside world about to pay them a visit, or it was another one of Raymo's overreactions. Either way, he needed to investigate it himself. Standing in the doorway, he gave a loud, shrill whistle. It was the alarm that a hunter was in trouble. He didn't know if there were any hunters within earshot, but if there were, he wanted them at his side.

He climbed the limbs of Lookout Tree, expecting to find Raymo up in its platform, but there was no one there, just a pair of binoculars. He stepped up onto the deck and looked toward the northeast. He was glad he had the binoculars, but he didn't need them to see what Raymo had seen. Two dark spots off in the distance, and they didn't appear to be moving. He thought he could hear a faint noise coming from them, and it wasn't birdsong.

He looked down and saw Chad and Tawny wandering around. He gave the whistle again, and they looked his direction. Jarden shouted, "Chad!" He pointed at the two of them and yelled, "Up here!" He saw them disappear under the tree branches. He could see other people emerging from the Facility and figured Raymo must be alerting everyone. This day was about to be like none other for the Community. He prayed it would end well.

The helicopters stopped and hovered about five kilometers from the drop zone. The pilots of both units performed final checks between each other while Arcon and Elaina listened in. When they were through, they heard the pilots say, "Arcon, the crew is ready. If you're ready as well, we'll begin the final approach."

"I'm ready to go now," said Arcon as Elaina gave him a thumbs up. He looked, and got a nod from Victor. "We're all ready, sir. Proceed." He felt their helicopter start to move and watched the other one follow slower and move further away. He didn't notice his leg nervously bouncing up and down.

"Are you okay?" asked Elaina.

"I'm fine," said Arcon. Then he added, "I hope Jarden is there."

"So do I," said Elaina. "I can tell he's important to you, and I'm excited to meet him."

Arcon looked at her and said, "It may surprise you, but he'll be excited to meet you too."

Elaina tipped her head. "Why do you say that?"

"Because I talked to him about you. He told me I should try to find you, and he prayed I would."

"He did?"

Arcon thought about that and answered, "Yes, to both."

"What do you mean?"

He reached over and took her hand in his. "Yes, he prayed, and yes, God answered his prayer."

As Chad got up on the deck of the lookout, he was handed the binoculars by Jarden, who pointed to the dark shapes in the distance and said, "It looks like they're starting to move again."

Chad found them and watched for a moment. "What are they?"

"Aircraft of some sort," said Jarden.

"Let me see," said Tawny. He found the objects and adjusted the focus. "Wow. I can hear them, too."

"Hand those back," said Jarden. He trained the nocs on the crowd gathering outside the Facility. He expected Raymo to be among them, but he couldn't locate him. He turned his sights back on the objects in the sky. One was coming their way fast; the other was hanging back, moving much slower. There was a popping noise coming from them that was getting louder. Now it was obvious Raymo hadn't been seeing things. He could only hope Arcon was in charge of whatever was coming. He still wanted to believe Arcon wouldn't bring in the outside world unless it was the right thing to do.

Raymo burst into the Room of Remembrance and hurried to unlock the room of Ancient Evil. He lifted the rifle he'd staged, the one with birdshot in its clip, off the wall. He started to leave, then stopped, grabbed the clip full of bullets off the other rifle, and stuck it in his pouch. He ran out of the room and dashed out the east exit. He snuck around to the back side of the generator shed, away from the crowd gathering on the east side of the Facility.

He could hear rushing, popping sounds coming from the sky to the northeast and knew whatever it was, it was coming closer, and it wasn't any kind of bird. Whatever it was, he was fully ready to warn it off with gun shots. Or more, if necessary.

The people who'd gathered, stared in disbelief at the noisy object advancing in the sky over the Facility. It moved until it looked like it was centered right over their location. Many fled into the Facility, dragging the children with them. Others hid under the trees, while some stayed to watch—either out of defiance or utter fascination.

As it got close, Jarden recognized this machine as a helicopter, because he'd seen pictures of them in books and magazines. He also knew there should be people inside of it, so he adjusted the focus on the nocs as he trained it on an opening in its side. He hoped one of those people was Arcon and that he had some kind of control over the actions of this machine and its occupants.

He watched closely as the machine hovered directly over the south courtyard and faced different directions, appearing to be maneuvering itself for something. The opening slowly turned his direction and he saw movement inside. Then something that looked like a branch swung out of the opening, and it appeared to have a hemp rope attached to it, with a platform at the bottom. A person sitting in the opening suddenly grabbed the rope and stood on the platform. *That person is wearing a hunter's vest.* "It's Arcon!" he exclaimed to the two hunters. "He's come back!"

When Arcon first stepped onto the foot camera platform, it waved around radically until he got his feet centered on it and stood up straight. "I'm ready to go now!"

"Can you hear us clearly?" asked the co-pilot.

"I can hear you clearly," said Arcon. "I'm ready."

As the co-pilot disconnected the safety line from Arcon, Elaina said, "I'll join you soon!"

Arcon felt the rope drop, and his heart begin to race. He tried to stay focused on the training he'd received, but the excitement of the moment was hard to ignore. "I'll tell you when I'm there and ready for you," he responded to Elaina. Then he added, "I love you. Pray for me."

"I will," said Elaina, as she remembered they didn't want idle chatter on the radio during the operation. Then she quickly added, "Love you."

Arcon looked down at all the people below and wondered if they recognized him. They looked like ants, and their legs looked strange when they walked. He glanced around, surveying the familiar buildings. He was getting closer to the treetops. Three people were standing on the platform in Lookout Tree. He waved to them, and they waved back. He couldn't tell who they were yet, but the exchange reassured him this would be all right.

Raymo knew it was time. Whoever it was, they were dropping people into the Community. He had to let them know they weren't welcome. He stepped out from under the tree where he'd been hiding and pointed the rifle toward the body of the machine. He didn't want to hit anyone because that may elicit a violent response from them. He just wanted them to know the Community was armed and would defend itself.

He could see the person hanging from the rope, and he could see the spinning parts of the machine. He aimed carefully to miss them all. Then he pulled on the trigger. It wouldn't move. He remembered reading about a safety button. He located it, changed its position, aimed again, and pulled the trigger. Still nothing, but this time the trigger moved. Then he remembered the bolt and something called chambering a round. He'd practiced doing this without ammunition, so he did it quickly. This time, he knew it would work. He aimed once more and pulled the trigger. He heard a loud crack sound as the gun fired. He lowered the gun to see how the strangers would react.

Jarden heard the familiar noise of a gun being fired—a sound he hadn't heard in over fifty years, but his trained ears could still recognize it. Those ears also knew that the noise came from the ground, not the sky. "Did you boys hear that?" he asked the other two as he turned his nocs to scan the area.

"I heard it," said Tawny. "What was it?"

"It was gunfire," said Jarden, "Somebody in the Community is shooting at them." He turned in the direction that his ears told him the noise came from. "Chad, climb down and head toward the generator shed. Listen for my whistles. We need to find out who's shooting and stop them. They probably don't know it's Arcon." As Chad climbed down the tree, Jarden continued to scan the area. "Tawny, you stay here. If I spot someone, I'll need you to help Chad stop him. Don't worry; the guns can't kill you."

"How do you know that?" asked Tawny.

"I'll explain later."

Arcon felt his descent lurch to a stop. "What's happening?" he yelled over the noise of the helicopter.

"We think we just took some fire," said the pilot. "Hang on."

Arcon listened as the helicopter crew tried to figure out where it came from and how to proceed. He recognized Roberto's voice and heard something about a small building. He turned to look down at the generator shed. Then he looked below him and saw someone emerge from under Lookout Tree and run toward the shed.

As he looked back toward the shed, he saw a figure step out from under some trees near it. Then he saw a flash of light and immediately felt a stinging sensation on his right calf, like he'd just walked into needle brush. His legs reacted by dropping him to a crouched position on the platform, and he heard his own voice in the earpiece scream with pain.

He heard the co-pilot say, "We're bringing you back," and felt the rope rising.

"No, no," Arcon yelled as he stood up. "I'm okay." He started bouncing up and down on the platform to let them know he wanted to continue dropping. The platform kept rising until he was close enough to climb back into the helicopter.

"Roberto, tell them to drop me down there!"

"It looked like you were hit," Roberto responded. "We need to assess the situation before we continue. Let the medic check you out."

Arcon pounded the side of the helicopter with the palm of his hand.

"C'mon, Arcon," said Elaina, grabbing his arm. "Sit down. Are you hurt?"

"It's nothing. I need to go down there."

The medic put his hand on Arcon's shoulder. "Sir, you're not going anywhere until I examine you. You have blood on your leg. Let me look at it."

Arcon plopped himself in a seat. The medic grabbed his foot and turned it until he could see a wound on the side of Arcon's calf. "Arcon's correct, Mr. Gonzalez. I see minor lacerations and a few welts. It appears to be a low-energy buck shot weapon—small caliber, maybe even bird shot." He swabbed it with alcohol.

"It doesn't hurt that bad," said Arcon. "Let me go!"

"Arcon, listen to me," said Roberto. "Even bird shot can kill you if you get hit in the face, or it knocks you off the platform. It's your call if you want to risk it, but Elaina and Victor can't go until you secure the site. Do you understand?"

Arcon got to his feet. "I understand, Mr. Roberto. I'm going."

"Arcon!" yelled Elaina. "Are you sure?"

"I trust my people," said Arcon. "You need to trust *me*." He reached for the cable and stepped back onto the platform.

Elaina grabbed his arm. "I trust you," she yelled over the sound of the helicopter.

He grabbed her hand briefly, then gave her a thumbs up. "I'm ready. Drop me down."

"At least make yourself a smaller target," said Roberto in his earpiece. "Crouch down. Guard your face."

"Understood." Arcon crouched, burying his head in his arms as the platform dropped.

Jarden thought he'd spotted movement near the trees on the other side of the generator shed. When he focused the nocs on that spot, he saw a flash followed almost immediately by another loud crack sound. "I see him," he said to Tawny. "It looks like Raymo, and he's at the edge of the trees southwest of the generator shed. Stop him any way you have to. I'll signal Chad on where to go. Now hurry!"

As Tawny climbed down, Jarden looked around for Chad. He spotted him near the northeast corner of the generator shed and let out a loud whistle to get his attention. When Chad looked his way, he gave another whistle that meant 'head south.' He saw Chad glance at the sky to get his bearings and then dash around to the other side of the shed. Then he saw Tawny running full-tilt out from under the trees, right past Chad.

Turning his attention back to Arcon, he saw him stepping back into the helicopter. He waited but saw no one in the opening where Arcon entered. He looked back to where he'd last seen the shooter. He didn't see anyone at first, then saw Raymo step out from under a tree, a rifle in his hand. Jarden could see Chad and Tawny searching the area. He let out another whistle that told them to head west. He saw them turn to each other and realized the noise from the helicopter was making it difficult for them to discern the signal. He tried again. They had to move fast.

Raymo thought his last shot worked because he could see the person went back into the machine. He watched from his hiding place, expecting the machine to leave. Instead, it remained hovering in the sky. After a few moments, he saw the person step out of the machine again. *It's time to get serious. I can't allow my*

Community to be invaded. He knew his next action may ultimately cost him his life, but the people were worth the risk.

He pulled off the clip containing the birdshot and replaced it with the clip of bullets. He remembered to chamber a new round. Stepping out from under the trees, he took aim at the body of the machine, hoping not to hit anyone. He pulled the trigger.

He'd expected an even louder noise when he fired, but heard nothing. He pulled the trigger again, and still nothing. He grabbed the bolt, ejected that bullet, and chambered another. He aimed carefully at the machine again and pulled the trigger. Still nothing. He chambered another round, and this time when he aimed, he could see others moving around in the opening. He didn't want to have to do it, but he pulled the trigger again. As he did, he felt the full force of being hit bodily by a charging Tawny.

When Tawny hit him, the gun went flying from his hands. As they tumbled to the ground, Chad jumped for the gun and was able to keep it out of Raymo's clawing hands. As Tawny kept him pinned to the ground, Chad raised the gun over his head, waved it toward Lookout Tree, then threw it into the trees. Then he jumped on Raymo himself, just as he was about to wrench himself free from Tawny's grip.

As soon as Jarden saw Chad had the gun, it convinced him Raymo was no threat, and he climbed down the tree. He quickly weaved his way through the people who were gathering around the three struggling young men. He found the rifle Chad had tossed and looked it over. Then he walked over to where Raymo lay on the ground. Chad and Tawny each had an arm pinned down, while two other men were now holding his legs.

"Hang onto him, boys," barked Jarden. Raymo stopped struggling when he saw Jarden standing over him. Jarden looked the gun over some more. Chad handed him a palm sized metal box and said, "We found this on him." He looked at it and realized it was a clip full of birdshot. He pulled the clip off the rifle and saw it was full of bullets.

Jarden looked squarely at Raymo and asked, "Murder? You were willing to bring the ancient evil of murder into our Community?" As he snapped the clip back into the rifle, he said, "You need to understand something. The Bible says an eye for an eye and a tooth for a tooth. He who lives by the sword will die by the sword." As soon as he said that, with an action almost too fast to see, he chambered another round and pointed the rifle right between Raymo's eyes. "I hope you know Jesus," he said, and he pulled the trigger.

Gasps and screams surged through the gathered crowd, but only a click was heard from the rifle. Most hadn't seen Jarden pull the gun up from Raymo's head at the last second. Jarden had no intention of accidentally doing what he'd just accused Raymo of.

Still pointing the rifle at the ground near Raymo's head, Jarden chambered bullets and pulled the trigger until he'd exhausted what was in the clip. It never fired. He glared at Raymo. "You also need to know that we removed the gunpowder from these bullets over fifty years ago. I thought it was a bad idea at the time. I was wrong." Then he said, "Let him up, boys. We've got company."

Most of the crowd started moving to the other side of the generator shed, walking slow enough for Jarden to pass into the lead. As he rounded the corner of the building, he could see a rope hanging down amidst the crowd, and someone taller than the others looking his direction.

When their eyes met, Arcon ran in his direction. When he got to Jarden, Arcon hugged him hard enough to lift him off the ground. "Have I ever got a story to tell you, boss."

"The name is Jarden, son," he responded.

CHAPTER TWENTY-EIGHT

Arcon looked around at the familiar faces in the crowd. He saw Tawny standing by himself near the corner of the generator shed, and yelled, "Hey Tawny, come here."

Jarden rested his hand on Arcon's shoulder. "I think he feels bad that he tried to stop you from leaving. Hope you don't mind, but we gave your new swingway to him. He's got your build, so it suits him." As Tawny approached, Jarden added, "Besides, he's the one who figured out your route and almost got you caught."

"You're kidding," said Arcon, giving Tawny a hug. "You figured out my swingway? I thought I'd made it more difficult than that."

"Well, I really just figured out the last part," he responded.

"How's it been working for you?"

"Great. I've started adding a second swing set so I can have a partner."

"And when he's done, his partner will answer to him," Jarden added.

"Unless I'm his partner," said Arcon.

Tawny's eyes lit up. "You mean you're coming back?"

"Maybe," said Arcon. "Oh, wait. Jarden, I have something for you to see." He turned to the side and spoke into his microphone, "Package one to Chopper one, Drop zone secure. Send in Package number two." He turned to Jarden. "Follow me."

The two men, and the rest of the crowd, followed Arcon back to where the rope still hung from a noisy machine overhead. As they approached, the platform he'd dropped in on lifted part way up toward the helicopter. Another rope dropped to Arcon's feet. He gripped the rope with one hand and pointed straight up with the other.

As they all looked up, they could see a shape sliding down the rope. As it got closer, they could see it was a young woman. "Is this that outsider gal?" whispered Jarden, but before Arcon could respond, Jarden smiled and guessed, "Elaina?"

"You remembered!"

"How could I forget?" asked Jarden.

Arcon stepped away so Elaina wouldn't land on top of him. As she unhooked from the rope, Arcon took her hand and said, "Elaina, I'd like you to meet Jarden Merrick, my best friend."

Elaina held out her hand to shake his, but Jarden took her hand and kissed it. She blushed. "Hi, Jarden. Arcon speaks highly of you."

"As well he should," said Jarden with a smile. "Thanks for bringing him back."

A radio voice in Arcon's ear said, "Package One, do you copy?" He also felt Elaina tap his shoulder. He gave her a nod and said, "Arcon here. Go ahead."

"Arcon, we need everyone to step away from the drop zone so we can deliver package number three."

Arcon turned to Jarden. "Can you help me get everyone to move away from this area? There's a big package coming down."

"Sure," said Jarden, and addressing the crowd, said, "Hey, everyone. Arcon needs you to step back, away from this rope. The onlookers drifted away from where the rope was. As they did, the rope rose back up to the machine. Jarden gestured for more room "A little further would be better." Then he put his mouth to Arcon's ear and asked, "What's coming down?"

"You're the head of procurement yet, aren't you?" asked Arcon.

"Of course."

"Well, these are just a few supplies the outside world wanted to share with the Community. It'll be your job to distribute them."

As the box landed, Arcon disconnected the cable, and Jarden asked Tawny and Chad to get it opened up. Then he looked at Raymo, still guarded by two men, and asked, "Raymo, would you care to help?"

Raymo looked sheepishly at Jarden. "Is it ... is it okay?"

"I don't know, let's find out." Jarden turned to Arcon. "This is the guy who shot at you. Should we let him see what the outside world has to offer?"

"I should have guessed it was him," said Arcon, angrily. He braced his leg up on the box so Raymo could see the wound. He looked sternly at Raymo, then smiled. "You're a good shot."

Raymo hung his head. "No, I'm not. I was trying to miss you."

Jarden looked at Raymo, who, judging by the set of his shoulders, was now a broken man. He turned to Arcon. "What should we do with him?"

Arcon thought about that for a moment. "I believe he was trying to protect the Community. For that, we should not condemn him. But Raymo, you were wrong about me, and you were wrong about the outside world. They're all good people. In fact, out there, the rules to guide society begin with grace and forgiveness. So, I forgive you for being a pain in my side—and my leg—and I extend grace to you to start over. Is that agreeable?"

Raymo grimaced but said, "I agree to your terms. Thanks."

Arcon pointed at the box of supplies. "But you'll have to earn my trust again. You can start by helping Jarden."

People were extracting things from the box, and some were even weeping at what they discovered. Jarden looked in the box himself, and his eyes welled up with tears. He withdrew a box of pencils. He turned to a woman standing near him and said, "I think your students need these." Then he turned to Arcon and asked, "So the outside world truly is good, just as we thought it might be?"

Arcon smiled at him and said simply, "Jesus is ruling from Jerusalem." Others within earshot heard this, dropped to one knee, and bowed their heads. Soon, the news was spreading like wildfire through the crowd. For over a hundred years, the ArcPoint people had waited to hear those words, and Arcon was well aware of that. He'd planned to make that announcement at a formal meeting, but somehow this seemed far more powerful.

Suddenly, a spontaneous song of praise erupted in one area near the building and spread to everyone there. Others heard the singing and streamed out of the Facility. As the news of Jesus having returned spread through the Community, more joined the chorus. Some of them started skillfully imitating musical instruments with their voices.

Arcon had heard this song done before, but never so beautifully. It was like their hearts held more joy and love than ever before. *Maybe it's the timing. Tomorrow is the annual vote on whether ArcPoint should rejoin the outside world.* In his own heart, Arcon knew that wasn't the reason. What had always sustained them in this place was God's peace. Now they knew the Prince of Peace was sustaining everyone on the planet. The freedom of that fact was overwhelming.

He turned to Elaina and saw her weeping. He desperately wanted to hold her but realized Jarden was the only person who knew who she was. Then they both heard in their earpiece, "Excuse me, could you two face the crowd again? We need to record this. It's unbelievable!" They individually turned in different directions as the cinematographer instructed.

Arcon knew the song well, and what was coming. As the song neared its end, the voices began to crescendo. They grew louder and louder as the singers repeatedly sang the phrase,

"He is Lord." On the last time they sang it, they held the last note for an incredibly long time. Then suddenly, without direction, it abruptly stopped, and there was a deafening silence, except for the whoop, whoop, whoop of the helicopter blades—and the cheers from the control room that only those wearing an earpiece could hear.

The silence was brief, and the people gathered there discussed the news. Then Arcon heard in his ear, "Arcon, package four is ready for delivery. Acknowledge."

"Hold back for a moment," replied Arcon. He let the crowd carry on their conversations for a few minutes and then said, "Excuse me, everybody. There's one more package to be delivered." As the people stepped back, he said into his mic, "Deliver the package," and pointed to the sky again. All eyes were on what looked like another person descending. Arcon distracted Jarden, saying, "At the bottom of this box is a bunch of literature for the lab workers and the leaders of the Community. It appears our ArcPoint trees are very valuable."

"They are?"

"Yes, they are. So, in that box is an offer to help us develop them for use by the outside world. I think it's an important offer that should be taken seriously." As Jarden looked in the box, Arcon glanced up and saw that Victor was getting close. "Oh, and there are also some technical papers in there for our medical staff. They think they have a cure for the infertility problem."

"You're kidding," said Jarden. "Really?"

"Yes," said Arcon, as Victor stepped off the platform. "Oh, and one more thing. I'd like you to meet this young man. His name is Victor Merrick, and he's one of your relatives."

Jarden's mouth dropped open as Victor walked toward them. said Arcon, "Victor Merrick, I'd like you to meet my good friend and your no longer lost relative, Jarden Merrick."

As the Merricks embraced, Arcon looked for Elaina so they could do the same. He saw her moving around Jarden and Victor, taking direction from the cinematographer.

Arcon walked over so the camera could get some shots of the ArcPoint dwellers and their excitement over the supplies that had been delivered. Then he remembered something. He walked back over to Jarden and whispered, "Can I interrupt this family reunion for a moment?"

Jarden whispered back, "Of course you can."

"That's good," said Arcon. "There's something else at the bottom of this box. Along with the technical papers, there are a bunch of letters and information about other relatives. Jarden, I've met other Franklins and other people related to us. We need to get this box unloaded as soon as possible so people here can find out about their relatives in the outside world. I'm sorry we didn't find more, but I think we may later."

"Hey, you three!" Jarden yelled to Chad, Tawny, and Raymo. "Get some people to carry that box into the Facility. Don't let anybody take anything until I get there. Now hurry!"

In his ear, Arcon heard Roberto say, "Big D to Package One, we're through with the operation on our end. Are all needs satisfied on your end?"

Arcon spoke in his microphone. "Mr. Roberto and crew, all is well in the ArcPoint Community. You may take away the helicopters now. Elaina, Victor, and I will stay in touch and will look for your return in two days."

Roberto interjected, "Arcon, we have one more question for Jarden. The medic is asking what they shot your leg with."

Arcon asked Jarden, "What did Raymo shoot my leg with?"

"It should have been .22 caliber bird shot," responded Jarden.

"Okay, that's good," responded the medic, who'd overheard. "He should be examined by the local medical personnel periodically, but unless he's in a lot of pain, I see no urgency. Roberto, those folks should be able to handle the problem. We're clear to leave."

As the spoke, the people on the ground saw the platform rise back up to the helicopter. Then Arcon got emotional and said, "Ranger Dan, please thank everyone for all they've done for me and my people. We're very grateful."

There was a brief silence; then they heard Ranger Dan say, "Thank you, Arcon, for making the Mojave Forest interesting for me in a *good* way. We all look forward to what the future holds, and to know what plans Jesus has for your people. See you in two days. Dan out."

Arcon looked at Elaina, smiled, and said, "Tarzan and Jane out." Once again, Arcon had to refrain from pulling her close.

The noise from the helicopter startled some as it suddenly grew louder and moved away. As the noise subsided, Jarden asked Arcon, "Who were you just talking to?"

"When? Just now?" Arcon responded. "I was talking to Ranger Dan. He saved my life at the Rift. I was also talking to Roberto, Elaina's dad, telling him the helicopters can go away now. Oh, and a medic who was in the helicopter."

"Were the Ranger and Elaina's dad in the helicopter too?"

"No, they were back at base camp."

"Where's base camp?"

Arcon looked around to get his bearings, pointed, and said, "About 20 miles in that direction, on the other side of Soda Lake. In an abandoned town."

Jarden's face scrunched as he asked, "In Baker? How can they hear you that far away?"

"You know about the town of Baker?"

"Sure. When I was young we took the Griffin tractor there, looking for supplies. But how can someone hear you from that far away?"

Arcon pulled a small device out of his ear and handed it to Jarden. "When I stick this in my ear, I can hear them. And they can hear me when I talk. Here, try it," he said, and helped him position it in his ear. Then he leaned toward Jarden and yelled, "Roberto, do you read me?" He waited a second and asked Jarden, "Do you hear a voice?"

"Someone just said, *Roberto to Package One, go ahead.*"

"Good, that's Roberto. I'm Package One. Say hi and tell him who you are. You don't have to yell."

"Hello, Roberto, this is Jarden Merrick."

"Well, hello, Jarden," responded Roberto. "Arcon speaks highly of you. How is your day going?"

"I'm a little shaken out of my normal routine, but I'm doing fine. Thank you for returning our prodigal son to us."

"And thank you for not shooting at my daughter."

"But ... I wasn't the one that—"

"I'm just kidding, Jarden. We watched the whole thing happen. I was concerned, but Arcon told us there was nothing to worry about."

Jarden asked Arcon, "I thought you said he was in Baker. How did he watch it happen?"

"I can see you right now," interrupted Roberto. "Arcon has a camera on him, and so does Elaina. We also had one on the platform we dropped him down on. We don't mean to invade your privacy, but we thought this was a very special occasion that needed to be documented. Don't worry; none of what we're recording will be made public without your permission. If you want, you can tell Arcon to turn off his camera. Elaina has already turned hers off."

Jarden said to Arcon, "You can turn off your ... wait a minute. Roberto, can you take still pictures with that camera?"

"Absolutely," said Roberto.

"Good. I'd like you to get one of me with Victor. Oh, and get Arcon and Elaina in it too." Jarden put his hand on Arcon's arm and said, "He's telling me Elaina needs to connect."

Elaina turned on her earpiece and showed Tawny how to hold Arcon's camera. While Jarden got everyone to pose, Elaina told Tawny where to stand as she relayed instructions from her dad.

When they were through with that, Arcon shut off his microphone and whispered to Jarden, "Can I talk to you privately?"

"Sure. What is it?"

They walked away from all the commotion and conversations. "Our arrival has been so, I don't know—"

"Shocking? Abrupt?" offered Jarden.

"More like noisy and chaotic," said Arcon. I'd like to formally introduce Elaina and Victor to everyone. Would you do it?"

"That seems like something *you* should do."

"I'd planned to. I was going to have you call a big meeting." Arcon reached into his hunters' pouch. "But I need your help. Here, look at this." He handed Jarden a folded slip of paper.

Jarden unfolded it and looked it over. "Official Request for ... oh, my. You've been busy while you were gone. Is this how they do it out there?"

"No, not at all. But it's how *I* wanted to do it. When we tell everyone about the outside world, could you explain how I've actually communicated with Elaina for many years? I want ... they need to know ... I don't know how to say it."

"I think I understand, son. You want the Community to know you're committed to each other, and that Elaina's father recognizes that commitment."

"That's right. I want them to accept Elaina as having the same Holy Spirit that we have. I believe that of Victor as well. In fact, everyone I met in the outside world seems to have a heart for our Lord. Isn't that what we expected when Jesus is ruling?"

Jarden nodded. "Would you like me to arrange for that now?"

"For Elaina and Victor's sake, yeah, I would. But could you do one thing first?"

"What's that?"

Arcon reached into his hunter's pouch and pulled out a pen. "Could you be one of my Life Guarantors?"

"Wondered when you'd ask."

Jarden signed the Request form, and they walked back to where Elaina and Victor were standing. Arcon gazed at those milling around the boxes. Many were waiting patiently to see what was in them. Others still had hands lifted in praise. Inside, the Facility became crowded, as word of the day's events continued to spread. Danner and Derik were missing, as were a few from the dye house, but Arcon couldn't wait for them. "Can you announce it now, Jarden?"

"Sure, as long as ..." They both saw Brina walk into the Facility with her family. "We can do it now." Arcon nodded in agreement.

Jarden cut loose with one of his shrill whistles, and the crowd fell silent. "I need to make a quick announcement," he yelled. Arcon helped him get up on one of the tables, so everyone could see and hear what he had to say. "As you are all aware by now, Arcon has returned to the Community."

A rumble went through the crowd, with many of them applauding. Jarden allowed the din to continue for a minute, then waved his hand for them to quiet down. "Arcon's brought two of the outsiders with him. I hope they don't mind me calling them that." The crowd roared. "First, I'd like to introduce this fine, handsome lad." He waved Victor up onto the tabletop with him. "His name is Victor Merrick, and here's a surprise ... he's a distant cousin of mine."

The applause for Victor was tremendous. He waved to everyone, then stepped off the table. As the noise died down, Jarden cleared his throat. "Now I want you to meet someone special. Unbeknownst to us all, she's had a connection with this Community for over eight years ..." A collective gasp went through the crowd, so Jarden held up his hand. "She and Arcon have been communicating behind my back for that long. But don't blame her. I am convinced—as are they—that God initiated this connection and has kept them safe and blameless through it all."

Once again, the room got noisy. Jarden let it happen and asked a young woman near him for a glass of water. After he took a swallow, he raised his hand. "Quiet, please. To show everyone gathered here that they are committed to each other and to the traditions of this Community, I hold in my hand a signed Request for the Daughter's Hand!"

As the crowd roared their approval, Jarden beckoned Elaina up onto the tabletop. When she got up there, she waved to everyone. Someone near the front yelled, "What's your name?"

Elaina blushed, and Jarden yelled, "Sorry. Her name is Elaina!"

"Welcome to our home, Elaina!" yelled someone else.

"Thank you," she replied. "Glad to be here."

As the applause died down, Elaina climbed off the table. Jarden cleared his throat again. "I'd like to get Arcon up here to say something. After all, he's the one who has completely disrupted our day." Arcon waved him off, but Jarden insisted. "You need to tell them what's in the box."

"Oh, right." Arcon stepped onto the table, receiving applause as well as a joking "Throw the bum out" by Chad. Arcon looked around the room. "I didn't expect this." His chin started to quiver, but he shook it off. "But then, I didn't expect to get shot at, either." He pointed at the wounds on his calf, then smiled at Raymo. "Forgive him, everyone, for he knew not what he was doing."

He got a mixed reaction from the crowd as they discussed the gun situation. He waved his hand. "Seriously, everyone, there's something I need to tell you. It's not about the outside world. That's a long story I'll save for later. It's about that big box over there." He pointed to where the box dropped from the helicopter was now on another table. "In it are some much-needed supplies, gifts from the outsiders, and messages from a few of your relatives." Arcon waved his hand when it began getting noisy. "I need to apologize," he yelled. The room got quiet. "In order for us to track down relatives, we needed information from the

Founder days. I didn't have enough of that in my head. Many of you will be disappointed, but please take hope. We'll use whatever information you can give us, and we'll search for more of your relatives."

This time, Arcon let them talk to each other for a while. He watched their faces and tried to read their lips. There was no denying that the majority wanted to know more. *I'm not where I'm supposed to be.* He had an idea and jumped down from the tabletop.

"Where are you going?" asked Jarden.

"I'm going to rip open the other boxes and dig out the personal information. Are you with me?"

"Right behind you," said Jarden as he got down from the table.

"Me, too," said Elaina.

When they reached the box, Arcon dug through the supplies until he found a sealed box labeled Family Info. He picked at the shipping tape. "Wait," yelled Elaina. She grabbed the multi-tool out of her pants pocket, pulled out one of the blades, and sliced the tape. "Always be prepared," she said.

In not too long, Arcon was pulling large envelopes out of that box, then handing them to Elaina, who divided them up between the young ArcPoint men who'd been guarding the box. Meanwhile, Jarden helped spot the recipients of the envelopes in the crowd.

When Arcon ran out of envelopes, he grabbed Elaina's hand and led her out of the Facility. He found a tree and sat in a shady spot under it. He patted the ground next to him. "Have a seat."

"Why did you leave?" asked Elaina as she sat down.

"Same reason I left before."

"What do you mean?"

"When I left the Community, I wanted everyone to move on without me." He hung his head and stared at the ground. "Many people expected me to be the next great leader of ArcPoint. That should be Jarden, not me. I'm better at working with someone than I am at leading." He looked up at her. "When I stepped up on that table, it felt like I was back to the old me—before I left ArcPoint and met you." He grabbed her hand. "I don't want to go back to being that person. If I have to, I'll lead them just far enough to get them started. Then they're on their own."

Elaina nodded. "I think you've done enough… for now."

"Meaning what? Are you talking about the ambassador thing? I still don't know what that means or what I need to do."

She turned his head to meet her eyes. "Don't worry about it. Jesus knows. Trust him to work out those details, according to the plan He has for you."

J.W. GILBERT

MOJAVE
ROCK

MOJAVE ROCK

Book 3 *of the* ArcPoint Series

CHAPTER ONE

The ArcPoint Facility was a cacophony of conversation. Jarden stepped out of the large Quonset hut style building and into the quiet of the sunny south courtyard. His nerves could still feel the disruption that had shattered the peace in this place only an hour ago. No one had ever seen a machine that could fly, let alone one that hovered like an enormous hummingbird— its spinning propellers scattering dust and frightened residents everywhere. Everyone in the Community had seen pictures in the library's old books and magazines, but the real thing had been absolutely exhilarating. And terrifying, Then, to watch Arcon step out of its innards ... *this is not a normal day for the laid-back people of ArcPoint.*

Jarden shook his head and surveyed the forest. It's towering trees and impenetrable thorns had created a protective cocoon around ArcPoint—like a shelter in a storm. Until the outsiders stormed in from above. Even now, with the helicopter gone, many people still hid behind trees, some clutching their children.

Those brave enough to come to the Facility after this intrusion were being rewarded with news of their family in the outside world—relatives they hadn't known existed. Arcon had

279

recruited three of his peers, Chad, Tawny, and Raymo, to deliver the bulky envelopes of letters and pictures into the hands of their rightful owners.

Where had Arcon run off to?

Jarden stepped back in and rescanned the crowd, but didn't see the young man he considered a son. He couldn't help but smile with pride at the sight of Arcon's recruits working side-by-side. *Less than an hour ago they'd been fighting over the gun Raymo fired at Arcon. These men truly know how to forgive.*

By his estimates, over half of the families had received one of those blue envelopes. He'd gotten his, plus an unexpected bonus—the arrival of a distant cousin. Victor Merrick, stocky, square-jawed, and with a receding hairline, was the spitting image of himself in his thirties. He was pleased to see that Victor was visiting and getting along well with people but it was time for them to shift gears. Jarden sent a youngster over to retrieve him.

Soon Jarden and Victor were sauntering out of the Facility like old friends. His youngest hunter, Tawny, joined them. "Have either of you seen Arcon?" asked Jarden.

Tawny pointed toward the forest. "There he is, under that tree near the goat trail. See the vest?"

Jarden shaded his eyes from the high noon sun. "Okay. Yeah, I see him." He waved his arm to get Arcon's attention. Arcon saw it and nodded. "Let's go see how he's doing."

Arcon stood and pulled Elaina to her feet. As Tawny and Jarden approached them he asked, "Did everyone get their envelopes?"

"There's a few dozen left," said Tawny. "Chad has people searching for the stragglers."

Jarden chuckled. "They need to check behind trees. So why are you and Elaina out here all alone?"

"Aahh, you know I don't like to be the center of attention," said Arcon.

"You won't escape that," piped in Tawny. "You wander away to the outside world, then fly in here on a big noisy machine with two outsiders? Don't expect us to ignore you."

"Well, right now, I just want people to know they have connections on the outside. Sorry I couldn't find some for you."

"That's okay," said Tawny. "You might be able to later on though, right?"

"Yeah, but I need old names from the Founder days. Arcon turned and asked Jarden, "Can you get the word out for families to scrounge up some information about other relatives that didn't come here? That'd help, too."

"I'll let *you* orchestrate that. You've probably got other things to discuss with the leaders anyway." Jarden saw Arcon's countenance fall as he looked toward Elaina.

Elaina gave Arcon's hunter's vest a tug, interrupting. "When do we get to go swinging?"

Tawny heard that and asked excitedly, "Are you going to take her to one of the swingways?"

"We were talking about it," said Arcon.

Tawny couldn't contain himself. "Let's go to the new one. I want to show you what I did to it."

"Maybe someday. Beginners have to start out on the Sunset trainer." He pointed west and when Elaina looked away, put his finger to his lips to tell Tawny to keep quiet. "It's tradition. Besides, that's the first one that Jarden made, and it's where he taught me."

"That sounds perfect then," said Elaina. "But can't we at least just go in the forest? I can't wait to be in there. To walk and climb among those flowers. They smell so good."

"I want to, but we have so much to discuss with Jarden, and people are bound to be confused. We should have a talk with the leaders."

Jarden spoke up. "How about if I arrange a meeting for tomorrow morning? That way, you kids can spend some time

281

together. But I'd like to tag along with you to the trainer. You know … for safety reasons."

"Safety reasons?" asked Elaina.

"It's just protocol," said Arcon. "On a person's first jump, we always err on the side of caution."

"Can I come too?" begged Tawny.

"I suppose," said Arcon reluctantly. "At least until she gets comfortable with it. Then we'll swing away from you both. Maybe all the way to the Sunset outpost."

"Really? Has a girl ever been to an outpost?" asked Tawny.

"It's a whole new world out there," said Arcon. "You won't believe what girls can do." Then he hugged Elaina and said, "Especially this one. She can go farther in one day than you have in your entire life."

Tawny turned to go and said, "Wow, then let's get going. This'll be fun."

"We can't go out there right now," said Jarden. "We need to get back to helping Chad and Raymo empty those boxes. We should at least let them know before we go."

"Okay, I'll hurry them up," said Tawny.

"And Tawny," added Jarden, "open the roll-up doors. It's getting stuffy in there."

"Yes, sir," said Tawny. He ran off like a hunter chasing a rabbit.

When he was out of earshot, Jarden grinned and said to Elaina, "I think you've lit a little fire under that boy."

"How so?" asked Arcon.

"Well, think about it. You go away for a few weeks and come back with the perfect girl for you. He's at that age. I bet it won't be long before he'll want to see what might be out there for him."

"I understand," said Arcon, and pointed at Elaina. "I'll explain to him it took me eight years to find this one."

Victor, content to listen like a spectator, added, "I still haven't found the right one for me."

"Well, ArcPoint isn't necessarily the best hunting grounds for that sort of thing," said Jarden. "Anyway, if you three would like to get started toward the trainer swingway, Tawny and I'll meet you there in a bit."

"Okay," said Arcon.

Jarden was halfway across the south courtyard when he glanced back and saw that Arcon was jogging to catch up to him. He yelled, "I need to explain about a couple of the supplies that came in the box."

Jarden stopped. "You said something about technical papers if I remember right."

Arcon came alongside and the two of them walked on together. "I wanted to say that Victor's not as comfortable being off the ground as we are, so I don't think he really wants to go to the swingway. But he likes machinery, so can someone show him what's been done to keep this place going?"

"Sure. Who do you have in mind?"

"How about Luther? He's familiar with the mechanical things. Plus, I don't think I have any family stuff for him. It'll distract him from that disappointment."

"Understood," said Jarden. He whistled toward Elaina and Victor while Arcon waved for them to join him and Jarden.

"Anyway, about the boxes of technical papers—there's one marked Medical. It contains research the outsiders did on the infertility problem. They need more information from us to know for sure what's happening, but it sounds promising. Someone needs to run those papers over to Minda Polk at the Med Shack and tell her to look them over. She'll have questions—she needs to know we'll link her up with the outsiders later."

"I should probably handle this myself," said Jarden.

Arcon agreed. When Elaina and Victor arrived he said, "Slight change of plans, we've one quick stop to make before we go swinging—and Jarden, there's another box marked 'Trees.' It seems the infertility problem comes from the ArcPoint trees.

They're pulling certain minerals out of the ground, and we're eating them. That's the *bad* news. The good news is those minerals are valuable to the outsiders. They're working on a plan to extract those minerals and rid us of the needle-brush as well."

Jarden's eyes got big. "Are you saying they can solve the infertility issue, and take away that cursed needle-brush at the same time?"

"Well, yeah, sort of," said Arcon. He walked over to the roll-up doorway and scanned the crowd who were still milling around.

Elaina added, "It's a lot more complicated than that, but that's the end result they're hoping for."

"I think I like you outsiders already," said Jarden.

Arcon spotted who he was looking for. "I see Luther. Let's have him take the tree information to the shop people. It's mostly mechanical stuff, anyway. Maybe Victor can go with him. He understands what it's about, right, Victor?"

Victor shrugged in response and said, "Mostly. You just need them to look it over anyway, right? They don't need to act on anything right now."

"No. Yeah. They only need to try to figure it out. I need to meet with the leaders of the Community before we do anything. This is all just information. I'll go get Luther."

As Arcon jogged off to the other side of the Facility, Jarden said, "Victor, would you like to join us in swinging through the trees, or can I have Luther show you around our Facility? You'll see a lot of worn-out machinery that's been creatively kept running. Arcon tells me you like machinery."

"That sounds like fun, the machinery that is," replied Victor. "The authorities wanted me to find out what you folks may need in your shops. I might as well get started."

"I'll talk to Luther and have him give you a tour of our shops."

"Sounds great," said Victor with a sigh of relief.

Arcon searched until he located a muscular, middle-aged man wearing an oil-stained leather vest. As he got closer to Luther, he noticed Brina standing with her grandfather, away from everyone. As their eyes met, he nodded to her, but she looked away. His heart sank. Besides Jarden, no one in the Community had been a better friend to him. *She always cared about my well-being, and I betrayed her friendship. I need to talk to her soon, but now is not the time.*

"Hey, Luther! Are you busy?"

Luther spun around to look at Arcon, then held out his empty hands. "Wish I had one of those blue envelopes, but you didn't bring me anything."

"Sorry about that. If you tell us names of some of your relatives, I'll see if the outsiders can find something."

"That'd be righteous. How can I help you?"

"I want to introduce you to Jarden's distant cousin, Victor. Would you have time to walk him around the Facility? He's mechanical. Knows all sorts of stuff. You'll like him."

"Sounds like it."

"Then follow me."

When they got back to Jarden, Tawny had rejoined their group. Victor was holding the box marked Trees. "I see you found it," said Arcon. "Victor, I'd like you to meet Luther. He's one of the main reasons a lot of our machinery still works. Luther, this is Jarden's cousin."

"I see the resemblance," said Luther. "Glad to meet you."

As they shook hands, Arcon said, "By the way, there are some papers in this box I'd like you to give to Firsten for the shop people to look at. It's a design for a machine to chew up the needle-brush. See if they can figure out how it works. If they have questions, they can ask Victor."

"What if I don't know the answer?" asked Victor.

"Then fake it," said Arcon. "That's what Luther does." He laughed and added, "We both learned that from Jarden."

"Time for you boys to leave," said Jarden jokingly. He turned to Arcon. "I see Minda over by the kitchen. I'll take her this medical information and meet you at the Sunset trainer. Are you going with them, Tawny?"

"For sure. If he's going to teach her to swing, I gotta see it."

Arcon saw Brina and her grandfather go into the Franklin meeting room. He said to Elaina, "Could you and Tawny wait outside for a few minutes? There's something I need to do."

"Sure, of course. We'll wait for you by the woods where we were before."

Arcon gave Elaina's hand a squeeze. "Great. I won't be long."

Arcon walked across the Facility until he saw Tawny open the south man-door for Elaina. When she was out of the building, he stopped, opened up his backpack, and pulled out a bulky blue envelope. In the Franklin room he found Brina talking with her Grandpa Lars at one end of the conference table. Standard ArcPoint behavior was to let a private conversation run its course before interrupting, but he couldn't wait. He walked into the room. "Can I show you two something?"

"Sure, you can," said Brina, gesturing for Arcon to take a chair. "Grandpa just needed to sit down for a few minutes."

"Hi, Lars. I think you'll want to look at this." Arcon sat and handed Lars the envelope.

"What is it?"

"It's information about some of the Ashford family in the outside world."

"Really? I didn't think there was one for us," said Brina.

"I had it. I wanted to give it to you myself. I don't know everything that's in here, but I know there are letters and pictures from some of your family members. I've even met a few of them. They're all good people, and they're happy to know that we are too—and that we're still alive. Go ahead and open it."

Lars Ashford slowly opened the envelope and carefully pulled out a sheet of paper. He saw a picture of a smiling young man and started reading aloud what was written with it. "Dear Ashford Family. My name is David Bryzinski." He looked at Arcon. "Who is David Bryzinski?"

"I met him. He's the grandson of an Ashford that is related to your father, Norm. He really wants to hear about all the things Norm did for our Community."

Lars set that letter aside and slowly reached into the envelope again. Brina said to him, "Grandpa, can I do that for you?" He handed her the envelope, and she dumped the contents out on the conference table.

Arcon stood and said, "I should let you two look this over on your own. I'm leaving now."

He was two steps away when he heard Brina say his name. He turned just in time to see her wipe a tear from her cheek as she said, "Thank you."

"For the letters?"

"For coming back."

"I had to," he said, as his chin quivered. "This is my home." He had to look away from them. He hadn't planned to make that confession, and wasn't really sure where his ultimate home would be. But he knew ArcPoint would always be one.

His thoughts were interrupted when he heard Lars say, "Is it true what they're saying? Is Jesus ruling in Jerusalem?"

He turned to face him. "Yes. Jesus is on earth again and ruling from Jerusalem. I haven't seen him, but he appeared to someone I know just a couple of weeks ago. He has a whole network of judges and authorities governing the world. Things have changed a lot out there since the evil times. Like the Bible says, there are no more wars or lawlessness."

"That's good to hear, Arcon."

Lars went back to looking at some pictures, so Arcon smiled at Brina. "I really need to go now. I have things to attend to."

"I want to meet her," she said, matter-of-factly. They both knew who she meant.

"She'd like to meet you. But right now, I promised to show her the Sunset swingway. She'd like to try swinging."

"Uh-oh. Maybe I should meet her before you leave, and give her fair warning. You know, just in case something happens."

That statement confused Arcon, but then he saw a smile creep across her face and said, "You promised not to tell anyone."

"I haven't," said Brina. "And I won't. But as soon as you get back, I'll ask her how the training went."

Lars perked up. "What training?" he asked. "What are you two talking about?"

"It's nothing, Grandpa. Arcon's just going to give his girlfriend a few swinging lessons."

"Sounds mighty unwise, if you ask me," mumbled Lars.

Brina smiled at Arcon. "You'll probably be back in an hour or so?"

"Maybe a little longer."

"I'll be watching the trail and praying for her."

Arcon laughed. "I'm sure she'd appreciate that, but I'm not going to tell her why you're doing it." He winked at her and said, "Thanks for understanding. I'm leaving now."

There was a buzz of conversations in the Facility, especially near the dining area. Arcon assumed they'd want to find a private place to browse the family material. Instead, they were excitedly sharing their discoveries with each other.

He stopped for a moment to take in the scene and feel the relief—glad those who didn't receive envelopes weren't upset. He'd not been able to recall the last names of more than half of the ArcPoint Community. Compounding his guilt was knowing every single person knew who he was. None of that seemed to matter at this moment.

As Arcon worked his way through the Facility, several people held up their blue envelopes and smiled at him. *What made me think returning to this place would be unpleasant?*

Arcon looked away from everyone and hustled to get back to Elaina and Tawny. As he approached them, Tawny was grinning ear to ear. "Is she going to get the full training?"

"That'll be up to Jarden," said Arcon. As soon as Elaina wasn't watching, he whacked Tawny on the shoulder and motioned him to keep quiet.

Tawny just smiled.

MOJAVE ROCK is Book 3 of the ArcPoint Series, the final book in J.W. Gilbert's uplifting post-apocalyptic story. The community of ArcPoint is in the midst of more change and upheaval than ever before. Their prayers have been answered ten-fold but the disruption is almost unmanageable.

Arcon has returned to ArcPoint-reluctantly. Going back was not part of his plan. A butterfly should not return to its cocoon or a baby chick to its shell. Sightseeing with Elaina was more to his liking. The comfort of familiar surroundings at ArcPoint could not overcome the excitement of discovering new things ... Elaina's search and rescue training hadn't prepared her for milking goats. Arcon told her this would just be a visit, but what had she just heard him say to Jarden? He wants to find a spot to build a home? ... Ranger Dan has no training in governing humans. Plants, animals, and the land they use-this he understands. To make matters worse, he's never known people like those in ArcPoint. What he wouldn't give for a standard operating procedure manual.

To learn all of their fates, they must travel to Jerusalem and face the most powerful people on earth, Central Authority, keepers of world peace, whose judgment will be swift and final. Beyond them, appeal can only be made to one individual-Jesus himself.

Inspired by actual people, places, and events from the Bible, *Mojave Rock* - Book 3 of the ArcPoint Series weaves together authentic Biblical Scripture and original storytelling to create an entertaining and spiritually uplifting must-read. This fun, feel-good tale of community takes readers through remarkable moments as Arcon learns the true meaning of what it is to lead and includes a peaceful, humble reveal of the world after the second coming of Jesus Christ who walks with us all.

MOJAVE ROCK
BOOK 3 *of the* ARCPOINT SERIES

Visit JWGilbertBooks.com for more about your favorite ArcPoint characters and the world they live in.
Subscribe to our mailing list for FREE STORIES, book releases, and blog updates from the author.

ABOUT THE AUTHOR

JOHN WOZNIAK IS A CHRISTIAN FICTION WRITER with a knack for stories, research, and rock hunting. He and his wife are life-long Oregon residents with a passion for discovering the beauty in rocks and the One who created them. John's goal is to create rather than destroy, conserve rather than waste, hope rather than despair, and to laugh rather than weep. These goals have served him well, even when he was determined to remain an atheist.

Life altering experiences drove John to write his second book: *Escaping Ignorance—Pursuing Wisdom: More Than 150 Stories Revealing God's Grace, Guidance, and Goodness in the Life of a Former Atheist.* He's been writing ever since, honing his skills, and making headway with editing and self-publishing.

Before retiring, John worked as an international trouble-shooter for data-center cooling. He now draws readily from his years in research to shape realistic environments for his characters. *Mojave Rift*, the award-winning first book in his post-apocalyptic series, takes place many decades from now in the once desert regions of California. John has spent thousands of hours researching science trends and comparing them to Bible prophecy for this series. *"I've sought expert advice in computers, energy, climatology, genetics, botany, geology, transportation, and other fields."*

John is also having a lot of fun creating characters who are admirable without being super-human. He writes characters who lend a helping hand rather than a swift kick. He's met those kinds of people, and tries hard to emulate them. Many of their positive traits are portrayed in the characters of John's books. *"In the Bible, I discovered predictions for a time when these attitudes would be normal, without being forced. My desire is for the reader to discover the same hope I did."*

To learn more about J.W. and the saga of Arcon, please visit:

JWGilbertBooks.com

www.ingramcontent.com/pod-product-compliance
Lightning Source LLC
Chambersburg PA
CBHW070834250626
47159CB00003B/776